FIXER

Roderick C. Lankler

ISBN (Hard Cover Edition): 978-1-09830-474-4

ISBN (Soft Cover Edition): 978-1-09831-259-6

ISBN (eBook Edition): 978-1-09830-475-1

This is a work of fiction. Any resemblance to actual events or persons, living or dead, is entirely coincidental

Dedication

To Barbara

who's greatest gift has been staying married

to me for sixty years

and

to her second greatest gift, our four sons,

Andrew, Douglas, Gregory, and Stephen

.

FIXER

RODERICK C LANKLER

1

After Judge Hastings took his seat overlooking his courtroom, the court clerk shouted, "Be seated." As everyone in the courtroom took their seats, Hastings waited for complete silence. He looked around his courtroom, and then down at Assistant District Attorney Ian MacDonald.

"Mr. MacDonald, you may make your opening statement."

Ian rose from the prosecutors' table and walked directly to the jury box where the twelve jurors and four alternates were seated. He carried no notes or other papers. He knew what he wanted to say. He was ready.

"Ladies and gentlemen of the jury, this is a case of rape and murder. A brutal, violent, forceful rape in the back of a van and a murder by strangulation. The victim of this murder, you will learn, was a beautiful, bright, twenty-six-year-old young lady named Mary Rusk. Mary lived on Staten Island with her mother, father and two siblings. Mary worked as a summer intern in one of the large banks headquartered in lower Manhattan. This was a summer job. In the fall she was to begin her first year at the Wharton School of the University of Pennsylvania, one of the nation's leading business schools.

"You will learn and the people will prove that, on the night of July 30 of this past year, Mary worked late. It was her custom to take the ferry to Staten Island, and on this night, she took her normal route to walk to the ferry. Only it was much later. The streets of lower Manhattan were empty. Empty except for one man—this defendant, Gino Conti. Conti sat in a Dodge Grand Caravan in a vacant parking lot at Cedar Street. As Mary Rusk drew abreast of the lot, this defendant grabbed Mary and forced her into the back of the van. He ripped down her skirt and pantyhose, and he raped Mary. He then took the pantyhose, wrapped it around Mary's neck and pulled tighter and tighter until Mary was dead.

"At around 5:00 AM the next morning, a sanitation truck was moving east on Rector Street when the driver saw what he believed to be a mannequin lying in the middle of the street. As he slowly approached the object, he realized it was not a mannequin. It was a human body. Mary Rusk's half-naked body had been dumped in the middle of Rector Street. You will hear that the driver of the truck called his supervisor who, in turn, alerted the police. Upon closer inspection, the pantyhose was found so tightly wrapped around Mary's neck, it was embedded in her skin. You will learn and the people will prove that, as the police responded to Rector Street and began their investigation . . ."

Two-and-a-half weeks later the trial ended. It was a disaster.

2

The first bombshell came at about 3:00 PM, two hours after the jury got the case and began its deliberations. The court officers notified everyone that the jury had sent out a note. The judge would be taking the bench in ten minutes.

Word spread fast throughout the Homicide Bureau. A senior trial assistant asked, "What the hell is this all about? Isn't it a little early for a note?"

"Beats me Al, but duty calls." Ian grabbed his suit coat and his trial file. The smile on his face betrayed the feelings in his bowels.

"You better wash your face; you got some mustard there from your sandwich."

"Thanks Al. I'm my usual mess."

The fact was that Ian was not usually a mess. He was in good shape: 6', 150 lbs. He ran marathons and played a respectable game of golf. He was not a fancy dresser, but his suits fit, his pants were pressed and his shoes were well shined. As far as he could see, there were no mustard stains on his tie. His greying temples were striking against the pitch black of the rest of his hair. He was nicely tanned from running and playing golf. There was a distinctive scar by his left ear where a kid threw a fire cracker at him when he was younger. It gave him a bit of a macho look that women loved. They also loved his steel grey eyes and his brilliant white teeth. He was single. He would make a great catch.

He had been in the Homicide Bureau of the New York County District Attorney's Office for the last seven years and was clearly recognized as the top trial lawyer. He was well respected by the senior pros in the bureau, and the younger assistants loved him. He was always looking for ways to involve the junior people in his trials. Taught by some of the best, he knew it was his duty to pass it on. He got a healthy share of "Good luck" as he went down the hallway toward the elevator bank.

He was trailed closely by Detective Joseph Jackie, known by all as Robbie, and Detective Eustice H Smith. Smith was never, ever called Eustice. He was just plain Smitty. These were the two detectives who originally caught the mannequin case. They had invested a large portion of the past year finding Conti and getting the case to trial.

Bringing up the rear, scrambling as fast as he could, juggling papers everywhere, was Louie Balzo, a rookie in the Homicide Bureau. This was Louie's maiden trial voyage, and he looked like he was going to throw up.

When Ian's group got off the elevator on the twelfth floor, they were met by Nails Ballen, Conti's lawyer. With Nails was Bunny, his ever-present associate wearing her ever-present mini skirt. Ballen's real name was Hopewell J. Ballen, but everyone called him Nails. He seemed to like it. He looked like a nail—tall and skinny—with thinning black hair swept back, and reading glasses that he always wore down at the end of his nose.

"What do you hear, kid?" demanded Nails.

"Nothing, Nails. I just got a call that there was a note from the jury and to come up to court."

"Bullshit. Those court officers are always giving you ADAs little hints. What have they told you?"

"That there was a note and the judge would be taking the bench in ten minutes. That was nine-and-a-half minutes ago. I went to the bathroom."

"Despite the bathroom you are still full of shit, and besides, what is confidential about a note? Someone's got to read it."

"I have no idea what is going on, but it's too early for a verdict. They probably want some part of the charge explained to them. Bunny, don't you think Nails should be more careful of his language in front of you?" Bunny rolled her eyes.

Ian went into the austere wood paneled courtroom. It, like the rest of the Criminal Courts Building, reflected the art/deco style. It bore one of those telltale depression era murals all along one side of the courtroom, featuring, naturally, the blindfolded Lady Justice and her scales.

Instead of going to the prosecutor's table with Louie and the detectives, he went over to Davey Garr's desk. Davey was the clerk of the court. He'd worked in the courts for a hundred years.

"What's going on, Davey?"

"Bad news," Davey said. "Bad news," he repeated slowly, and left to get the judge. Ian had heard Davey the first time.

When all the jurors were seated, Judge Hastings said, "I am in possession of a note submitted to me by Juror Number 1, your foreperson, which I ask be marked court's Exhibit 21."

"That would be 22, your honor," Davey Garr said. "We are up to 22."

"Whatever. Mark it as court's Exhibit 22 and hand it to me." It was clear that Judge Hastings was not happy. Hastings took a long, exasperated breath and continued, "The note reads as follows:

'Your honor, as soon as we began our deliberations, one of the jurors got up from the table and said, "You people are on your own on this one," and he pulled a chair over by the window and sat. We asked him what was wrong and he wouldn't say anything to us other than "You are on your own." The rest of us started to discuss how we felt about the case and he just sat there and looked out the window. We asked him if he wanted to share any thoughts or opinions and all he said was "You are on your own." We would like some help about what we should do. This note was written by the other eleven of us.'"

Ian, and everyone else in the courtroom, watched the jury as Hastings read the note. Most of the jurors were looking at juror number 11 who sat with his head down and his eyes shut as if he were sleeping.

Louie whispered, "I think it's number 11. He is sitting in the back row toward the right." Louie was proud of himself.

"Yep, thanks Louie," Ian acknowledged.

Hastings was clearly pissed. "Now listen to me very carefully, ladies and gentlemen of the jury. Each one of you took an oath and swore that you would listen to all the evidence as it was being presented to you in this courtroom. You swore that you would diligently consider that evidence and try to determine where the truth lies. You swore that you would respectfully listen to your fellow jurors, consider their arguments and their positions, calmly and carefully present your own arguments and positions and that you would all attempt to come to a unanimous decision. Now I am charging you that you have an obligation to live up to those promises. You are to go back to the jury room and do just that. All of you. You are now directed to continue your deliberations." The jury filed out of the jury box and out the courtroom door to the jury room.

At 5:30, there was another note. It was essentially the same news, except it was obvious that eleven jurors were in agreement. Nails saw his client going down if juror number 11 caved in and immediately moved for a mistrial. Hastings knew "11 to 1s." He'd experienced them many times before. He denied the motion for a mistrial, and ordered the jury to continue deliberating, confident that the holdout would buckle.

Two days, six notes and eight mistrial motions later, it was clear that number 11 was not budging. There would not be a verdict, and a furious Hastings declared a mistrial and excused the jury. Two-and-a-half weeks of trial went down the drain.

Ian asked his detectives to bring the Rusk family down to his office.

3

Maggie Rusk, Mary's mother, led her family into Ian's office. She was a wreck. She'd been crying, and kept running her left hand through the left side of her hair as if she couldn't get it back far enough. She was a fragile woman weighing barely a hundred pounds. She was an immaculate and meticulous dresser, which made her present condition all the more striking. In Ian's many dealings with the Rusk family, she was always courteous and pleasant. She treated Ian as if he were her son. Ian thought that she was probably in her late forties or early fifties. Her three kids were born one right after another: first Mary, then Adele a year later and Brian a year after that. Pete Rusk, Mary's father, told Ian that he received special permission from their parish priest, Father Joe, to get a vasectomy in order to keep Maggie's sanity. Maggie's sanity was not doing too well at the moment. She had a white hanky in her right hand. She had coiled part of it around her thumb, and when her left hand wasn't busy with her hair, it was winding and unwinding the hanky.

Ian was scurrying around trying to make room for people to sit.

"My God, this is never going to end, is it?" Maggie asked no one in particular. "Does this mean we have to start all over at the beginning again?"

"Ma, let's let Ian catch his breath and then he can explain everything to us." Adele was patting her mother's busy hands as she spoke. Adele was twenty-five, in the second year of her medical internship at New York Presbyterian Hospital and a knockout. Detective Smith would say, "She is hot," but Ian had asked him to control himself and to stop using that expression to describe her. Besides having a great body, Adele was pretty. Her long blond hair was pulled back in a pony tail with a blue band that matched the blue of her eyes. Her face was striking. She was a Grace Kelly look-alike. In addition to all of that, she was brilliant, caring and kind.

Everything that Adele was, Brian wasn't. Overweight and unkempt, he possessed a big mouth from which very little of any worth spouted. He was the personification of "ready, fire, aim." Over the months, Ian had become very impatient with Brian, not because he was stupid, but because he was stupid and thought he was smart. It was hard to believe that he was the brother of two such bright and talented girls as Mary and Adele. Ian could see, as a fuming Brian entered the room, that this wasn't going to be pretty.

Pete Rusk was the last of the family to take a seat. In typical fashion, he immediately said, "Ian, before you say anything, we just want to say again how grateful we are to ya for . . . not only the tremendous professional job ya did with this trial . . . but the incredible way ya have treated my family. I personally am beholden to ya and don't know how I can ever repay ya."

He rose from his chair and went over to Ian's desk and extended his hand. Ian grabbed his hand and said, "Pete, thank you. I don't know how this happened, but something's fishy. We will get to the bottom of it."

"I know how it happened. You never should have picked that idiot juror," blurted out Brian. "Right after you picked him, I told you you shouldn't have picked him and I was right."

"Brian, you also told me I should not have picked three other jurors and they all obviously voted for conviction, so give it a rest."

"Yes Brian, this is no time for ya comments. Just button it," said Pete. Brian turned away in disgust and concentrated on a piece of peeling paint on the window sill.

Pete was retired from the New York City Comptroller's Office where for the last twenty years he had run the police department's pension program. He essentially made sure that the retiring New York City police officers got what they were supposed to get when they retired. All the police knew him, knew what he did and they all loved him. Mary's murder resonated among the police force as if she were one of their own.

Pete was a massive man. He played football when at Fordham University and had stayed in shape since graduating many years ago. Over 6'6" tall, he kept his weight at around 200 lbs. by daily visits to the gym not far from their home in a pleasant section of Staten Island. Pete's one fault was not that he was devoutly religious, but that he wore his religion on his sleeve. This sometimes caused others discomfort. "Ya know, Ian, that I believe the Good Lord works in mysterious ways, and this little setback today is just Him testing us. We have to let His will be done."

"You may be right, Pete, but that doesn't make it any easier," a depressed Ian replied.

"It's all right, Ian. The Good Lord sent ya to help Mary and us, and ya doing a wonderful job. God bless ya."

"Thank you, Pete. Let's talk for a minute about what all this means. First of all, Conti is back in his cell. He is not going anywhere. Secondly, Judge Hastings has put the case on for Monday morning at 10:00 AM. He is going to ask what our intentions are, and I am going to tell him I am ready to move the case for retrial immediately. We have no idea what Nails might do. He is going to want more money for another trial. He may look to get out of the case. He will be begging for a plea. He and Conti know they barely escaped a conviction."

"But why would he think he could get a plea?" Adele asked softly. "He knows that we would all be against a lesser plea."

"Let him plead to murder and rape with consecutive sentences," chimed in Brian.

"Lawyers are always looking for a plea. Nails will now tell me that he has the advantage of knowing our entire case. Which is true. I know how awful it is reliving Mary's death. I just want to make sure we are all on the same page and that we are going to trial again. No plea. Correct?"

"Correct," was the almost unanimous reply.

"I don't know if I can stand it," Maggie Rusk whispered. "It is so horrible to hear that testimony about finding her and the autopsy. Why not take some sort of plea and get out of here? Get on with our lives. Nothing is going to bring her back." She started to sob. Adele ran over to put her arm around her mother.

"Shit," said Brian as he walked out of the room.

Mr. Rusk leaned forward in his chair, arms on his knees, hands clasped as if in prayer and just shook his head.

Detective Smith came into the room and asked Ian, "Could they just have a seat out in the waiting area for one minute? There is something I should tell you." When the Rusk family left, Smitty closed Ian's door. He explained, "After you left, I stayed up in the courtroom because I heard Judge Hastings direct the court officers to grab juror number 11 and bring him into the courtroom. I wasn't sure what was going to happen. Hastings cleared the courtroom, but he let me stay. He asked 11 to explain himself. I got to tell you, Ian, it was as if a lawyer wrote out the answer for him. Hastings was ready to carve him a new asshole, but when 11 was finished, Hastings was speechless."

Ian collapsed in his chair. "Damn Smitty, what did 11 say?"

"He covered himself. He said that during the jury selection process, he listened very carefully, and when he was questioned, he answered all the questions truthfully. He said that when he was sworn in as a juror, he took the oath seriously and he believes he lived up to his oath. He said that as he watched the evidence being presented, a feeling grew that there was a conspiracy going on to frame Conti because he was of Italian heritage. He said that he became convinced of this when he heard your summation, Ian. The judge's charge put him over the top. He knew when he went into the jury room that only *his courage* could keep Conti from being railroaded. Now what do you do about that? He may be nuts, but you can't lock him up for that."

"No, you can't. I'll be damned. What did Hastings say?"

"Nothing at first. Then Hastings shook his head and said, 'That is ridiculous. You have wasted everyone's time. Get out of here.'"

"When 11 left the courtroom, there was a man and a woman waiting for him, and they all went down in an elevator together. I took another elevator down to the lobby and saw the three of them get into a limo out on Centre Street and head north. I tried but couldn't get a plate number."

4

The driver of the limo carrying number 11 and the two others took a convoluted route to the north-bound entrance of the FDR Drive at the Brooklyn Bridge. He was making sure that he wasn't being followed. Twenty-seven minutes later, he pulled up to the door of a warehouse a block away from Arthur Avenue in the Bronx. Almost immediately, the overhead door began to rise. The limo was inside before the door reached the top, stopped and began to make its descent. Once inside, the three passengers headed for the elevator that took them to the fourth-floor offices. Number 11 was left in the reception area, while the man and woman went into the inner office.

"He is perfectly calm and cool," the woman told the rotund man seated in an overstuffed recliner. "Nothing to worry about from this end."

The rotund man grunted and said, "Give him this attaché case and get him up to our plane at Westchester County Airport. Get him on it and out of here. Tell him to follow the instructions, and in a week he will get the balance of his money."

In less than an hour, number 11 was walking up the steps of a private Gulfstream jet parked at the general aviation hangar at Westchester County Airport. He had his own crew and flight attendant.

No one else was on the plane. In a little over four hours, he was pulling up to the entrance of the Crescent Moon Cove Resort in Jamaica, West Indies, and a half hour after that, he was in his ocean front villa. An attaché case full of money lay on the bed. He was reading an instruction sheet:

"If you expect to live and to receive the rest of your money, you will do the following:

1. Check into the villa that has been provided for you. Don't go off the property. Don't make any phone calls. Don't write any letters. Don't generate any form of contact with anyone.

2. Eat all your meals at the resort restaurants. Charge them to your account, which you will pay in full when you leave, using the cash we have given you.

3. If you want to purchase anything, you will purchase it at the resort store and charge the items to your account.

4. On Friday, you will go to the resort store at 4:45 PM. Don't be late. The store closes at 5:00 PM. You will ask for a fifth of Dewar's Black Label scotch. After you receive it, you will ask for some Bruner's pretzel snacks and for the package that has been left for Mr. Ralph. That package will contain the balance of your money.

5. On Saturday, you will pay your bill and check out of the resort. You will go wherever you want to go as long as it is not back to New York City.

DESTROY THESE INSTRUCTIONS."

The details about picking up the package at the resort store were new. The rest of the instructions had been drilled into him. He had been promised enough money to keep him comfortable for the rest of his life.

5

Leroy P. Hastings was the most senior judge of the trial court. His twenty years on the bench would soon end. He would be retiring at the end of the year. There was very little he hadn't seen. He'd paid his political dues as a young lawyer working with the Legal Aid Society, been appointed to the lower Criminal Court bench by the mayor and then promoted to the top trial court.

Because of his seniority, he occupied the largest and grandest chambers on the top floor of the Criminal Court Building. He was seated behind his large desk smoking a cigar. There was a scotch on the rocks in a fishbowl-sized glass sitting at his elbow. He always wore bright red braces in addition to a wide brown leather belt and claimed, "You can never be too sure when it comes to keeping your pants on."

He also wore an oversized bow tie that he tied himself. His ties made a loud paisley statement under his wrinkled chin. The only things larger than his bow ties were his eyebrows. They almost ran up to his receding hair line. Judge Hastings' eyebrows reminded Ian of Brillo Pads.

When Ian called, the judge invited him to come up for a chat. Ian had tried several murder cases before Judge Hastings. Both men respected each other.

"There is something that doesn't pass the smell test about this, Ian. I have seen holdouts on other juries, and they are nervous and scared. This guy was just too cool. Most holdouts think they are about to have the shit kicked out of them by the other jurors. It was as if this guy knew that if he kept his mouth shut and just sat there, nothing would happen to him. He also knew that if he gave me the right answers, there would be nothing I could do about it. It is almost as if he'd been coached."

"Maybe he was—I mean, coached. If you were going to put someone on a jury, to hang that jury, you'd want him to be prepared. You'd want him to know how to go about it, to know how to resist the pressure from the other jurors. Most of all you'd want him to know what to do when the judge starts leaning on him. This guy seemed prepared."

"So what do you propose we do about it?" asked the judge.

"I thought I would meet with the boss of Manhattan South Homicide over the weekend and see what we can dig up. I just wanted to confirm that you felt the same way."

"Absolutely." Hastings slammed his scotch on the desk. "And anything you need: search warrants, wire taps, subpoenas signed, anything, come to me. I'd like to help. I feel like a number has been done on us, and I am pissed."

When Ian got back to his office, there was a call from Captain LoMurko. Jim LoMurko was in charge of Manhattan South Homicide, a terrific detective and Ian's good friend. Ian called him back, and they set up a meeting for the next day, Saturday, in Ian's office.

"Whatever you want. Whatever you need. You got it," said LoMurko as he strolled into Ian's office eating a hamburger from one hand and a popsicle from the other. For a 6'5" tall, totally fit ex-marine, his crew cut belied his fifty-two years. Captain James LoMurko was a poster boy for the New York City Police Department. "You need extra men? You got them. You need overtime authorized? You got it. You need cars, guns, sirens, women, I got lots of sirens and women, flashing lights—"

"I got them," Ian interrupted. "What I need are your brains. I want to know everything I can about this damned juror who screwed us, and I want to know what we can do about him."

"Well, my fine friend, that is what you will get. Give me your jury file and any other information you may have on this guy. The magical powers of the New York City Police Department will soon be at work. There will be no stone left unturned."

Ian gave LoMurko his jury selection file and explained the randomness of the jury selection process to him.

LoMurko looked out the window for a few seconds, and then said, "So that means that they—whoever they are—were required to wait until the jurors were called, questioned, survived challenges and were selected. Right?"

"That's right, Jim, if there is a 'they.'"

"They waited until the jury was picked, and then they started to check on each sworn juror to find the one they could get to. Elementary, my dear MacDonald. So if these 'they' could find him, doth thou not think New York's finest can find him?"

"No, I'm sure you can, Jim. That's why we're spending our Saturday together."

"Ok," added LoMurko, "so now that I have finished my lunch and we are no longer talking silly, here's the plan. We locate this guy and find out all we can about him. This is not going to take long. We then meet and figure out how we want to go about getting the truth out of him. I got a buck that says it goes back to the Conti family."

"You may be right. We never did go any further than doing a little background on Conti's connections because this had no elements of a mob crime. It was treated as a straight rape and murder."

"So let's see what we can dig up."

LoMurko called Ian on Sunday night and left a voicemail that they should meet first thing Monday morning before Ian went up to court. He had some information for Ian. LoMurko would bring the blueberry muffins.

6

Ian bought several cups of coffee because he didn't know if the bureau coffee urn was perking yet. Nor did he know how many others would be showing up with LoMurko. Smitty and Robbie were there when Ian arrived, eager to start doing something about 11. 11 possessed a name, but, forevermore, he would be just plain 11.

LoMurko showed up with a blueberry muffin half eaten in his left hand. His right hand was busy running around the room shaking everyone else's hand. He'd already been in contact with Robbie and Smitty.

LoMurko was in charge of the briefing. "11 has been divorced for the last seven years. He has no children. His mother and father are both deceased. He has a brother, Austin, who is a correction officer at San Quentin State Prison in California. The brother has not seen 11 in more than five years. The last time was when they both attended their mother's funeral service. They do not like each other and have little to do with each other. Austin knows very little about what 11 does for a living. He thinks he is some kind of a bookkeeper. He likes his former sister-in-law more than he likes his brother and touches base with her around the holidays. He says the divorce was very bitter. The ex claims 11 is vengeful, resentful and abusive. We have not talked to her yet, but she shouldn't be too difficult to locate. We think she is in the Chicago area. She is not the person he would run to if he were hiding. We will find her and check her out.

"11 is employed at the Citi main office in the bookkeeping department. Les Harris is over there this morning to talk to his boss, and we should be hearing from Les shortly.

"We have learned from his neighbors that 11 was not looking forward to serving on any jury. He'd been complaining ever since he got his summons. This was, of course, in keeping with his high sense of civic duty. He told a couple of neighbors that he was selected to be on a jury and that it sounded like it was going to be a murder case. So that part fits. The neighbors all say that there came a time when he disappeared. No one was certain when, but one day, he was no longer around. He stopped coming home in the evening and leaving in the morning. At least no one saw him do that. One neighbor swears he saw 11 get out of a car and run into his house a few days ago. He waited, was going to ask him how the case was going, but 11 ran out of his house carrying a suitcase, jumped into the car and left. The neighbor said there was nothing particularly distinctive about the car. He remembered it was green and kind of new and shiny. He is no good on makes or years. No one else saw that happen, and no one from the neighborhood has seen him since. So we need to hear from his job and figure out what we can learn from his ex."

At that moment Ian's phone rang. He picked it up, listened and said, "Put him on." Covering the mouthpiece, he announced that it was Les Harris. He handed the phone to LoMurko.

They all replenished their coffees as Les reported to his boss. After a few questions, LoMurko hung up.

"Well, it seems that when 11 didn't show up for work today, his immediate supervisor called the number at the courthouse. He heard on the news that there had been a hung jury in the mannequin case last Friday, and he expected 11 at work today. He got a confirmation that the case ended late Friday. He thought that 11 would be in for his paycheck before the weekend. The boss will call Les if anyone sees or hears from 11. I'm betting that isn't going to happen."

Ian's phone rang again. This time it was another detective from Manhattan South Homicide reporting to his boss. A check of all outgoing commercial flights from all the airports in the area turned up nothing. Photos of 11 obtained from the DMV were shown to ticket agents at Penn Station, Grand Central and the Port Authority Bus Terminal with no luck, but that was an iffy move at best. They all agreed to up the intensity of the search for 11. They notified the usual authorities, distributed his picture by wire and started alerting some of the other contacts that only good cops know how to use.

As they were breaking up, Ian received the annoying news that Nails Ballen was in the reception area hoping to see Ian before he went up to court. Ian told Robbie and Smitty to stay for the meeting. Jim LoMurko hung around until Nails came in and Ian introduced him. LoMurko gave him that withering "I'm going to slice your nuts off" look he reserved for very select few.

"What was that look all about?" asked Nails. "You'd think I neglected to bathe for a month. And what are these detectives doing here? Can't we have a lawyer-to-lawyer conversation about what we are going to do without cops being here?"

"Nails, we have known each other for a long time. I am not going to bullshit you. We think there was something fishy about that hung jury."

"You don't think I was involved in anything like that, do you?"

"I'm not saying you were; I'm just telling you what is going on. If there was some hanky-panky, the hanky is going to come out of the panky, because I am pissed."

"Well, I hope that isn't going to cloud your judgement on where we should be going with this case. You have always conducted yourself in a professional manner, and I wouldn't expect you to act any differently because of your suspicions, no matter how ridiculous they may be."

Smitty got up from his seat and walked toward the door. "You're going to have to excuse me. I'll be outside if you need me. I want to prepare some subpoenas to serve on Nails' bank accounts."

Ian told a startled Nails that Smitty was only kidding. "What do you want, Nails?"

"I want you to see if we can't dispose of this case with some sort of a plea. I know your entire case now and it is going to be much easier for me to defend it."

"Nails, even if I wanted to offer you a plea, I could not. It would be an insult to the Rusk family and to the memory of Mary Rusk. As far as knowing my entire case, you are mistaken about that also. We have other evidence in this case which we will present in the second trial that we didn't in the first because we thought it was superfluous. Now we know nothing is superfluous, so prepare yourself for the long haul."

"If I can't get a plea, I will probably get out of the case. I can't afford to spend more weeks on trial on this case. It is already costing me."

"The fact that you may not have gotten a large enough retainer is of no concern to me nor will it be to Judge Hastings. You may try to get out of the case, but I'm betting the judge is not going to permit that."

"He will if you consent."

"So that is what this is all about. You want my consent for you to be able to get out of representing Conti for a long retrial. Well, forget it. If you are prepared to give us some information on this juror number 11 thing, I would be very interested, but short of that, as I said, forget it."

"I know nothing about juror number 11 other than that he was smarter than the other jurors."

"*Ok*, Nails. I'll see you in court in a few minutes."

"You may want to change your mind. It turns out Mary Rusk wasn't all you made her out to be."

If that parting remark was intended to get Ian's attention, it worked.

1

"PLEASE HELP ME"

That was the last line of the letter Ian found stuffed in his IN box. The mailroom had delivered it to Vince O'Rielly, Ian's bureau chief, and Vince routed it to Ian with a yellow Stickum attached to the envelope. On the Stickum was written, "What's this?" Ian turned back to the first page and started to read it again. He stopped and reached for the envelope.

The letter was written on yellow legal paper, but the envelope looked like it came from a stationary set. In the upper left-hand corner was the word "Handy," and underneath that were the numbers "4773908586." The third line said "DSH," and the fourth line, "Dannemora, NY." There was no zip code.

Ian got up from his desk and walked to Vince O'Rielly's office. Vince's secretary, Mable Heath, was at lunch, so Ian looked into the office. He found the boss in his easy chair to the right of his large desk. Vincent O'Rielly was a twenty-two-year veteran of the office. He had been recruited right out of Fordham Law School, and soon became a top trial lawyer. He was a short man, but well built. Vince possessed all the positive traits of an Irishman: an overwhelming smile, sparkling eyes, quick wit and a sharp sense of humor. If an Irishman had any negative traits, he possessed none of them. He would take a drink now and then. He was loyal to his men to a fault. He believed none of them ever did anything wrong. He was known by the entire New York City Police Department. They loved him, and he loved them. He frequently said that he would have been a cop instead of a lawyer, but he was too short to pass the physical. He would leave the office early only occasionally to take his wife for chemo treatments. It was colon cancer, and the prognosis was not good. Unfortunately, his son and daughter were grown, married and on the West Coast. They were not around to help.

"Got a second?"

"Sure, Ian. Come on in."

"You routed this letter to me," Ian said waving the letter. "It is from an inmate up at Clinton State Prison in Dannemora. Actually, he is in the State Hospital for the Criminally Insane attached to the prison, so I guess he is technically a patient. He writes that his doctors tell him he will have a better chance of getting well if he confesses his sins. He writes that he is responsible for the bludgeoning murder of a man in the hallway outside his apartment in a building in lower Manhattan. From what I can see, I think it may be the Freeman case."

"The TV news guy? Didn't he produce one of those TV News magazines?"

"That's the one."

"How old is that case?"

"It's old. I think I was a raw rookie in the bureau when it happened, but I'm having Mike pull the file. I thought I'd call LoMurko. He loves these old cold cases. Ok?"

"Great. Use my phone."

LoMurko wanted to come right over to Ian's office, and in a half an hour, he was there. Finishing his popsicle, he said, "I love it. Nothing better than breaking a cold case. Shows we never quit, we never give up, we are the best."

"Easy, captain. Here, read the letter."

LoMurko sat down to read. "I see the tip-off is that he mentions the hose nozzle. There was a hose nozzle in the Freeman case."

"Yup, without that it could be any case. And don't forget, this guy is nuts. He may have no idea where the murder took place. But I would start with the Freeman case. I'll bet that's it."

The Homicide Bureau has a duty chart. Each of the rookies and even some of the middle-level assistants are assigned a twenty-four-hour period. The duty ADA will respond to the police precinct if there is a homicide committed in Manhattan and a perpetrator is apprehended; or, if there is no one arrested, but the police need some legal assistance, like getting a search warrant; or, if it is just a big deal, heavy duty case, which is translated as meaning the press is interested, and the Freeman case was one of those. The duty ADA was no longer in the office., but he had started an investigation, and the case file was now being delivered to Ian's office.

Ian looked through the file and picked up the phone to call LoMurko. "I think you got a bit of a break. I just got our file and the squad detective from the Wall Street Squad, who caught the case, was Fred Starvins."

"That's no break. That's awful. He is a great detective. I can't steal a case from Freddie."

"He retired last month. He has a job with Wells Fargo. His retirement dinner is a week from Friday. I suggest you buy a ticket."

"Really? Freddie Starvins has retired?"

"Maybe he'll come back when he hears that one of his cases is about to be solved by you. Anyway, the original homicide detective, I think, is also out of the picture—Pete Higgins. Doesn't he have cancer?"

"Yeah, Pete is not doing well. But I'll let him do anything he wants to do, or is able to do. It might help him to be involved even if from home."

"No matter what else we do, I should respond to this letter. I don't want this guy to think we are ignoring him. Nor do I want him to change his mind about talking to us."

An initial check on the letter writer revealed that his name was Roger Handy. He was a thirty-year-old with a history of burglaries. He was arrested about a year after the Freeman killing for another burglary on the east side. The apartment owner came home and found Handy sitting on the floor of his living room. He was looking at a large framed photograph of the apartment owner's grandmother. He was sobbing. The owner, terrified, ran next door and called the police. When the uniformed officers arrived, Handy was still sitting there sobbing. He kept saying "Mommy" over and over again as he stared at the photograph. He was taken to the psych ward of Bellevue Hospital where he maintained that he didn't realize he was burglarizing his "mother's apartment." Eventually, after sufficient medication, he was declared sane enough to stand trial. He pleaded guilty and, because of his prior record, was sentenced to ten years in state prison. Shortly after being sentenced, he suffered a further breakdown and was transferred to Dannemora State Hospital.

Handy put some significant details in his letter including, most importantly, that he had not been alone. So there was another person out there who took part in this murder. Another person who'd killed once and was obviously capable of killing again.

Another telling fact in Handy's letter was that the nozzle of the hallway fire hose was used to bludgeon the victim. This fact wasn't reported publicly. It was the kind of thing only the killer would have known. Ian was convinced that the letter was legit and worth following up.

Later in the day Ian called LoMurko. "Hi, Jim, have you found the homicide squad file?"

"We have."

"Is it the Freeman case?"

"Sure looks like it."

"What do you want done?" Ian asked.

"Go get a confession from him."

"Ah yes! A confession from a crazy man in a hospital for the criminally insane. That should stand up in court. There's no problem with that one."

"So what are you saying? We don't have enough to arrest this guy even if he talks?"

"I guess you might need the skills of a legal magician here. Maybe a little hocus pocus, a little alla kazam, a dash of Hey Bob E Re Bob from your Dear Waspson."

"You're as mad as Handy."

"For openers, we need some detectives. We need some guys to go over the files from beginning to end. I have no idea what the crime scene guys found at that apartment. Handy's prints may be all over the place."

"They are not. No prints."

"Ok. You know that; I don't. What I'm saying is we have to put this thing together. There must be some evidence. It was a big case at the time. The press was all over it."

"Do you want any particular detectives?"

"Well, you might give some thought to assigning Smitty from your squad, and maybe we could get Robbie assigned from the Wall Street squad. They are already detailed here to me on the Conti case. They could pick up the Freeman case and work on it."

"Done. I'll call Tim at Wall Street." Tim was Captain Timothy MyGott, the commanding officer of the Wall Street Precinct. "So let's say by the end of the morning, you have Smitty and Robbie. What else do you need?"

"We need all the files. We need a meeting with everyone. We have to find out what the docs upstate can tell us. What are they allowed to tell us? Is there a privilege that exists between a prisoner and a state doctor? I don't know the answer to that question. Let's get Louie Balzo working on that. Louie," Ian yelled down the hallway and Louie came running in. Ian gave him a two-minute summary about what was going on and told him to get up to the library.

"We need to make arrangements to get up to Dannemora. It's at the ass end of the earth. We need to get authority to talk to Handy. We need a stenographer to be there with us. Lots of stuff."

"You're exhausting me," declared LoMurko. "I gotta go take a nap."

Ian reached out to Dr. Felix Herman. Flex Herman was the go-to shrink for the office. Whenever there was an insanity defense raised, Flex would conduct an initial examination and give the trial assistant a good idea whether the defense could be overcome. He knew everyone in his profession worth knowing.

Flex was a wee bit shot in the ass with himself. He was pompous and a little arrogant. With a huge head of grey hair, he dressed conservatively, often sporting a vest, even on warm days.

Ian wanted Flex to call the chief doctor at Dannemora. He was betting that Flex knew him and was sure that Flex could pave the way for their visit. He was right. Ian asked Flex if he thought it would help for Flex to come with them when they went to talk to Handy. Flex declined. He believed the Dannemora doctors had probably established a rapport with Handy and they would be more help than he, Flex, would be. Ian got the sense from Flex that the doctors were going to be helpful and that doctor-patient communication privileges were not going to be a problem.

LoMurko was taking care of the transportation issue. A New York City Police Department helicopter would get them there in a little under two hours. The chief of detectives had approved the helicopter.

He felt a moral obligation to get the second killer off the streets as soon as possible.

There are a group of stenographers who are assigned to the Homicide Bureau. Like the ADAs they have a duty chart. When an Assistant responds to the precinct, a stenographer also responds. The stenographer is responsible for taking a stenographic statement if the defendant chooses to waive his right to remain silent. He might also take a statement from witnesses.

Ian called the steno pool and asked for David Sean, who was in charge of the group of stenographers assigned to the Homicide Bureau. David was a young rookie at the same time Ian was. They grew up in the Homicide Bureau together and were good friends. Ian always believed that there were people who could make your life miserable and there were people who could make your life a joy. He cultivated a friendship with both groups. David fell in the joy category. Ian explained what was going on and that he needed someone to come to Dannemora with him. As a stenographer, in addition to the stenographic statement, David would also be responsible for making a video of the Q and A.

"This sounds like a job for the boss," declared the boss.

"I was hoping you would say that."

"Yes, we wouldn't want to leave this to anyone but the boss. When might we be taking this trip?"

"Don't know yet, but it could be soon. We are putting it together. It will be a one day up and back, so we don't have to pack."

"Rats, I was hoping to spend some time in the North Country."

"David, to you Yonkers is the North Country."

Flex called Ian to say that they were ready at Dannemora whenever New York was.

9

Ian needed to make one other call. Jim Vacco picked up his phone on the third ring.

"Vacco", he growled.

"Jim, it's Ian with a question."

"The answer is no."

Ian ignored him and plowed ahead, "Let's say you represent a guy who is convicted."

"Not possible."

"I know, but humor me. Let's say the guy is convicted and sentenced to state's prison for life. Does your representation of him end upon sentencing, or do you continue to represent him while he is serving his time, like for the rest of his life?"

"I can't talk about such a sensitive subject over the phone," claimed Vacco, looking for an excuse to have a drink with Ian. "We should meet at our usual place at six this evening."

Jim Vacco was the senior supervising attorney for the Legal Aid Society. The society had entered into a contract with the City of New York to represent the great majority of indigent defendants who trudged through the criminal justice system. Most of the defendants claimed to be indigent. Very few possessed the resources to retain the quality attorney most mortals would choose to have representing them in such an important matter as their freedom.

Just as some rookies right out of law school went to the District Attorney's Office, others went to the Legal Aid Society. Probably because of their upbringing, some were more comfortable defending and some more comfortable prosecuting. None of them knew anything.

These neophyte lawyers gained experience together, accepting their victories and defeats more calmly and stoically as time went on. As adversaries, they learned to have respect for each other. In due time, the zealousness of the adversarial position was tempered by the knowledge that they all were trying to do their best, irrespective of what side they were on.

There were exceptions. There were some ADAs who saw everything in black or white. There was never any grey area. There was never any doubt. If the cops arrested you, you deserved it and you were guilty and should be locked up for as long as the law allowed. They usually didn't make very good assistants.

Similarly, there were some legal aids who were "bomb throwers." They saw their mission as destroyers of the social order. No laws were good laws. The sole purpose of all authority was to suppress freedom. They usually were so busy hoping to overthrow the government, they did little to protect their individual clients.

As Ian and Vacco aged and gained more experience, their defeats were accepted with more grace and their victories with less exuberance, for they knew that the next time out, their roles could be reversed. They genuinely respected each other. Ian told many of his colleagues that if he ever got in criminal trouble, he would want Jim Vacco to defend him.

Vacco was a bit of a bull dog, both in appearance and demeanor: short, about 5'5", stocky, maybe 180 lbs. His voice was gruff, kind of hoarse. He was well tanned. He spent his weekends and spare time out at the paddock of Belmont Race Track. Vacco loved the ponies. Whether in court or at the race course, he was always well dressed. He spent a lot of money on clothes, and it showed. He was able to stay at the Legal Aid Society because his wife, whom he adored, was an heir to a popcorn fortune.

The Criminal Courts Building was on the west border of Chinatown in lower Manhattan. There were plenty of bars and restaurants in the surrounding neighborhoods. Vacco and Ian liked an unspectacular hunan restaurant a few blocks into Chinatown. Most people didn't even know it had a liquor license. It was generally patronized by tourists. The spicy hunan food was to die for, and the bar was usually empty.

Ching Chang, the owner, loved both Ian and Vacco. Ching did nothing to spiff up his place. You walked down a narrow staircase to get into the restaurant. Along the far wall was the bar.

It was understood that Ian was required to pay for his drinks. He was a public servant, and the DA would fire him if he thought he was drinking "on the arm," or free. Ching knew that rule didn't apply to Vacco, so Ching would make Vacco buy most of the rounds. Ching Chang bought about every other round.

Ching respected their privacy and would leave them alone, but would always accept an invitation to join them and "chew fat." This evening he would wait to be invited before he joined in.

Ian had arrived first and was seated at the end of the bar when Vacco came bounding in, shouting, "Set 'em up, Ching," at the top of his lungs.

"How come all of your arrivals are like a train wreck?" Ian asked.

Vacco slammed Ian on the back and said, "Quiet! Can't wait to have a drink with you. Haven't seen you since you started your latest hung jury. Have you recovered?"

"No, I'm still pissed."

"Get over it. It is only a trial."

Ching set beers down before his two friends and, as he retreated, said, "Call me when you need another."

Vacco thanked Ching, and then said to Ian, "The answer to your question is that our representation ends at the conclusion of the case and the case is considered concluded when final judgement is pronounced. So most judges after some dippy speech say, 'And therefore I sentence you to five to fifteen years in state's prison. Is there anything else?' When the defense attorney says there isn't, the judge says, 'That ends the case. Advise your client he has thirty days to file a notice of appeal.' Our job is finished."

"What about the appeal?"

"We do not automatically represent the defendant on appeal just because we represented him at trial. The defendant has to request us to represent him for the appeal. If we do, it is an entirely new case. Now tell me, which of my former clients are you about to screw over?"

"So, hypothetically, let's say you represented a guy who was convicted and he is sentenced to state's prison. His appeals are over, and five years later, I have evidence he committed a murder. I can go question him on that new case without worrying about the fact that you were his lawyer? I have no obligation to notify you?"

"That's right. You still have to give him his Miranda warning and he has to waive his right to be represented by an attorney, but that's right, in your hypothetical. However, you and I are friends and you wouldn't do that without telling me which of my former clients you are about to screw over."

"I am not screwing over anyone but I would like to talk to a guy Legal Aid represented, a burglar named Roger Handy."

"Roger Handy? I don't remember Roger. Did I represent him?"

"No. One of your colleagues named Emmit Soul represented him several years ago. I don't think I know Emmit."

"He didn't stay with us long. He went out and made money. He was a smart guy."

"Interesting," said Ian and then he told Vacco about the letter and the Freeman murder.

10

Some patrolmen are just interested in being patrolmen. That's all. Maybe because they grew up respecting the local cop on the beat—the jovial, if somewhat feared, Officer Murphy who kept peace in the neighborhood and took care of all the kids.

Other patrolmen are interested in advancement. As soon as they are eligible, they study for and take the sergeant's exam, then the lieutenant's exam, then the captain's exam, always studying and taking exams and hoping for a promotion up the civil service ladder.

Other patrolmen want nothing more than to get into the detective division. Some get there by showing an aptitude for investigative work while patrolmen. Some go into specialized bureaus like narcotics. Some have a "rabbi." They know someone who knows someone. Like all other areas of life, the New York City Police Department has its politics, its favorites. Who you know is usually more important than what you know.

Robbie was a case of cream rising to the top. Early on, because he was a youthful looking, slight, 150 lbs., 5'5" African American, he was recruited by the narcotics division and trained to be an undercover officer. He looked like a high school student and was easily able to worm his way into student bodies and purchase drugs from the shit head dealers who were enticing kids to get hooked.

He was a fitness freak and spent hours at the police academy gym working out, lifting weights, running and taking martial arts courses. He was rock solid and fast. He could take care of himself in a fight and run like hell if he had to.

He was raised by his mother and grandparents. His dad was killed in a drive-by shooting in Harlem when Robbie was ten. It happened as Robbie and his father were walking down 3rd Avenue. A car came around the corner of 132nd Street, and pulled up by a guy who was walking down the street. The guy started to run. The car chased him and someone in the back seat started firing an automatic weapon, spraying the street with bullets. The running guy was shot several times. One stray bullet hit Robbie's dad in the head. It killed him instantly. Robbie sat next to his father's body on 3rd Avenue holding his father's hand until the police arrived. He saw the man who was firing the automatic weapon and swore he would become a police officer someday and kill the man.

Robbie and his mother moved in with her parents. His mom worked for the New York City Transit Authority, made a respectable living and believed that education was the key to getting a better life. With the help of the grandparents, Robbie studied, got a scholarship to Fordham Prep and then Fordham University. Much to his mother's dismay, he turned down a chance to go to graduate school and entered the police academy. He graduated with honors.

It wasn't long before his undercover skills led him to work on other major investigations. He escaped with his life after a nine-month stint infiltrating the Black Panthers. After that, the department kept him under wraps for a while until they thought it was safe for him to return to regular detective work. He was assigned to the detective squad of the Wall Street Precinct. By then he was one of the youngest second-grade detectives and, if Ian had anything to say about it, he would soon be the youngest first-grade detective. The only time Robbie would beg off an assignment would be if his mother needed him. Clearly, he was cream.

Smitty was another matter. Born in the lower east side, he was given the unique name of Eustace Helper Smith after his father's probation officer Eustace Riley. His father called his probation officer "Eustace my Helper." Most of the kids Smitty grew up with became robbers, not cops. He went into the army after high school and found that, because of his service, he could get a pass into the NYPD.

The toughest part of the academy, for Smitty, was the physical regimen. He was a mess. He'd always loved food. His mother was Italian and a great cook, and Smitty didn't let her down. When most cadets were popping off twenty or thirty pushups, he could barely do two. Whether he would be able to pass the physical became an issue. He realized that he was in jeopardy of being busted out, and got three of his body-builder friends to get him in shape. He actually looked great by the time he graduated and became a probationary patrolman.

As time went by, though, his mother's cooking won out. To add to his woes, he married his grade school sweetheart, Ethel Ranzzoni, another Italian, who considered it her mission in life to make Smitty forget about his mother's cooking. She was accomplishing that mission. Weight was always going to be a problem for Smitty, but contentment was his mainstay. He was a happy man.

Smitty may not have been book smart, but there was no one who had more street smarts. He knew New Yorkers. He particularly knew New Yorkers who lived on the lower east side. As a patrolman, he was forever being brought in by the precinct captain to solve a local dispute. There seemed to be an innate fairness about his solutions, and he got few arguments. All this was done with a great sense of humor.

As his reputation flourished, an old-time deputy inspector, who knew Smitty's father, jumped at the opportunity to get Smitty into the detective bureau. He was assigned to Manhattan South Homicide where he excelled. He knew everyone south of Houston Street, and if he didn't know an informant with information on a case, he knew someone who knew someone. He was brought in, out of rotation, on the Mary Rusk case because of his familiarity with lower Manhattan.

When Ian was a rookie in the Homicide Bureau, Smitty was the homicide detective who caught Ian's first case. Smitty took pity on Ian, showed him the ropes, kept him out of trouble and they became fast friends. They worked several cases together mainly because Smitty's bosses in the PD finagled the work chart so that Smitty ended up on duty when Ian was too.

Smitty didn't always play by the rules. Maybe it was his upbringing, maybe it was that most of his friends and neighbors were borderline bad guys, maybe it was because some of the rules were stupid and no one knew that better than Smitty, but whatever it was, keeping him out of trouble was a time-consuming endeavor. Sometimes Smitty needed a lawyer; sometimes he needed Ian. All Ian knew was that Smitty was worth the effort. Also, quite honestly, there were times when it made sense to bend the rules.

11

There was a concern Ian wanted to share with Smitty and Robby. "Nails Ballen implied that he might have some information about Mary Rusk that he would drop at the retrial. I know we have done our due diligence, but I thought I owed it to the family to give them a heads up—"

"And you thought that the best way to do that would be by speaking to Adele," interrupted Smitty. "I would have thought you would seize this opportunity to spend some quality time with Brian. He is obviously the gate keeper of the family and the one who should know. Shouldn't you be talking to him?" Smitty's rotund face was lit up like a lighthouse beacon, his grin at least two feet wide. He loved to needle Ian. "So this is just some little scheme for you to feast your eyes on that little hotty," Smitty laughed.

"Smitty, give Ian a break," Robbie insisted. "He works here twenty-three hours a day. Let him have a little field trip every now and then. The fresh air will do him good."

"Don't misunderstand me, Robs. I'm all in favor of the man showing he might have some testosterone."

"Come on Smitty, it's time for me to buy you a beer. Is LoMurko sending over a car and driver?" Robbie asked. Ian confirmed that he was.

Smitty reached into his pocket and pulled out a wad of bills. "Need some extra cash?"

'I'm meeting her at the doctors' lounge, and I'll take her to the cafeteria for a cup of coffee."

Smitty threw his hands up in the air in disgust. "Now that is a really dumb idea. Why don't you ask her to take a walk with you, and when you get outside, ask her if there is a favorite place she has in the neighborhood? Then take her there and buy her a drink. Maybe even dinner. This is just plain, old-fashioned, good investigative technique. She is going to feel much more free to be honest with you if she is some place private rather than the crowded hospital cafeteria."

Robbie added his agreement as he pulled Smitty out of the room.

The honest truth of the matter was that Ian wondered why he was doing this. He was only mildly troubled by Nails' remarks. He was confident that they were dealing with a perfect victim, if there was such a thing. All their background checks confirmed that. Still there was always the possibility of some kind of problem. After all, Mary was a very attractive lady who enjoyed a normal dating life. There was also the possibility that Nails was up to no good.

Ian admitted that he liked the idea of getting out of the office, of going uptown and of being able to go home after the meeting instead of staying in the office. He also liked the idea of seeing Adele. She was easy to look at. She was clearly bright, and Ian admired the way she took care of her mother. He also liked the way she was handling herself through this awful ordeal. *What the hell*, Ian thought, *let's enjoy the trip.*

When Jim LoMurko heard what Ian was planning on doing, he insisted on providing his car and driver. He knew that, otherwise, Ian would take the subway. Ian was not one to take advantage of the perks of the job—all the more reason to help him out.

The unmarked squad car pulled into the circle in front of New York Presbyterian Hospital. Danny Wright, LoMurko's driver, was a rookie detective in the homicide squad. "Do you want me to wait for you and give you a ride Mr. MacDonald?"

"Danny, I appreciate the respect, but please call me Ian. Mr. MacDonald is my father. And no, I don't have any idea how long this is going to take. I'll get myself home."

In less than a minute after Ian arrived, Adele came walking down the hall. Ian didn't know anyone could look so stunning in a white doctor's smock. Her blond hair was pulled back in a pony tail. She wore a stylish pair of glasses that she never wore while at court. She had put on make-up. The obligatory stethoscope hung around her neck. There was a smile on her face. "Hi, Ian," she greeted.

"Hello, Adele. I've never seen you with glasses on."

"It's more important that I see things here at the hospital. Should we go to the cafeteria and get a cup of coffee? I only have another forty-five minutes to go before my shift is over."

"Sure. How long is a shift?"

"They vary, but this one started at 8:00 AM yesterday."

"Oh my God! You must be exhausted. I wish you'd told me. We can do this another time."

"I'm ok. This hasn't been a bad shift. I actually got some sleep last night."

Ian stopped as they were walking down the hallway to the cafeteria. "Look Adele, how about this? How about we see how the next forty-five minutes go, and if nothing comes up, we go for a walk. You tell me your favorite place in the neighborhood and we talk there." Ian was proud of himself for remembering Smitty's lines.

"You wouldn't mind waiting a few more minutes?"

"Not at all."

"Honest?"

"Honest."

"I would love to do that. Wait for me here in the doctors' lounge. I'll be able to sneak out a little early unless there is some kind of disaster. We are all pretty good about covering for each other. I should be back in a few minutes. Don't be looking at all the nurses while I'm gone." Adele blushed. "I'm sorry, I shouldn't have said that. You can look anywhere you want." She turned and hurried off.

Down the street was the ER Bar and Grill. They found an empty booth toward the back of the bar room area and sat down. It was obvious that this was a doctors' and nurses' hangout since Adele was greeted by several of the patrons. She seemed to be happy to be seen with Ian.

"They have great Swiss Beer on tap here. Want one?"

"I didn't know the Swiss made beer."

"Everyone makes beer. Even my dad makes beer."

"Technically, I am working and, technically, I am not supposed to be drinking when I'm working, but I guess if I drink one Swiss beer in the interest of advancing my investigatory techniques, it wouldn't hurt."

"And I won't—what's the word—rat on you."

"Honest?"

"Honest."

Adele said nothing until the waiter left the beers and moved on to another table.

"So tell me, what's happened. I feel like something bad has happened."

"It's probably nothing, but I felt I should let your family know and you were the best one to tell. Mr. Ballen—"

"Nails," Adele interrupted, smiling.

"Yes, Nails, he came out with a remark before court the other day when I told him that we were not offering any plea other than to the entire indictment. He said, and I am quoting him, 'You may want to change your mind. It turns out Mary Rusk wasn't all you made her out to be.'"

"Oh my God! What's that supposed to mean? It sounds like he's discovered something about Mary."

"That's exactly what he would like us to think. Keep in mind that he was saying this in the context of attempting to get me to offer a plea. I think it's all a big bluff on his part, but I felt obligated to tell you. I have been through this before with your parents, but not with you. If there is anything about Mary, anything at all, that you think I should know, please tell me. Forewarned is forearmed or whatever that saying is. You know what I mean? If I know about something, maybe I can head it off. I don't want your family being hurt any more than they already have been."

Adele shook her head very slowly. "I can't think of what there could be, Ian. To me, Mary was a saint. She told me everything. I heard all about her dates, about the guys she fought off, about the old lechers at work. She never mentioned that she slept with anyone and we were so close. I think she would have told me." Her eyes started to tear up, and she grabbed her purse and found a hanky. "I'm sorry. I guess I'm a little tired. I just can't stand the idea of them trying to do this to Mary. Isn't raping her and murdering her enough? Now they want to make her out to be some kind of slut."

Ian found himself reaching over the table and gently touching her hand. "I will not let them do that, Adele. I promise you." Adele left her hand in Ian's. He realized what he was doing and released her hand. "Look, this is all probably a lot of crap. Suffice it to say, if you think of anything, no matter how off the wall it might be, tell me. Let me decide if it has any importance or relevance. Don't think of something and neglect to tell me because you think it isn't important. You are too close to this."

"I will tell you Ian, and thanks, you have been the best. I am so grateful."

"Do you want to get a bite to eat?"

"I don't think so. I'm kind of beat and I don't think I would be very good company. I would love a raincheck. Any chance of that?"

"Absolutely!"

"Honest?"

"Honest."

They walked slowly back to the intern dorm. It was only two blocks. Ian was wishing it were longer. He bid her good night and started to walk over to the subway on Lex. There was a bounce in his step. He felt good.

His thoughts were interrupted by the *beep-beep* of a car pulling up to the curb. The passenger window went down and Danny Wright said, "Hop in, Ian. I'll give you a ride home."

12

They were all at the East River Heliport by seven forty-five in the morning.

Robbie and Smitty had all the police reports produced since the inception of the Freeman investigation. There were two files, each about seven inches thick. They'd been reviewing them since the previous afternoon. David Sean was wrestling with all his equipment.

At 7:55 AM, the *thump-thump* of the police helicopter rose up from the south and descended into the East River Heliport. By 8:00 AM, they were all buckled in and ready to take off. Smitty announced that this was his first helicopter ride. He wondered if helicopter passengers ever got sick. The co-pilot gave him a bucket.

A little under two hours later, they set down at the Plattsburgh Airport. Smitty opened his eyes for the first time. Ian swore he heard Smitty praying. Smitty denied it and said, "Piece of cake." A state police car pulled up to the helicopter, and they all got in for a cramped twenty-five-minute ride to the prison hospital. The trooper said, "Welcome to Plattsburgh, New York, where the weather is the fourth of July and winter."

The north side of Cook Street, the main street in Dannemora, New York, is dominated by a huge cement wall, maybe twenty-five or thirty feet tall. It runs along the south side of Clinton State Prison. At the east end of the wall, there is an old stone house that is right out of a Charles Addams' cartoon. A circular drive takes you to a portico and steps leading up to the front entrance.

Superintendent Dr. Maurice Heller was waiting for them on the top step. He insisted that everyone call him Mo. After all the introductions, he invited everyone to his office, a huge room, on the main floor. He introduced Bella, his secretary, who took orders for coffees and showed everyone to a large box of donuts they had purchased for the occasion, going all out on Southern hospitality. It was much appreciated after the long helicopter ride.

"We have things set up for you. I have Dr. Dick Broderick, Handy's primary doctor, alerted to come whenever you are ready for him. Handy has signed a waiver of confidentiality, giving us permission to answer any questions about his condition, his treatment, his future prognosis—in a word, anything. It is the broadest possible waiver. He is looking forward to speaking with you, and I think he will tell you everything. There has been a marked improvement in his demeanor ever since he decided to get this off his chest."

"Thanks doctor. This is very helpful and you have already answered some of our questions," Ian added. "We were concerned about the privilege, and we are concerned about his present mental capacity in the unlikely event that we are ever to prosecute him. Would we be in a position to use any confessions he might give us today?"

"I can't answer what some judge might rule. I can tell you that Handy suffers from schizophrenia and is presently being medicated for that disease. The medication is helpful, but I would not want to see him leave a psychiatric hospital. I think he might be a danger to himself and to others. He is generally lucid. He usually knows where he is and why he is here. But there are times when he is delusional and takes on some other personality. He firmly believes that if he makes amends for what he did, he will be better. We happen to believe the same thing. One's conscience can be a weighty matter. You will have a better sense of his condition after you speak to him. The bottom line is that he is not going anywhere for the foreseeable future. We do not intend to send him back to the general prison population. I guess that could change, but I think that is unlikely."

"Is there some way that we could be notified if that were contemplated?"

"We will put it in his file that you are to be contacted."

David Sean was set up in the stark conference room. There was a long conference table with chairs around it. The walls were painted grey, and the floor was a grey linoleum. It was depressing. Dr. Broderick, a skinny bespectacled bald man in a white doctor's coat, spent about half an hour briefing everyone on what Handy would say. It was agreed that Broderick should be present during the questioning and that he should feel free to interrupt if he thought that was necessary. Broderick warned Ian that Handy would probably cry, but that should not stop Ian from asking questions and insisting that Handy answer. He said that Handy likes to be dominated and ordered about. It gives him a sense of security. Crying was one of Handy's traits. He cried whenever he talked about the crime.

Ian was curious about how much Handy would talk about his accomplice.

"You are going to get an earful."

13

Handy must have liked the hospital's food. The mug shot taken at his most recent arrest about five years ago showed a wiry, gaunt guy with a pronounced chin and nose. Sitting in front of Ian was an obese man without any chin. Just a huge neck that ran from his forehead to his chest. Ian spent the first few minutes making sure they were all talking about, and to, the same guy. This was Handy.

He was grinning, all bouncy and full of cheer. "Hi guys, so nice of you to come and see me. Where do you want me to begin?" He was like a puppy about to be taken for his morning walk.

Ian spent the next few minutes running through the Miranda warning. It was so obvious that Handy wanted to waive his rights that Ian felt it safe to emphasize his right not to talk to anyone. But nothing was going to stop this guy.

"Suppose we start by you telling us what you did."

"Well, I went with Hal to this rich guy's apartment and we killed him. That's about it. Excuse me." He started to cry. "Every time I talk about what we did, I cry. Can't help it. Please forgive me. For crying I mean. I don't expect you to forgive me for the killing part. I didn't do the hitting. Hal did the hitting. But I did do the holding. I held him while Hal hit him. I told Hal to stop the hitting, but he just kept on doing it. Hal is a little crazy."

Hal was the main culprit, but Henry was not denying his own involvement. He kept crying. It was Hal's idea to go to this guy's apartment, but Henry went along willingly. More crying.

"What can you tell us about Hal? Who is he?"

Henry thought his last name might be Jackson or Johnson. He really only knew him as Hal. When Hal worked, it was usually as a super or a super's helper in an apartment house. He hung out around the Port Authority Bus Terminal over on 8th Avenue. He loved to pickpocket or otherwise scam the tourists coming off the buses into the city. He always worked the long-distance buses.

Hal knew about Freeman from working as a super's helper in the same building a few years before the killing. He only worked there for a day or two, and then he quit. Freeman's toilet needed to be fixed, and Hal got a good look at the apartment when he was up there. Hal said that they would be able to get valuable jewelry because Freeman was always wearing bracelets and a lot of gold.

That was how Hal worked. Whenever he accepted a super's job, he would always take a good look at the apartments to see what the tenants owned. He would make a note of it and then figure out how to burglarize the place. Henry burglarized several apartments with Hal.

"Why did you kill him?"

Handy was silent for almost a minute. He kept looking at Dr. Broderick, then his hands and then back to Dr. Broderick. Ian was afraid he was going to clam up. He decided to suggest that everyone take a break when Handy started to talk very quietly, almost in a whisper.

"That is the part that makes no sense. I thought that Hal tied the guy up. He was lying on the living room floor. We told him to remain quiet. He seemed scared to death. He was shaking and whimpering 'Please don't hurt me.' We told him we wouldn't as long as he was quiet and remained tied up. We were collecting everything we could in two separate pillow cases. We finished grabbing everything we wanted and were leaving. As we got out in the common hallway and the apartment door was about to close, there he is. He got loose. He is standing there looking at us. Another five seconds and we would have been gone.

"Why did he come after us? He freed himself and was coming after us, calling us names, really vile names. The three of us are out in the hallway. Hal shuts him up by putting his hand over the guy's mouth. He tells me to hand him the fire hose that was in one of those enclosures you see in some apartment house hallways. I grab the nozzle and hand it to Hal and Hal starts hitting, and hitting, and hitting, and hitting." Tears and more tears. "I was holding the guy at first, but after the first hit, I didn't have to hold him. He slumped to the floor and Hal kept hitting." Henry kept sobbing.

Henry said he panicked and ran for the stairwell. He left Hal, the guy and the pillow case behind. He ran all the way downstairs and got out onto the street and ran from the building. He said he ran for days. He doesn't know what happened to Hal. He doesn't know what Hal did with the stuff they took.

He thought he saw Hal one more time, about a month later, and when he saw him, he ran again for days. He told Ian that if Ian ever saw Hal, Ian should run because Hal is crazy. He has a violent temper and is nuts.

After Ian was finished, he made sure that Henry would be able to write to him if there was anything else he wanted to tell him. Henry cried and told Ian how much better he felt.

Ian helped David pack up all his equipment and the trooper took them to the airport. From the time Smitty got on the helicopter to the time they landed at the East River Heliport, he never once opened his eyes.

14

11 had enjoyed his week at Crescent Moon Cove. The accommodations were great. He'd assumed that he was being closely watched and, for that reason, had followed the instructions meticulously, except for one—he didn't destroy the instructions. He figured they would be his ace in the hole if they were stupid enough to try and cheat him out of his money. He'd hid the one-page instructions under a removable liner in his suitcase. In another thirty minutes, he would go to the resort store. As soon as he got his money, he would check out, pay his bill in cash, take a taxi to the airport and look at the flight board. He would pick a country and buy a first-class ticket. He wasn't going to wait until Saturday.

The resort store was at the far end of the property, out of the way and inconvenient. In a resort like this, if a vacationer wanted something, he called room service. Few people used the store. 11 hopped on his bike and peddled along the beach. He wanted to be down there by four thirty so that he could enter the store at exactly four forty-five. That was exactly what he did.

There were only three people in the store. Two men were checking out the wine section, and a clerk was behind the counter. 11 approached the clerk. "A fifth of Dewar's Black label please." The clerk reached up, grabbed a bottle of Dewar's and handed it to him. "I'll also have a bag of Bruner's pretzel snacks and I believe you have a package for Mr. Ralph." With those words, the two men checking out the wine pulled guns and shouted, "This is a stickup. On the floor." Cradling his Dewar's, 11 hesitated and turned toward the men. The taller of the two fired three shots into the middle of 11's forehead. Then they emptied the cash register and fled.

The terrified clerk lay on the floor with his hands over his eyes. When he was certain there was no one else in the store, he slowly got to his feet and looked around. He saw his customer lying on the floor in an expanding puddle of blood. The back of his head was missing. The clerk passed out.

Ian was in a meeting with Vince O'Rielly. It was six thirty, but both men had been busy all day and this was the first chance they had to talk. Mable Heath, O'Rielly's secretary, reluctantly opened the door and stuck her head in. There was instant silence. "Ian, urgent," she said, and she disappeared. O'Rielly knew that only the most important calls got past Mable during a meeting so he waved Ian out of the room.

It was LoMurko.

"I got good news and I got bad news; which do you want first?"

"Jim, you know I hate it when you do that. What's up?"

"I take that as wanting the good news first. We think 11 has been located."

"Fantastic! Where is he?"

"He is in the morgue. That would be the bad news."

"In the morgue? What do you mean he's in the morgue? Is he dead?"

"Wow, Mrs. MacDonald didn't raise any dummies. We have to talk. I should be over there in ten minutes unless there is bad traffic."

LoMurko came into Ian's office followed by Smitty, Robbie and two other detectives from Manhattan South Homicide. Ian knew there was trouble when he saw that LoMurko was not eating anything.

"What the hell happened?"

'Well, there is this snazzy place in Jamaica. That's Jamaica, West Indies, kid, not Queens. It's called the Crescent Moon Cove Resort. There was a robbery there this afternoon in the resort store. A customer was shot and killed. Right after the hung jury, we sent 11's picture to some of our guys in a narcotics task force down in Jamaica. When they got the word that a guy from New York was shot, they hustled out to the cove. The body had been removed to the morgue. They went to the morgue with their picture and made the match. They immediately informed the locals, and 11's villa has been sealed. I have hinted to them that there might be a drug connection and they have agreed to go over to the villa with some DEA agents and babysit the place. The question is what do you want done and the answer is for us to get somebody down there ASAP. So why don't you give Smitty and Robbie a kiss goodbye and wish them luck."

Ian took LoMurko with him into O'Rielly's office and explained the problem. O'Rielly picked up his phone and asked Mable to get "Seth in Washington." Ian didn't know who Seth was, but when he got off the phone, O'Rielly said, "I don't think anyone will touch that villa for a while, but get your asses down there now."

Fortunately, there was a Jet Blue flight leaving for Montego Bay in an hour. The detectives would be able to get on it even if they sat in the galley.

Crescent Moon Cove was not accustomed to murders, and they were not handling it well. The yellow police tape surrounding the store and the villa was a constant reminder of the tragedy, and management wanted it out of there as soon as possible. The narcotics task force guys did a great job of keeping everyone away. The local police were pissed and were making frantic phone calls to get the Jamaican big wigs involved.

Robbie and Smitty were met at the airport They were transported to the resort with sirens blaring. As they came up to the villa, the narcotics boss said, "Do what you got to do as fast as you can. I don't think we are going to be able to hold this place secure for much longer."

Robbie told Smitty to get to work inside; he would schmooze with everyone outside.

There wasn't much for Smitty to do. The place hardly looked lived in. There was one suit hanging in the closet. There was some shaving equipment and other toiletries in a Dopp kit in the bathroom. There was a suitcase opened on the bed and an attaché case over by the desk. Smitty tried to open the attaché case, but it was locked. He reached into his pocket for his jackknife, but thought better of springing the lock. He put the case on the bed next to the suitcase and then dumped everything out of the suitcase. There were only items of clothes, underwear, socks, some light weight shirts, two pairs of Bermuda shorts and a floppy hat. There were no papers, no airline tickets, no money.

Smitty muttered "Amateur" under his breath as he found the loose edging of the suitcase lining. He worked it up and out, and found the instruction sheet. Smitty quickly read it. He pulled up his shirt and shoved the paper into his boxer shorts and then tucked in his shirt. He reset the lining, and replaced the clothing. He picked up the attaché case and walked outside. "This is the only item of interest," he said holding up the attaché case. "Contrary to our information, I didn't find any hint of narcotics, but you guys should take a look."

"We will be happy to relieve you of that case," a smiling Jamaican police officer said. There were all kinds of ribbons and medals on his chest and down his sleeve. Smitty figured he must be a general. At that moment, a Mercedes limo pulled up, the driver got out and ran to the passenger side rear door. As soon as he opened it, a huge man in a black suit with a white pearl cane got out of the car. Smitty's general bowed so low, it was clear that this was the boss of bosses.

The boss looked around, and there was silence. "We have done all we can do to assist you and cooperate with your State Department. We are deeply sorry that you have lost one of your citizens in this reprehensible felony murder. You may be assured that we will locate and apprehend the perpetrators. Now I have been instructed by our prime minister to take control of this investigation, the crime scene and this villa. He has informed your State Department of our decision."

"Excuse me, sir," interjected Smitty, "but I found that attaché case by the desk in the villa. I tried to open it and found it locked. We have reason to believe that the case has narcotics or money which would be evidence in a major investigation we are conducting in New York. It would be most helpful if we could be present when you open the case. Do you think that would be possible?"

Robbie thought he would faint. He'd never heard Smitty be so polite and solicitous.

"Of course," the huge man replied. "Baker, get your equipment and open the case." The man called Baker took some wedge like tool, slipped it in the end of the attaché case and sprung it open. Several thousands of dollars spilled out onto the ground, only money, nothing else.

"That would be the evidence we are looking for," declared Smitty.

"It will be counted, vouchered and secured in our property clerk's office."

"Any chance we could take it back to New York?"

"No, there is no chance. Absolutely none."

Robbie and Smitty checked the flights back to New York, and decided that they could speak to the store clerk in the morning. After they got in their hotel room and locked the door, Robbie said, "Ok Smitty, what's up? You gave up that attaché case much too easily."

"This is what's up." He pulled up his shirt, reached into his boxers and pulled out the paper. "11 was set up. He was sent to his death. Whoever hired him had no intention of paying him and didn't want to have to worry about him talking."

Robbie spent a few minutes reading and rereading the instructions. "It's late, but let's call Ian and give him a briefing. He'll want to hear these developments."

Ian was glad that Smitty found the instruction sheet, but uncomfortable about how he did it. He told Robbie to find some place to make a copy, then get it to narcotics and tell them to figure out some way for the Jamaican authorities to "find it."

After the shooting, the clerk had been taken to the hospital, given a quick exam and cleared to go home. The resort gave him the next day off. Narcotics gave Robbie and Smitty a ride out to his home.

The clerk said that he'd seen the victim several times during the week before his death. He thought the victim was an alcoholic, because he seemed to buy a fifth of scotch a day. He was surprised when he asked for Dewar's Black Label because he had always ordered Chivas Regal.

He thought he remembered the victim asking for some pretzels and some sort of package just before the shooting. The clerk knew nothing about a package. He never would agree to accept something that was to be delivered to someone else. He would tell the person to leave the package with the front desk.

He never saw the two stickup men before. He didn't see much of them this time because he hit the floor as soon as he was told to. No, he would not be able to identify them. Yes, he is sure no one gave him a package that one of the vacationers would come and pick up. No, he doesn't know a Mr. Ralph and has never heard of a Mr. Ralph.

They left the clerk's home and arrived at the airport in time for their return flight to New York. LoMurko sent a car to pick them up at the airport. With sirens blaring, they were at Ian's office in forty minutes.

Ian was amazingly calm. "Well, my father would say, 'The Lord giveth and the Lord taketh away.' We found 11—that's the giveth. He can tell us nothing about who hired him, who promised to pay him and who killed him—that's the taketh away. But we do know this wasn't some accidental killing during the course of a robbery. It looks more like a phony robbery that was concocted to cover up a murder. It certainly explains three shots to the forehead."

"Where do we go from here?" asked Smitty.

"I think we should let LoMurko handle the communications with the Jamaican authorities. He can watch and see what they do and what they tell us. I would be shocked if they catch the assassins, but if they do, he can tell them we will do whatever we can to help the police down there. Anything anyone can do to find out who hired them sure would help."

15

A second letter arrived from Handy. Unlike the first, this one was addressed directly to Assistant District Attorney Ian MacDonald. Ian stared at it as it lay in his IN box. Handy's return address was clearly printed in the upper left-hand corner of the envelope. What was this all about? Was Handy about to recant his confession? Was he writing to tell Ian he made everything up? Ian picked up the letter and started to read it.

"Dear Assistant District Attorney MacDonald:

I can't tell you how happy I am for you coming to see me. I am a new person. The docs tell me I am getting better. Anyway, there is something else I would like you to know. I think telling you about it will make me feel even better, but I'm hoping you won't let me get into trouble.

Anyway, I have a cousin. He is my mother's (dead) sister's (dead) son. As far as I can tell, he is my only living relative. He is the only person who writes to me. Guess what? He is in prison down in New York. Some family we got huh!

Anyway, you should talk to him. I wrote to him and told him that you were a good guy. He is being held in New York for murder—your specialty. I told him how you came all the way up here to help me and that I was sure you would help him.

Anyway, you should talk to him. His name is Adam Peters. He says he knows why you lost the case you just finished. He says you were screwed and will be again.

Anyway, I hope this helps you the way you have helped me. Any luck with Hal yet? Don't forget he is crazy—be careful!!!!

Most Respectful

Roger Handy"

Ian read the letter again, and then one more time. "I'll be damned," he said to himself, as he picked up the phone to call Louie Balzo. Louie came running down to Ian's office. Ian asked him to find out everything he could about Peters.

Ian then called Dr. Mo Heller up at Dannemora.

"Dr. Mo, it's ADA Ian MacDonald calling from Manhattan. How are you?"

"Great Ian, I was expecting to hear from you. Dick Broderick told me Handy was sending you a letter. I assume you got it."

"I sure did."

"And I'm assuming you are wondering if Handy keeps letters he receives from Peters."

"You are way ahead of me Dr. Mo. What's the answer?"

"The answer is that he does not. But you are in luck. He still has the last letter from Peters. He hasn't thrown it out yet. Broderick has it. Handy gave it to him. All on the up and up. There's no detail in it. I think he might have worried about the censor. As you know, all their mail gets screened. But it is clear he knows something."

"Fantastic, Dr Mo. Any chance I could see it?"

"We will email you a copy now. We will keep the original in my safe in case you need it."

Louie Balzo came into Ian's office with a Redweld folder under his arm. He was closely followed by Brady Smith, one of the junior assistants in the bureau.

"Not only is the Peters case one of ours, but here is one of your favorite ADAs who is assigned the case."

"Thanks, Louie. Hi Brady. Have a seat. Let me check my emails and see if something has come in." There was an email from Mo Heller with Peters' letter attached. Ian read over the brief letter to Handy, and then he took five minutes to get Brady up to speed.

"What kind of case have we got against Peters, Brady?"

"It is pretty much of a slam dunk. Peters is in a bar in Hell's Kitchen when he claims this guy insults him. He picks up a chair and smashes the guy over the head with it. The guy is lying unconscious on the floor. Peters grabs one of the legs that broke off the chair and proceeds to beat the guy's head with it. Peters then asks for a shot and a beer and says he will sit at the bar until the police arrive. They arrive and arrest him. He is arraigned and legal aid is assigned. Their senior guy, a guy named Jim Vacco, is assigned the case. I don't know him, but he is supposed to have a lot of experience."

"I know him. You got your hands full even if it's a slam dunk case. Are there any witnesses from the bar?"

"At least six, in addition to the bartender who owns the place and doesn't want any trouble. He does a good business at his bar. The State Liquor Authority guys tell me he runs a pretty clean place. Peters is supposed to have a terrible temper."

Louie Balzo added, "Ian, there is one more thing you should know. I checked with the Department of Corrections. Guess who Peters' cell mate is."

"Give me a hint."

"Gino Conti."

Ian thanked Louie and Brady and, as they were leaving, picked up his phone.

"Vacco," Jim growled into the phone.

"Jim, it's Ian. This time the drinks are on me."

Ian bought a round of beers. He even bought Ching a beer, which Ching accepted, after appropriate protests, before he went into the kitchen.

"So," Ian began, "Adam Peters."

"Ian, Adam Peters is not a nice individual."

"None of your clients are nice individuals. They are all despicable scum of the earth."

"In fairness, this client is a little worse than most. But just listen for a minute and let me tell you what I have found out. Peters has been in pre-trial detention for several months. About a month ago his cellmate gets convicted and sent up-state. He gets a new cell mate. Gino Conti.

"You know—or you should know—that when these bozos get a new cellmate, they are very suspicious of each other. They think all sorts of things are possible including death. Among the things they think are most likely is that this transfer has been made because one or the other is a planted rat, an informant put there by the man to gain information."

"I know what a planted rat is, Jimmy."

"So, my guy and Conti are very suspicious of each other, but it is all for naught because neither of them has any mission other than to survive another day. But they don't know that, so they don't speak to each other for weeks. Then Conti's trial begins. Each day they take him out to court, and each night they bring him back to his cell. My guy is being nice, being solicitous. He knows the pressure Conti is under being on trial for murder. Anyway, they start to warm up to each other."

"And Conti eventually tells your guy the jury is fixed," Ian interrupts.

"Be quiet. And Conti eventually tells my guy the jury is fixed. And, just for you, gives details."

"Like what?"

"Like how."

"I want to draw up a court order to have him produced in my office as soon as possible."

"You've got a problem, Ian."

"What's that? Won't he talk to me?"

"I think he'll talk to you because he knows his goose is cooked. But he is going to want to know what you can do for him. Do you have an answer for that one? He brutally murdered a human being in front of witnesses."

"I'll think of something."

16

Jim Vacco knew that Ian would be reasonable. If his guy, Adam Peters, gave Ian some valuable information, Ian would make it worthwhile for Peters. Peters would want to know two things: one, that he was going to get some sort of a break, and, two, that he was not going to get killed. Ian made it clear that the only thing he would do about the "break" part would be to bring the extent of his cooperation to the attention of the sentencing judge. He thought the "kill" part was pretty well covered.

Vacco got to the meeting a few minutes early in order to take Ian's temperature. Ian told Vacco about the Jamaica developments. Vacco's response was simply, "Figures."

"So what's today's game plan, Mr. Public Servant?"

"The detectives have gone next door to the tombs to get your guy. They will bring him here. I thought we would let you have a private chat with him. We'll use the conference room. There is only one door in and out, and we will be right outside. You all right with that, or are you a scaredy cat?"

"Go on."

"I'm going to tell him the usual stuff: Gotta tell the truth, gotta tell the whole truth. No such thing as being a little bit pregnant. If we catch him lying to us—"

"Yeah, yeah. Yada yada yada."

"Yup, yada yada, but I am going to have him sign the usual 'Queen for a Day' agreement. Go over all that with him when he gets here so that we don't have to waste time haggling." The "Queen for a Day" agreement is the nickname given to a limited immunity agreement. It essentially says that, as long as the person being questioned answers the questions he's asked, and answers them truthfully, whatever he says cannot be used against him later on. It also makes it clear that there are no promises being made other than that the extent of the individual's cooperation would be made known to the sentencing judge at the time of sentencing.

"I will, but we have pretty much already done that. He is finished and he knows it. He has enough smarts to figure out that he should do whatever he can to help himself. His main concern is his safety. He knows that Conti is connected."

"Let's see what he has to say and whether we are going to be able to use it. Then we'll cross the safety bridge."

There was a knock on the door and Robbie stuck his head in. "He's in the conference room with Smitty. Do you want us to take the cuffs off?"

"Not while he is in there with Jim. You can take them off when we are all together. Ok? Let's go."

Peters was a white guy, so white that he was as pale as a cadaver. He weighed about 140 lbs., and on his tall, six-foot-plus frame he looked emaciated. Being incarcerated had done little for him. His hair was thinning and swept back. It was hard to get past a prominent, mean-looking fresh scar that ran down from his left eye to his chin.

It was the product of a fight with an inmate during his first week in the tombs.

"You have met Detectives Jackie and Smith. I am Assistant District Attorney Ian MacDonald. I am the one who drew up the court order to have you produced here in our offices. I did that at the direction of your lawyer James Vacco. He said you have something to tell us. You know Mr. Vacco?"

"Of course."

"He is your lawyer?"

"Of course."

"And you consent to being here today and talking to me?"

"Of course."

"Good. We will give you a moment with Mr. Vacco, and he will go over the ground rules controlling our meeting today. We will be right outside."

"Could you take the cuffs off? They are kind of tight."

"Smitty, loosen the cuffs, but leave them on until we get back."

They waited outside, leaving the door ajar. Smitty couldn't help himself, so he sidled over by the door and tried to listen. Ian shook his head and, smiling, said, "Smitty get over here."

"What do we know about this guy?"

"Not as much as we should or as much as we will if he gives us anything. He is charged with murder. He got in a fight in a bar over in Hell's Kitchen and beat a guy senseless. Then when the guy was lying unconscious on the floor, he picked up a chair and smashed it over his head about twenty times. It would appear he has a bit of a temper.

After he beat the guy to death, he asked the bartender for a shot and a beer and waited for the cops to come."

After a few minutes, Vacco came to the door and said, "Let's go." Everyone gathered around the conference table. Ian asked Smitty to take off the handcuffs. A tape recorder was set up on the conference table. David was there with his steno machine. Robbie turned on the recorder. Ian went over the ground rules again. Peters signed the agreement.

Ian asked, "What can you tell us?"

"I can tell you that you never stood a chance. You were had and you're going to be had again."

Peters told them that Conti didn't talk to him until the trial started. After the jury was selected, he noticed a marked change in Conti's disposition. He seemed more talkative and at ease. One night, after lights out, they were in their bunks and Conti whispered, "That cocky DA fuck is going to get a bit of a surprise." Peters seemed to be telling the truth, even if what he said was incredible. It all seemed to fit.

Ian was eager to get Peters back to his cell. He thought if Peters was gone too long, it would look suspicious. Vacco and Peters agreed, so they all planned to have another meeting.

Peters was to tell Conti that the ADA was fishing for information, but only about Mary Rusk's killing, that the ADA was hoping Conti had told him some details about how and why he killed her. He was also to tell Conti that he'd told the ADA to go fuck himself, that he knew nothing and that, even if he did know something, he wouldn't tell the ADA. He wasn't a rat and never would be a rat. If Conti asked about the jury tampering, he was to simply tell Conti that it didn't even come up.

Ian told Peters that, when he got back to the tombs, he would find that both he and Conti had been moved to another cell in a different wing of the prison. He would be told that a pipe sprung a leak from their toilet and the floor was dug up to get to it. A maintenance crew would be in their old cell with a jack hammer digging up the floor so it looked like they were actually making repairs. The real reason they would be moved was to get both Conti and Peters into a section of the tombs where the correction officers had received special training and could be trusted to protect Peters. If anything threatening or even suspiciously threatening happened, Peters could get help. Besides being more secure, Peters would find life a little more pleasant in this newer wing.

Ian was hopeful that this ruse would keep the relationship going between the two prisoners. He promised Peters that the situation would be closely monitored, and Peters felt confident that, if he needed help, he could get it.

Ian asked Mable to fit him in with O'Rielly as soon as she could. She got him in there in five minutes. Ian asked that two other senior ADAs also be present. One was Ian's mentor, Frank Carney, the deputy chief of the Homicide Bureau. The other was Lem Schooner, the chief of the Supreme Court Bureau.

Once he had everyone's attention, Ian began. "I'll fill in the details as you need them, but the bottom line is that a former ADA has gone into the business of fixing juries."

17

The reaction was, as expected, shock and disbelief. The former assistant was Barry Bradford. He had left the office on the day his four-year commitment was fulfilled. He told everyone he was going into private practice to become a multimillionaire. He had joined the office after a bright academic career. He made no bones about the fact that he wanted to learn how to become a trial lawyer, and he had been a very capable assistant.

The downside was that he required extensive monitoring. All his superiors thought he was forever cutting corners, and several questioned his ethics. At one point, Lem Schooner, Bradford's bureau chief, received a confidential complaint from a trial judge that he thought Bradford might be messing with the evidence, possibly even suborning perjury.

"Damnit! I knew there was something about that kid that wasn't right," Lem burst out. "I'll be a son of a bitch." Lem seemed to be blaming himself that he didn't catch Bradford.

Ian ran through a brief summary of Peters' information. "Peters explained that Conti's family put out feelers to see if anything could be done about Guido Conti's predicament. Bradford must have gotten the word, made his pitch and was hired. Not as Conti's lawyer—that was

Nails Ballen—but to see what he could do about the jury. According to Guido Conti, as relayed by Peters, Bradford said that this was what he specialized in: 'taking care of jury problems.' He sold himself on being able to use his experience as a trial lawyer to identify the most vulnerable juror selected and find ways to put in the fix. I guess sometimes it was blackmail and sometimes it was just plain good old money or the promise of money."

Carney asked if Nails was a part of this.

"On the contrary, according to Peters, Conti said that Bradford was a loner. He insisted that no one else know what was going on. He was apparently working on his own, unconnected to Ballen. Probably a smart move. I don't think Nails has the stomach for this sort of stuff."

Ian went on. "Bradford further sold himself by claiming that he had hired a group of former NYPD detectives and federal agents who would stop at nothing to dig up whatever was needed to compromise the right juror."

A distraught Carney interrupted, "This goes right to the heart of our system. It is not just getting one guy in the jury room to hang the jury 11 to 1; it is having someone in there who can be an advocate. He could possibly sway others, even interject extraneous material, stuff that isn't even in the evidence. It introduces factors over which no one has any control. This is very serious. This could be a disaster."

Frank Carney was one of those uniquely special people, but not because of any particular physical characteristics. He was of average build, about 5'9" and maybe 175 to 180 lbs. He was not in particularly great shape. He had been a swimmer in college, but other than a few rounds of golf, he hadn't done much in the physical department for the last twenty years. That was because he was always in the office. He was a hard worker.

He didn't spend too much time worrying about clothes—everything was adequate, but nothing spectacular. He was closer to fifty-five than to fifty. His hair was thinning. He was combing it now, a habit he fell into whenever he got pissed.

Frank had had a good catholic upbringing. He had attended Catholic prep school, college and law school. He went to church. When he first obtained his driving learner's permit, he lost control of the car, went up onto the sidewalk and almost hit a nun. He never drove a car again. After law school, he went into the service, and from the service, right to the New York County district attorney's office. He was a natural in the courtroom and rose rapidly to be one of the top trial lawyers in the office. He was put in the Homicide Bureau and was immediately assigned the most difficult cases.

He shared his trial skills with others. He was a great teacher. Any rookie he picked to assist him on a trial was in for an outstanding learning experience. There was something he had immediately liked about Ian. Shortly after Ian arrived in the Homicide Bureau, Frank chose him to be his "second seat," the one who would assist him. They were a great team, and Frank picked him every time he could. Ian considered Frank his mentor.

Frank's family—his wife Dina and two daughters—was his first love. There were two other loves. He loved art. He could be found spending time with the impressionists at the Metropolitan Museum of Art. And he loved New York sports teams; he would root for any New York sports team. Inter-league play was a disaster for Frank. If the Jets were playing the Giants, he almost became bipolar.

Ian could see that Frank was very concerned. He knew that Frank would have a million questions, but continued, "Keep in mind we just learned all this about an hour ago. We haven't been able to substantiate any of it yet, but I got to tell you, it fits with what I have just been through with the Rusk case. Peters said Bradford is planning on doing the exact same thing on the retrial.

"I have my guys making some preliminary inquiries into Bradford's firm. We will find out who's working for him. That will give us an idea of what he is capable of doing. If he were to manage another hung jury in the Rusk case, I don't know what that family would do. Mrs. Rusk would just as soon take a plea right now and get out of here. There is no telling what the nutty son would do. The father seems ok, but something about him troubles me. The only one you can really count on is the sister. She is an intern up at New York Hospital. She has her head screwed on correctly."

After another half hour, O'Rielly wrapped up the meeting. "This couldn't be more serious. Let's give this the highest priority. I'll call Culkin and get the squad on it."

"There's one other item we should discuss before we leave," Frank Carney added. "Do we brief the DA?"

Ferris Harper was actually the interim DA, appointed by the governor when the previous long-time and revered district attorney had passed away after suffering a stroke. Harper had to run for election in the fall, and it was clear that his election was his most important priority. His thirst for publicity put several significant investigations in jeopardy. It was becoming increasingly clear that his appointment had been a mistake

O'Rielly immediately and adamantly replied, "Not yet; that's my vote. The fewer people who know about this the better. I'll take responsibility for this decision when the shit hits the fan. My reasoning is simple. One, we have just learned of this and we need to verify the information. Two, it is essential that the number of people who are aware of this be kept to a minimum so it can be controlled. Three, there is nothing else in this office that can possibly compare in importance, and it has got to be investigated promptly, thoroughly and professionally without political interference. We all know that will not be the case if the DA becomes aware of this. All of his decisions will be based on how does this impact his election chances. Am I not right? Any problem with this?" O'Rielly looked around the room.

Scofield said, "Not from me. I agree."

Ian said, "Ditto."

Frank was silent for a moment and then he added, "If I were the DA, I would want to know."

O'Rielly replied, "If you were DA, you would be told. Unfortunately, you are not the DA. Come on Frank, you know who we are dealing with."

"I do, and you are right. Let's keep this to ourselves for as long as we can, but we all know what is going to happen when we have to tell him. We should constantly keep that in mind. It wouldn't surprise me if he fired the four of us."

"That's an attention grabber," concluded Ian.

18

Inspector Richard Culkin was the commanding officer of the district attorney's squad. This was not only an elite group of detectives, but one of the plum assignments in the NYPD. Once you got into the DA's squad, you did everything you could to remain there. The squad was there to work on any ADA generated investigations. O'Rielly wanted the squad on this case.

Culkin, who insisted on being called Dick, had been commanding the squad for the past few years. He was chosen by the prior district attorney upon Frank Carney's recommendation. He was one of those police officers who took the civil services exam as soon as he possibly could. He was the youngest officer to ever take and pass the captain's exam. He had led a special task force that had uncovered widespread corruption in the police department. His successful investigative techniques also revealed scandals in two other city departments. Most people considered him worth his weight in gold.

Culkin was almost sixty. He had been eligible to retire many years ago, but never entertained the thought. He was in great shape, 5'11" tall, 175 lbs. of muscle and pure class. His ruddy complexion went right up to the top of his full head of hair. Even at three in the morning, he always looked like he'd just stepped out of a shower, shiny clean, with clothes to match, everything pressed, everything starched. He was one of those guys who smiled with his entire face. He also frowned with his entire face. You wanted Dick to be happy. He was better looking when he smiled.

What was so impressive about Culkin was that he was one of the coolest, calmest, most reserved men you would ever meet. No one could ever recall him raising his voice or losing his temper. People saw him get mad, but it was always a quiet mad. He would calmly go about redressing the problem. He was efficiently effective.

A graduate of City College, he passed on an opportunity to go to law school. He wanted to become a police officer like his father and three uncles. He was the type of man with whom you could leave visiting dignitaries: polite, dignified and articulate. The dignitaries would get the impression that all New York City cops were like him. They were not, but Culkin did nothing to disabuse anyone of that impression.

Inspector Culkin came down to Ian's office with his top sergeant. Ian had impressed upon Culkin the need for confidentiality. After Ian finished briefing him, Culkin was shocked. "I thought I had seen it all, but this tops everything. This guy could single-handedly destroy the justice system."

The group agreed to start learning everything they could about Bradford, his employees and his clients. It would be very helpful if a check of recent hung juries or acquittals turned up a Bradford connection. They would get someone digging into that. Somewhere there would be a weak spot, something they could use to get inside.

"Dick, while you're checking, see if by any chance Bradford might be hiring. If he is getting busy, maybe he needs another investigator. He might even need another secretary or paralegal. It would be nice to have someone working there. Like they say with the lottery, 'You never know.'"

"Good thought, Ian. We might even be able to generate some interest in an applicant. An impressive resume might tweak Bradford's interest. I remember him from when he was in the office. He was a guy who loves to have smoke blown up his ass. 'Dear Mr. Bradford: I have heard so many wonderful things about you' etc. etc. . . .'"

While Ian was in the meeting, he received two phone calls: one from Robbie and one from Adele. Neither was marked urgent.

He returned Adele's call first and waited while they paged her. She was on the phone in a few seconds and said, "I have here in my hand a rain check you gave me, and I wondered if I could cash it in."

"Of course. Name the time."

"Well, I'm about to finish my shift and thought I would get some rest. Are you doing anything tomorrow night?"

"I hope I am. I hope I'm having dinner with you."

"If you pick me up at the dorm, I'll show you a neat place with no doctors or nurses, and it's within walking distance."

"Is everything ok?"

"Everything is great. How is 6:00 PM?"

"See you at 6:00 PM."

"Honest?"

"Honest."

Ian hung up the phone. This was turning into a good day, a really good day. Next, he returned Robbie's call.

"Hi Ian. I'm sure you haven't checked it, but his website is The Bradford Law Firm and it says he does legal and investigative consulting. There is a glowing bio of Bradford, but interestingly it emphasizes the investigative stuff more than the legal stuff, the kind of thing you would see for a private detective rather than a lawyer. And here is the real kicker. It lists Garner Jost as his chief investigator."

"Jowls?"

"Yup. Good old Garner 'Jowls' Jost of Frederick Commission fame."

"Didn't he just barely avoid indictment?"

"By the skin of his teeth!"

"He was suspected of flaking?"

"Correct. There were a whole bunch of junkies the commission staff found who said Jowls planted heroin on them. Turned into a 'he said-she said,' only it was 'junkies said-cops said.' Cops won. No indictment."

"This is great. We have got to find out who else they have working for them."

"Correct again. We are going to sit on the place for a while, see who goes in and out."

"Great, Robbie. Anything else?"

"The website also lists a Barbara Banner as his associate."

"There is something familiar about that Banner name. She may have been legal aid. I'll ask Vacco. Call me if anything pops."

Ian confirmed that Barbara Banner had done a stint with legal aid. She was assisting Ralph Earlman, one of the lead legal aid guys, in a case he was trying against Bradford, and it was rumored that, while the case was being tried, she was having an affair with Bradford. Earlman confronted her, and she denied it. Earlman then confronted Bradford, and he, being the egotistical kid, boasted that it was true. Bradford was proud of it. They hadn't gotten their stories straight. She was asked to leave legal aid. She joined Bradford's firm.

19

One of Culkin's squad guys made a visit to Bradford's office dressed in a telephone company uniform. There was a desk for the receptionist that faced his office door. To the right of the receptionist, there was a waiting area for clients. It had a couch with a coffee table and two end chairs. There were two other easy chairs along the other wall. A table with impressive legal journals was wedged between the two chairs. Bradford displayed good taste. The office looked nice. There was a large dark wooden door leading from the waiting area to the other offices in the back.

He approached the young lady at the desk. "Hi, I'm with the phone company. There have been complaints about some static on the lines in the building and we are checking it out. Have you had any problems?"

"Not really. There have been occasional glitches, but nothing too unusual."

"Could you give me a clear line so I could take a listen?"

"Sure." She punched a couple of buttons on her console and handed him a phone. He took the phone and listened. "Can you try some of the other lines you have there, please? This one has nothing like what the other floors are experiencing." She did some more punching.

"We only have three lines in this office: one for the boss, one for Ms. Banner and one for the conference room. All the investigators are in the other office."

"Is that on this floor?"

"They aren't even in this building."

"Well, all your lines seem to be fine. You are lucky. Nothing for me to do here. Thanks for your help." He turned to leave

"Any time. Thank you for stopping in."

Just as he reached the door, he stopped. "You know what, while I'm here, I should check your inflow box for a block. Do you have a utility closet?"

"We have a broom closet with a lot of wires and stuff in it. Would that be it?"

"Could you show me where it is?"

"Sure. Right over there next to the coat closet." She got up, walked over and opened the closet door. The telephone man took a good long look, opened some gizmo-looking thing and closed it back up. He said, "Things look fine. Thanks again." He left the office.

Shortly after returning to the squad, the telephone man, aka Patty Verone, was sitting in Culkin's office with the office artist. They were drawing a diagram of Bradford's office showing where the furniture, telephone console, income box and all other relevant features were. Ian and several others were also there. Also in the meeting was Patty Verone's wife, Patricia Verone. Patrick and Patricia were a husband and wife team. They were both in the DA's squad, and they were both two of the best "wiremen" in the business. They were known as the Pats.

A wireman is priceless. When a judge signs a wiretap warrant authorizing electronic eavesdropping, it is the wireman who installs the eavesdropping device and makes sure it is working. Sometimes it's a bug, a miniature microphone, that permits anything that takes place in a given area to be heard; sometimes it's a tap, an instrument placed on a phone line that permits telephone conversations to be heard. In addition to being a technical genius, the wireman is usually a master at getting into places, breaking and entering, and making sure no one finds the eavesdropping device, hiding. Patricia was one such genius, but was equally adept at picking locks. There was yet to exist a lock that Patricia could not pick.

The inspector looked at the diagram. "Looks like a piece of cake."

"It will be. You get the warrant and we will have you listening that night," Patrick claimed.

"The problem is not getting the warrant. The problem is getting a warrant that holds up," Ian explained. "Judge Hastings is so pissed about this hung jury, he will sign anything. We have to make sure that we have enough probable cause so that when the warrant gets reviewed by some appellate court, it sticks. The last thing we want is to have whatever evidence we get on these bozos suppressed because some court says we didn't present enough probable cause."

Culkin asked, "You don't think you have enough with Peters' information?"

"We might, Dick, but a good argument could be made that, as an informant, he is not reliable. He is making up the information to save his own ass. He has no proven track record as an informant. He has never before given us information, upon which we relied, and which proved to be accurate. It's kind of close. If we could corroborate the information he has given us, we would be on much safer ground."

Patty looked at Pat and said, "I think we're on hold."

"I would feel much better if we could get a little more. I can get an adjournment of the trial for whatever length of time we need. Hastings will give us whatever we want. Nails isn't going to object. He wouldn't care if we didn't try the case in the next six months. We just need to have as much in place as we can by the time we start jury selection."

"So that's that. Let's go have a drink."

Ian demurred, "I have to be somewhere at six."

20

Adele looked great. She was quite stunning in a bright yellow sweater and skintight jeans that showed off her exquisite figure. She had given much thought to what she would wear. And she was well rested for a change.

"You look great. Where are your glasses?"

"I only have to see as far as you tonight. They are a nuisance."

"They look great on you."

"Wait right here. I'll run up to my apartment and get them." She turned to leave and Ian reached out to grab her arm.

Adele laughed and added, "Come over and meet two of my roommates. They have been hanging around hoping to get a glimpse of you. We might as well give them the whole nine yards." She took Ian's hand and pulled him over toward the fireplace where two nice looking women in white doctor's coats were checking him out. "Ian, this is Dr. Ober and Dr. Meyerson. Doctors, this is Assistant District Attorney MacDonald."

"Hi doctors, I'm not so formal. I'm Ian, and it's nice to meet you. Do you have first names?"

"Peggy," said Dr. Ober, "and she is Megan. It's nice to meet you and you are as advertised."

"All right. Enough. Go to your rooms and stop embarrassing me. Come on, Ian. We're out of here."

"Goodbye docs," Ian waved. "Do you ever use those things around your necks or are they just for show?" Adele pulled him out the door.

It was one of those balmy nights in New York, the kind that lets you stroll leisurely and enjoy the ceaseless activity of the city. Adele put her arm through Ian's as they walked together. "So what do you say we go Dutch so that no one can say we had a date and I don't have to worry about that anymore."

"Why are you worrying?" asked Ian.

"Well, first of all, I was worrying about whether I should even call you. I don't want you to get in any trouble and I don't know if there are any rules about prosecutors fraternizing with the victims or their families."

"There are. We are supposed to be friendly, polite, helpful, kind, sympathetic and courteous."

"That sounds like some kind of a scout pledge. Do you know what I'm talking about?"

"I do Adele, and I think that it is an issue. I would hate to think that you might think less of me if I were not successful in prosecuting your sister's murderer, and yet, it seems to me that that might be a perfectly logical conclusion. God only knows what Brian might think of me."

"Let's not even go there."

They arrived at Jimmie's, Adele's favorite restaurant named, after the owner and chief cook. "Hi Jimmie, do you have a table for two?"

"Hello Ms. Adele, I sure do. And who might this be?"

Ian stuck out his hand. "I'm Ian MacDonald."

"Well, Mr. Ian MacDonald, you take good care of this young lady. She is one of my favorites and she is special."

Jimmie found them a table off in a corner. He lit the candle, and handed them each a menu. "Can I get you something to drink?" Ian wanted a draft beer and Adele joined him.

"Look Adele, you were right to raise this. It could be tricky, but let's not worry about that tonight. Let's just have a good time. Who knows after tonight, you may never want to see me again and then we don't have any problem. If by some chance that is not the case, we'll figure it out. We are both intelligent adults, I think. What's your favorite dish here?"

After they placed their orders, Ian said, "There have been some developments that you should know about." He told her about 11.

"Oh my God. I'm glad it happened out of the country otherwise I would suspect my father. He was saying some pretty wild things about that juror after the hung jury. Stuff like finding his old army gun and blowing the guy away. Of course, I never took him seriously. Have you told my parents about this?"

"I haven't. I have decided that, whatever news that I think your family should know, I am telling you. You can decide what to tell them. This gives me an excuse to talk to you. You notice how I think it better to tell you things in person rather than over the phone."

"I definitely think that is the only way to go. The phone is so impersonal. I don't do well over the phone. All news must be delivered in person. I will tell my folks about the juror and that you believe he was bought. Anything else I should know?"

Ian decided not to give Adele the news about Bradford. At least not yet. "Not really, but the trial may be adjourned a couple of weeks. Just some logistics stuff. So tell me about your father's gun. Have you ever seen it?"

"I have, but not in a couple of years. Listen, I don't think I should have said anything about that gun. I am sure he doesn't have the thingy to have it—what do you call it?"

"A permit?"

"Yes, a permit. I think Dad brought it back from Korea and never told anyone about it. A couple of years ago there were some burglaries in our neighborhood. We were talking about them at the dinner table, and all of a sudden Dad got up and went down to the cellar. He came back in a couple of minutes and put the gun on the dining room table. He said, 'They come near this house they'll get theirs.' He then swore us all to secrecy because he said he didn't have a permit and he could get in trouble. There was a 3–2 vote for him to throw the thing away. You can imagine who voted for what. His response was 'Not a chance.' I haven't seen the gun since then, but I would bet my life he still has it, probably hidden down in the cellar."

"There are some very strict gun laws in New York state. He could get in serious trouble if he got caught with it."

"You aren't going to do anything about this, are you?"

"Of course not. I'm just saying . . ."

"I think if you were to arrest Dad, it would have a serious impact on our relationship, whatever that is."

"I should think it would, but that is not going to happen, and I would like to think we have a good relationship."

As they were enjoying the food, Adele said, "It's not fair."

"What's not fair?"

"You know everything about my family, and I know nothing about yours."

Ian agreed, "That is very unfair. What do you want to know?"

"Everything. Absolutely everything."

"Do you know what a PK is?" She didn't. "A PK is a preacher's kid. I was and am a preacher's kid. Do you know what PKs do?" She didn't. "They spend every waking moment trying to prove to everyone that they are not a goody two shoes. Their thesis is, 'Just because my dad is a minister don't think that I can't raise hell.' They get in trouble. They create chaos. That is what I did. I had a reputation to uphold, and it wasn't a good one. I drove my parents nuts."

Ian's father was the minister in the largest and wealthiest protestant church of a relatively prosperous dairy farming city in middle Pennsylvania, appropriately named Middle, Pennsylvania.

His mother was a fun loving, perfect minister's wife, who joined everything in town, loved everyone in town and was loved by everyone in town. She never let the good Reverend MacDonald get too full of himself, and she was the protective buffer when Ian was caught performing one of his stupid pranks. The Daughters of Saint Anthony Women's Club, which was a huge charity force run out of the catholic church in the Italian section of Middle, made her an honorary member.

She died of cancer after a horribly long and painful battle. Hospice care didn't exist in Middle, Pennsylvania, and her illness took its toll on Ian and his dad. The entire experience was sobering, and Ian realized it was time to stop messing around, concentrate on his studies and help his dad.

"I can't imagine losing either of my parents. I love them so much."

"You have great folks. But you lost Mary."

"What a nightmare. Do you have any siblings?"

"Nope. I was all they could manage."

"So how did you get to college, law school and become a prosecutor if you were so bad?"

"I always seemed to know when enough was enough. I knew I had to study for exams, and I got by. I was blessed with street smarts. I could lie my way through anything. Make up stuff. Come up with excuses. I would also take advantage of the fact that many of my teachers were part of my dad's congregation. They would help me get through."

"You sound like you were a thoroughly despicable kid."

"And then some. I was most unpleasant."

"When did things change?"

"In college. After Mom died. I had an advisor who was one of the greatest men I ever knew. He called me into his office one day and said, 'When are you going to grow up?' I felt like a real jerk and said, 'I guess right now.' I started to take college seriously and actually learned something. I decided to try to go to law school and took the LSATS, which are like your MEDCAPS. For some reason I did really, really well on them and got admitted to every law school I applied to."

"You did well on them because they test logic and native intelligence. You have both."

"Anyway, I went to Columbia Law School and hated every minute of it. All I wanted to do was graduate, get a job in the New York county district attorney's office, go to the Homicide Bureau and try murder cases. And that's what happened, not without some bumps along the way, but it happened. Enough about me. What about you?"

"It is not enough about you, but my story is short and boring. I was Ms. Perfect. Went to parochial school, got all A's. Went to a Catholic college for women, got all As. Wanted to go to Cornell Medical. Got in. Got all As. Wanted to intern at New York Presbyterian and got an internship there. Ms. Perfect and boring."

"Hardly boring. What's next?"

"I think I am going to do my residency in pediatric oncology."

"Isn't that kids with cancer?"

"Yeah. Kids with cancer."

When they reached the dorm, Ian took Adele's two hands in his and said, "I hope we can do this again."

"I hope we will do this again."

"We will."

"Honest?"

"Honest."

She reached up and kissed him lightly on his lips.

21

Robbie and Smitty wanted to do some record checking to see if they could identify Hal. A name and record check on Harold Jackson and Harold Johnson turned up too many hits. Robbie called Pete Higgins at his home to give him a summary of their trip north. He knew that Higgins dealt with the managers of the apartment building back when the homicide occurred. He wanted to give Higgins an assignment he would be able to carry out from his home.

"This guy Hal worked there as a helper for a day or two shortly after Freeman first moved in. Maybe they'll have some employment records and we can find this guy." Higgins was grateful for the job and congratulated the guys on developments so far. "Fortunately, I kept in contact with the building people over the years. Whenever we developed the slightest clue, I would give them a ring. I think they will do whatever they can to help."

Everyone agreed to meet the next day right after lunch.

They gathered in Ian's office. LoMurko sent a car to pick up Higgins. Ian, Robbie, Smitty, Higgins and LoMurko all sat around a six-foot-long conference table that was placed perpendicular to and abutted Ian's desk. Higgins looked like hell and tired easily, but was ecstatic about being out of the house and involved in work he loved.

They identified Hal. The building manager found an employment record for one Halyard Jackson who worked for them for two days during the second week that Freeman lived in the building. A check with BCI, the Bureau of Criminal Identification, produced a significant rap sheet. Jackson was a burglar with a series of assault charges—a dangerous combination. A mug shot on file was emailed to Dr. Boderick, along with seven other similar mug shots of other defendants. Broderick was asked to show Henry the photo lineup. Henry picked out Halyard. He then started to cry.

A call to the crime scene guys was also productive. "That explains why there was a pillow case full of valuable stuff found in the vestibule of the apartment. Your guy was probably planning on taking it, but left it there and took off when this Hal guy started the beating."

During the meeting, David came in with a copy of the Q and A that he took the day before. He had stayed up late to complete it. He distributed four copies. They made sure Higgins got one. "So," said LoMurko, characteristically taking over the meeting, "our job is to find Jackson and get him off the street before he hurts anyone else."

"Slow down, cap," Ian urged. "We have a pretty shitty case against him right now. We certainly wouldn't want to use Handy as our only witness against him. We would be laughed out of court. We have to give some thought as to how we can build a case against him."

"You are right. Let's find him. See what he is up to. Maybe we eyeball him for a couple of days and meet again." No one seemed to think locating Jackson in the city of New York would be a problem.

22

Jeanne Dalton didn't look a day over sixteen. She was actually twenty-six, and had been a cop for seven of those years. After graduating from the academy, she was put into narcotics, and she immediately started her undercover career. Like Robbie, she was a natural to pose as a high school student and she made buys from the pushers who worked the schools. Ian first met her when he was in the indictment bureau, part of the career path an ADA travels. On Narcotics Day, which occurred once a week, she would testify before the grand jury about her narcotic buys and her work with her backup team. The grand jury would vote an indictment. Ian would draw it up and file it, and the backup team would go out and arrest the pusher.

Jeanne Dalton was very good looking, possessed a great figure and could really lay on the charm. She loved flirting with the young assistants. Ian was a favorite target.

Ian had got her assigned to his office for a morning meeting. When she came in, she ran over to him and threw her arms around him.

"I haven't seen you in ages, but I keep hearing about your heroics. You are as handsome as ever. When I got the assignment to come down to your office, I figured you finally decided to marry me and I'm very excited."

"How does your husband feel about that?"

"Why do you always worry about details?"

"How is your family?"

"Pete is a deputy chief now and well on his way to becoming police commissioner, and the kids are six and five going on twenty-two. What are you up to?"

"Temporarily derailing your career."

"Oh yippee, that sounds exciting."

"We need to get inside a law firm, and I am hoping you will apply for a job as a paralegal there. Might require you to actually work for about a month."

"Sounds like fun. Always wanted to be a paralegal. Also always wanted to work."

Ian told her about the Rusk trial, told her about 11, told her about Peters and Bradford. The big issue was whether she knew Bradford when he was an ADA. Would he know her as a cop? "Not an issue. Never worked with him. But I think I've heard about him and believe it's because he has been recruiting narcotic cops to work for him.

"First of all, Ian, you know I would do anything for you, but above and beyond that, this is a serious and important case. Something needs to be done about this jerk. When do we begin?"

They talked about her schedule and when she could get freed up from her undercover duties. They decided that Ian would get her assigned to him starting next Monday. She would spend a few days with the office paralegals learning what they do and what she might expect. In the meantime, she would work with Office Logistics, the group that did special tasks like putting together irresistible resumes. Ian was confident that if he could get Jeanne an interview with Bradford, he wouldn't be able to resist hiring her whether he needed a paralegal or not. She would be an attractive addition to Bradford's staff.

LoMurko's own project was underway. He called it operation "One Last Deal" or "OLD." He was scouring the Detective Bureau for guys who were about to retire. He wanted him or her to go out in a blaze of non-glory. Ian told him that wasn't a word. LoMurko didn't care. OLD was simple. Find a detective who was planning on retirement. Get him to go along with the scheme by offering him additional benefits. Arrange for him to be charged with a corrupt act, preferably something like perjury. Let him resign from the department so that he can keep his pension and so that he can avoid referral for criminal prosecution. Get the word out. Get this guy hired by Bradford. LoMurko would straighten out the guy's reputation after the investigation was over.

Getting the word out was easy. In NYPD, if a cop in lower Manhattan said "Shit," a cop in the North Bronx would squat. There were no secrets, particularly when it came to policemen who were in trouble. LoMurko was sure that the word would get out, and he hoped that this would be the kind of detective who, in Bradford's mind, would have earned his stripes. The kind he would like to have on his investigative staff. He started making phone calls to his pals in the department to find out who was about to retire. He also called Pete Rusk. It turned out that officers contemplating retirement could request forms so that, when the time came, much of the paperwork was done. This was a great source of intelligence for LoMurko.

Robbie and Smitty were doing their own digging, and they had a pretty good idea of the people on Jowls Jost's staff. In addition to Jost, there were presently three investigators: a former Drug Enforcement Agency or DEA agent, a former patrolman who used to work in the

Bronx and, of most interest to Smitty, a former detective from the narcotics division by the name of Steve Upper.

"I think we have caught a huge break with this Upper kid. I think I know him from the neighborhood, and if he is who I think he is, we may be able to do some business," Smitty told Robbie.

"Please Smitty," Robbie implored, "don't do anything without checking with Ian. This is much too sensitive a case to be messing around."

"I know, I know. Let me do a little checking and then we will talk."

23

Judge Dickerson had retired several years ago. Ian was not sure how many, but he had never tried a case before him even though the judge had been a favorite of the Homicide Bureau. The homicide assistants, knowing he was an ally, shamelessly attempted to bring every heavy murder case before him for trial. He served on Dewey's staff, and his attributes propelled him to the bench. After years of service, at the age of sixty-five he retired. He didn't need to work. His father was a very successful investor and banker. Additionally, the judge had married a very wealthy woman. The judge and his wife lived in a 5th Avenue apartment that overlooked the Metropolitan Museum of Art and Central Park. When you took the elevator to their floor, you got off the elevator in the vestibule of their apartment and you were greeted by a butler. It was one of those apartments.

Frank Carney, Ian's mentor and deputy chief of the Homicide Bureau, had tried many cases before Judge Dickerson. They knew each other very well and were friends.

"He wants to meet you. It's as simple as that," Carney explained. "You had just come to the Homicide Bureau when he retired. You remember the Rosey case I tried before him. I think the guilty verdict came down shortly after you arrived. I grabbed you to do some of the gopher stuff, carrying my files and exhibits. That was when I realized what a great gopher you were."

"Thanks, Frank."

"You're welcome. You could have been a shitty gopher and we never would have become the friends we are today, but you weren't. You were really a great gopher. Anyway, Dickerson retired the day he sentenced Rosey to life in prison. His last words from the bench were 'I only wish the death penalty still existed.' I miss him. He was a great judge, and he is still a good friend. He asked me if I would see if you and your wife would come to his home with Dina and me, and I told him I couldn't do that because you weren't married. That didn't stop him. He wants you to come anyway. So that is that. Unless you are stark raving mad, you are going to come to dinner with us at the Dickersons' home. It will be a treat. You will get to meet one of the greatest judges to serve this city, you will get to see the most beautiful apartment you have ever seen in your life and, most importantly, you will meet Mrs. Dickerson, one of the loveliest and most gracious women you will ever meet in your life. This is a no-brainer. This coming Thursday evening. We will leave from the office, pick up Dina and get to the Dickersons by seven."

Growing up in Middle, Pennsylvania, did not prepare Ian for this. His mother and father had done their best to teach their rebellious son some social graces and his college and law school experiences had taken some of the hayseed out of his hair, but this night was a whole new experience. When the door to the Dickersons' apartment was opened by the butler who was dressed in tails, Judge and Mrs. Dickerson were standing at the far side of the foyer, which was about the size of Ian's apartment. The judge bellowed a warm greeting to Frank and Dina, and Mrs. Dickerson came up to hug both of them saying, "Two of my most favorite people in the whole world. What an absolute delight to see you two again. It's been months. And this handsome young man must be Ian MacDonald, the assistant district attorney of whom I have heard so much. This is an honor."

"Good evening, Mrs. Dickerson. It's a pleasure to meet you and you are so nice to include me. Judge Dickerson, also a pleasure to meet you, sir."

The judge puffed up and slapped Ian on the back. "Finally I get to meet you. I retired too soon. I knew if I held out long enough, a real trial lawyer would come along who would be able to carry on Frank's great reputation."

"You look great, judge. Retirement must be working," Dina Carney said hugging the judge and kissing both cheeks.

"Come on into the living room and let's have a drink before dinner," the judge suggested. "I want to hear all about that hung jury. Hastings is having a fit. He won't stop calling me."

As they walked into the living room, Ian was certain he saw works of art he recognized, and he was even more certain they were not prints.

Ian felt he survived the evening without making a fool of himself. It was very easy being with the Dickersons. They were charming people who put Ian at ease and made him talk about himself, something trial lawyers love to do. He formed a special bond with Mrs. Dickerson. Her father was a rabbi. She considered herself an RK. She also felt that she was compelled to raise hell. The big differences were that the rabbi was a millionaire, and her definition of raising hell was pretty tame compared to Ian's exploits.

The next day Frank Carney came down to Ian's office with a cup of coffee. "Congratulations, you have it made. Mrs. Dickerson loves you. That's all that matters."

"How do you know that?"

"The judge called this morning and said so. He is jealous. More importantly, he would like to have lunch with you. He is feeling me out about your schedule, about when you might be available. I think we should have a talk."

"I'm all in favor of that. I am not sure I know what is going on. Do you have time now?"

"I do. Come down to my office. We can talk easier there."

Ian filled his mug from the bureau coffee urn that held a thousand cups, and found a seat in Frank's office after moving a few files. "So, what's up?"

"You and I have been through a ton of stuff, Ian. Early on I saw things I liked in you, and I have not been disappointed. I think that we have made a good team and we have worked well together. I also think we have a mutual respect for each other."

"Stop it, Frank. My feelings for you go way beyond mutual respect. You know how much I admire you as a trial lawyer, as a leader here in the office and as a teacher. I feel like I have been at the foot of the master. I am so damned grateful for all you have done for me."

"Ok. We know where we stand. Enough dancing. Here is the scoop. The Dickersons are very important people here in the city of New York. They travel in the highest circles socially, politically, financially and every other *ally*. They have been big supporters of me, and now I think they will be big supporters of you. That is very, very important to you and your career. The judge likes to keep his finger in the pie of New York politics, both city and state. His wife knows that makes him happy, so she likes it also. They like to know what is going on, who is doing what and where they can contribute. If he wants to have lunch with you, that is good."

"Jeez Frank, you know I'm not good at this kind of stuff. I'm not a good schmoozer. I'm not a good politician. I'm just not comfortable doing this. I was really nervous about last night. I keep thinking I should take some etiquette courses or go to some sort of finishing school. I really am afraid what I might do would impact negatively on your relationship with the judge."

"You are selling yourself short. You did fine last night, and you will do fine at lunch. Just relax. Listen to what he has to say. He isn't going to put you in a compromising position. He is too smart and experienced for that."

"Do you know what he wants to talk about?"

"I honestly do not. I think he thinks I am getting a little long in the tooth and probably wants to establish some sort of a relationship with someone younger in the office so he will have someone to talk to and find out what is going on. You saw his interest in the Rusk case."

"Enough said. I get it. What should I do?"

"Well, he obviously doesn't think he knows you well enough to call you directly yet, so he is working through me. Let me know when you can make it and I'll set it up. I'm sure his schedule is flexible." Frank made a lunch date for Ian to meet the judge at the Yale Club in three days.

24

They sat at a table off in the corner of the Yale Club's top floor dining room. The judge was delighted to report that Mrs. Dickerson had enjoyed meeting Ian. He made no bones about how important that was. They both ordered a chopped chef's salad. The judge enjoyed a glass of wine, and Ian drank water.

"This city is very important to Mrs. Dickerson and me, Ian. Our parents came here when they were young kids with their immigrant parents. Mrs. Dickerson's parents were very wealthy. Her father's father was a banker in Germany. He was very successful. He wanted his son, my father-in-law, to take over his business, which he did, but upon his father's death, my father-in-law left banking and studied to become a rabbi. He left Germany and came to New York where he devoted his life to three things: becoming a Talmudic scholar, giving away his family money and raising my future wife. He was internationally recognized as one of the leading authorities on the Dead Sea Scrolls. New York City was very good to him, and he returned the favor.

"My grandparents were also Jews in Germany who had enough sense to get out of that country early on. They came to New York where my grandfather became a precious metal trader and was such a natural that he soon owned several companies.

"Lord only knows what their names were before they hit Ellis Island. I'm sure it wasn't Dickerson, but that was what it was when they left Ells Island and Dickerson it has stayed. Anyway, Dickerson is the only name I've ever known. My father was born shortly after my grandparents arrived in their new land. He grew up and continued in his father's business and was even more successful. He hoped I would join the line. I would have none of it. I knew from the day I was born I wanted to be a lawyer. But I also knew that I wanted to do something for this city which was so good to my family. My great chance came when I was able to join District Attorney Tom Dewey's staff and save the city.

"Of equal importance to New York City is the office of the district attorney of New York county. It is crucial to me that it remain a professional, non-political prosecutor's office. As one of your predecessors was proud of saying, 'You can't play politics with people's lives.' I know, from the way you talked at our home the other night, you feel the same way."

"I do, judge."

"I know you do. So, cutting to the chase, I am going to ask you a question. Before you answer, I want you to know that this conversation is strictly between us. I am mindful of the position I am putting you in, but you need not be concerned.

"Assuming there was a vacancy in the office of district attorney, what would you think of Frank Carney filling that vacancy? I am not talking about Frank running against Harper, the present district attorney. I am asking you to assume that Harper has moved on, kicked upstairs, made a judge, gets nominated to another public office, whatever. What are your thoughts?" Judge Dickerson sat back and took a long slow swallow of his wine.

"I appreciate the way you have framed the question, judge. I am not objective about Frank. He has been my mentor. He gave me my first witness to examine in front of a jury. I have learned trial techniques from him. But more significantly he is my friend. He is a wonderful human being. I have learned how to treat others from Frank. I have learned ethics. I have learned that things are not black and white; there is a lot of grey. That said, I think that Frank would make an excellent District Attorney and I know that he would run the office in a way that would please both of us."

"How would the staff react?"

"I think they would declare a holiday and celebrate. There may be some who don't like him, but I don't know who they are. There are probably some laggards whom Frank has taken to task, and they may not think fondly of him. The overwhelming majority of the staff would perceive this as preserving the great history of the office that started with Dewey. Now, I am proud to tell you that I know nothing of Frank's politics. I have never discussed with him whether he is a Democrat, and therefore electable in this county, or a Republican."

"Good point, Ian. I think I can handle the political end of things. Of course, if he is a registered Republican—how does the saying go—'The impossible takes a little longer.'

"I want you to know that Frank has no idea that this was what I wanted to talk to you about. I have not discussed with him the possibility of his running for DA. I didn't want to raise it with him until I could get some sense of his status in the office."

"Well, I have told you that I am not objective about Frank, but I would be willing to let you pick an ADA at random and ask his or her opinion. It will be the same as mine. I am sure that there are a few of the very senior members of the staff who would feel they are entitled to the job because of their years of service and experience, but that is bound to happen. I think that the threat of having another outsider like Harper being thrust upon them will quell their ambitions. They would gladly accept Frank."

"All right." The judge pushed himself back from the table and began to rise. "Thank you for having lunch with me, for taking the time to listen to me and for your honest and forthright opinion. I would only ask that you not mention this to Frank. There is a lot that would have to happen before this could become a possibility. What will be our cover?"

"How about that you thought Frank was getting a little long in the tooth and you wanted someone a little younger to tell you what's going on in the office?"

25

Three things happened on the Bradford case. Jeanne Dalton started work in the paralegal department of the DA's office, a detective came to see Captain LoMurko and Smitty had a heart-to-heart with Ian.

Jeanne was a quick study. She started working on her resume with Office Logistics. They made it foolproof, but the real kicker was the cover letter she was sending to Bradford. It contained such prose as, "While in school, I went down to see a trial and was told to go to the courtroom where you were trying a robbery case. They all said you were the one to watch. You were the best of the trial DAs," and then, "Wow, Mr. Bradford, they were right—you were truly awesome!" And then, "I heard you opened your own office and I would love to work with someone with your God given gifts." Ian thought he would puke, but those who knew Bradford said it would carry the day. It did. She got a date for an interview. Ian was confident that Bradford would hire her.

As for Operation OLD, while LoMurko was trying to find the right potential retiree. Bill Spence, a first-grade detective in the DA squad who worked exclusively as an undercover detective, was contacted by his boss, Inspector Culkin. They set up a meeting with LoMurko in Westchester, far away from the office, in order to protect Spence's cover.

When the situation was explained to Spence, he insisted, "You don't want to take some detective who has done his job and been clean, and turn him into a bum for this caper. You can use me. This Bradford putz doesn't know me. I posed as a corrupt detective in the Parker investigation out of the Bronx." He looked at his inspector and added, "You loaned me to them, but you never knew what was involved. I played the role of a rogue detective in the 20th Division. If Bradford ever checked my background, it will all be there. I was Detective Sammy Burns of the 20th Division. I was there for three years, which is three years more than most of the cops assigned there. They move them in and out of that division monthly. No one even bothers to learn the combination on their lockers. But the bosses all know me as Sammy Burns. They will vouch for me. We can use the same cover, only now I'm retiring and looking for a job. It is perfect and you don't have to go through the whole charade with some detective looking to retire. We ought to be able to put it in play pretty quickly. You give the go. I'll go to Office Logistics and see what they can set up."

LoMurko had his retiring detective.

Smitty closed the door to Ian's office and sat down opposite his desk. "Could you suppose a supposing?"

"Is that a hypothetical, Smitty? You want to give me a hypothetical?"

"I want to give you a supposing. I want to tell you a story which could be true, but I don't want you getting excited and doing anything because it may not be true. Deal?"

"Deal."

"Ok, supposing there is a guy who is working with Jowls over at Bradford's shop and supposing I know him and supposing I have known him since we were kids in the neighborhood together and supposing I know this guy did some things that he would not possibly want anyone to know he did and supposing I—"

"Stop Smitty." Ian held up his hand and paused. He pivoted his desk chair so that his back was to Smitty, and ten seconds later he pivoted around so he was again facing Smitty. "Tell me you have said nothing to this guy, Smitty. I'm begging you to tell me you have said nothing to him. Have you?"

"No."

"Now I'm asking you—are you telling me the truth, or are you telling me what you know I want to hear?"

"I'm telling you what you want to hear."

Ian slumped in his chair, his head on the desk.

"And it is the truth. I have said nothing to this guy."

Ian got up and walked over to Smitty who started to get up from his chair fearing that Ian was going to do something to him. Ian hugged him.

"Thank you, Smitty."

"You're welcome, Ian."

Everyone was making a very serious effort to keep the Bradford investigation on a need-to-know basis. Ian thought that the legal aid side of things was under control. Jimmy Vacco understood that the fewer people who knew about the investigation the better. All was quiet with Peters. He and Conti were happily settled in their new cell block, and Conti had accepted Peters' story about Ian trying to get information on Mary Rusk's death. "Shows you what a shitty case they have against me," was his reaction to Peters being hauled into

Ian's office. Culkin and LoMurko were keeping the number of NYPD personnel who knew about the case to a minimum, and those who did know were trustworthy. The people in the DA's office who were aware of it were sitting in O'Rielly's office: Ian, Lem Schooner, Frank Carney and O'Rielly.

Ian started with an update, "We know who presently works for Bradford. We hope to soon have Jeanne Dalton be interviewed for a paralegal job at his place. You all know Jeanne. If she gets her foot in the door, he won't be able to resist her. We have Bill Spence about to apply for an investigator's job. He is posing as a retired detective out of the 20th Division. If Bradford does a background check on him, he will see that he is smelly and he will like that. My bet is if we get those guys in place, we will be able to develop enough probable cause for an eavesdropping warrant. We can then make noises about starting the retrial of Conti and that should stir things up. Additionally, we have some leverage on one of Bradford's investigators, and we are betting that after Bradford is brought down, this guy will rapidly fold and tell us all. There is also an associate there whose house is built upon sand and should come tumbling down. If you'll pardon a reference to an old Bible school song."

"I can't tell you how happy I am to learn that," said O'Rielly.

"About the progress on the case?"

"No. About the Bible school song. Any thoughts or questions?"

Lem asked, "Does that Bible school song begin with 'Wise man builds his house upon the rock'?"

Ian started to sing it, and Lem joined in.

26

Robbie became an honorary member of the Port Authority Police Department. He went over to their headquarters at the bus terminal on 8th Avenue every morning on his way to work. They loved seeing him. The PAPD were familiar with Halyard Jackson. They'd arrested him several times for petty junk, like picking pockets and disorderly conduct. There were also a couple of assaults on his rap sheet. He had a bad temper. They thought he might be an alcoholic. They did not believe he was a drug addict. They were sure it would just be a matter of time before he would be seen and they would put him under observation. Ian gave strict orders that he was not to be arrested, and the PAPD said they would comply unless he was in the process of committing a crime on someone and they felt obligated to act.

After eight days, they spotted him and they called Robbie. Hal was doing his usual stuff in the morning watching the long-distance buses coming in. He was looking for a *mark* and found one getting off a bus from Toledo. The Port Authority police sent an undercover in to interfere before he could either do anything to the mark or get himself in trouble. They didn't want to have to arrest him.

Unexpectedly, he left the bus terminal shortly before noon and walked over to a high-rise apartment house on 35th Street just off Madison Avenue. It turned out he had a job as a super's helper and worked from noon to 8:00 PM. A relay team was set up to watch him at the apartment house and follow him when he left. Ian was brought up to date.

"I want whatever it takes to keep eyes on this guy. I do not want to lose him and I want to get someone close to him as soon as we can. How are we going to do this?"

Ian looked at Robbie and a big smile came across Smitty's face as he volunteered, "We have one of the best undercover cops right on this team. I hereby nominate Mr. Joseph Jackie, also known as the Robster."

"I knew this was coming and have been giving it some thought. It helps that Hal has a regular job. If I can get hired to work with him, we should have a shot. I'll start taking some of his work load. He will like that. We should get cozy and, if I can establish a rapport with him, we will see where that gets us."

Ian interrupted, "Except for one big thing, Robbie. This guy has killed. He has a temper. He can be violent. There is a substantial risk involved in all this, in getting close to this guy." The room fell silent.

After a few moments, Smitty said, "We can't just go and pick him up. He isn't going to admit to anything. Too much time has gone by, and there has been no contact with his accomplice. He probably figures the guy is dead and he has nothing to worry about. There is only one way we can do this. We hope Robbie can get close to him and we listen to everything while we are never far away."

"We listen?"

"Yup. Robbie, you've got to wear a wire when you are near him, and I've got to be in the vicinity listening so that if this guy gets frisky we can jump him and jump him fast."

Ian asked, "What do you think, Robs? It's your call."

"Hell, I think it will work, but first let's see if he keeps his job, if I can get hired, if I can start working with him, if we are in the same building or if there are multiple buildings, if a wire will work or are we dealing with heavy walls and a million other things. But at least we got a plan and we can start doing something. There'll be no more waiting. We got to get this guy off the street. We have no idea what he's done since he finished bashing Freeman. There've been a ton of apartment burglaries, robberies and assaults since Freeman. We've no idea how many he may be responsible for."

"You're right, Robbie. See what you can do. Let's get to work on who owns the building and their managing agent. We can pull some strings to get Robbie hired and then placed with Hal. Ok, Robbie? Let Smitty know whatever you need. He will relay it to LoMurko and me. Smitty, Robbie's safety is your number one priority. I don't care how you do it; just do it. If we get Robbie placed, we will then get the manpower and equipment we need. Understood?"

"Understood, Ian."

Oldmark Management had not been too thrilled with Hal Johnson's work ethics and was on the verge of firing him when the call came in from the police department that changed everything. Sure, they would find a spot for Robbie. Sure, they would have him work with Hal. Sure, the boss would see to it that Hal stayed on and helped break Robbie in. Sure, there were a ton of jobs that they could share and split the work on. Would it help to give Hal a small raise? At least a little pep talk about how his work was getting better. Oldmark could not have been more cooperative. The fact that the owner's cousin was in the DA's office didn't hurt. Robbie could start work whenever he was ready to.

The wiremen produced a couple of gizmos they could put on Robbie that would never be detected. Oldmark would give them a large closet that served as a receiver point for any conversations that took place anywhere in the 35th Street apartment except the top four floors. If there was work up there, they would have to scamper and make sure another receiver point was established. Ian was sure that, if needed, they could get an eavesdropping warrant for the locker room where the super and his staff spent their spare time. LoMurko got clearance for whatever additional manpower was needed to cover Robbie. Robbie was sent up to another Oldmark building on the upper east side. He spent two days working there in order to get "a crash course on supering." Hal's immediate superior was ordered to pull his fangs in and cut Hal some slack. No one wanted him pissed off and quitting just yet.

Ian felt things were all set and planned to have Robbie start work on Monday.

27

Jeanne Dalton's husband, the deputy inspector, told her she looked "very, very, very—that's three verys—sexy" and started to display a little more interest in the details of this latest undercover assignment. "There is no touching involved in this, is there? Just looking?"

"No touching on my part. Can't tell what bozo might do."

"Do you think you could show just a little less cleavage?"

"Nope."

"Do you think you could wear slacks instead of that micro skirt you have on?"

"Need to show bozo a little leg."

"That is not a little leg. That is a lot of leg."

"Maybe I'll change the skirt."

Her interview with Bradford was scheduled for 10:00 AM at his office in the Woolworth Building, and Ian wanted to go over a few of the details. "You clearly are prepared to elaborate on anything in your resume. What are you going to say if he asks you how you heard about him?"

"One of my girlfriends in the bowling league. Her husband is in law school and spends time in court. He watched Bradford try an assault case." Bradford had tried several assault cases. "So I went to court and watched him. He was fantastic."

"You are ready, Jeanne. You have the panic button on your charm bracelet. You are not going to need it, but remember it's there. If he gets out of hand or it looks like he knows you are a cop, just hit it and the guys will be there. We are right down the hall. The name of the game is 'flattery will get you everywhere'. You cannot possibly blow too much smoke up this guy's ass. He lives to greet himself each morning and to tell himself how great he is. Between the flattery and that outfit you have on, I am betting my salary you'll get the job."

"You should have seen the other skirt I had on."

"No, I should not have."

"Ian, you are such a prude. I'm off. Wish me luck."

When Rita, the receptionist, saw the paralegal applicant walking into the office, it looked like her eyes were going to pop out of her head, but she was immediately won over by Jeanne's friendliness. "Have a seat. He is on the phone, but he'll want to know you are here." She got up and went into the back.

Jeanne wished she could hear what Rita was saying to Bradford. They both came out in a matter of seconds, and Bradford was taken up short when he saw Jeanne. He turned on the charm and oozed the stuff all over her, "Come on into my office and have a seat. So nice of you to come over to see me. Can I get you coffee?"

After the interview, Jeanne reported to Ian. "So this guy talked to my boobs. He didn't get fresh. He never made any bad moves. He didn't say anything inappropriate. He just never took his eyes off my boobs. My legs never got a glance. I knew I shouldn't have changed skirts.

"All he wanted to know was when I could start so, as we planned, I told him on Monday. He wants me in a few minutes early because there is a retiring detective coming in at nine thirty to be interviewed for an investigator's position. Give me a picture of Bill Spence so I'll know if it's him when the guy comes in on Monday."

"Bill has an appointment to meet Bradford at nine thirty. But remember he is going in as Detective Sammy Burns. Now go home and change your blouse."

"Prude."

28

The Frederick Commission was ancient history, but still remembered with horror by anyone who cared for the NYPD. The corruption uncovered was pervasive and frightening. Two areas of police enforcement were particularly bad: the narcotics squads and the divisions. In a way, it was kind of explained by the fact that these two groups of policemen dealt with criminals who had tons of money. Additionally, it was ill-gotten money. Why not share the wealth?

When narcotics dealers were arrested, in addition to having drugs on them, they inevitably had lots of money. Why not voucher some of it and pocket the rest? It was not their hard-earned cash. It came from selling poison on the street to hopeless junkies.

The division officers dealt mainly with enforcement of laws on moral kind of stuff like gambling, prostitution and liquor. The mob was running most of those activities, so who cared if the mob paid a little money to the police to encourage them to look the other way. The boys running the numbers racket within that division would pay those police to be left alone. The street cop would pay some of it to his boss, and the boss would pay his boss. Everybody was happy. The gambler could play his number. The numbers runner made his money off the gambler, paid his boss and paid the division man and so the money went. No one was hurt, and no one cared. But it was illegal. It was a crime committed by those who were supposed to detect crime and prevent it, not join in.

Unfortunately, many honest cops who worked in narcotics, like Jeanne Dalton, or in the divisions were painted with the broad brush of corruption. They were forever having to prove that they were not one of the bad guys.

With Detective Sammy Burns, it was about to inure to his benefit. He was out of the 20th Division in the Bronx. He must be corrupt. Everyone in the 20th Division was corrupt.

Ian, LoMurko and Culkin agreed to meet at a conference room in a sub-basement floor of a Chinese movie theater in Chinatown. The conference room was called "the Hole."

Ian first entered the Hole with Frank Carney when the two of them were working on finding a guy who shot two police officers. Ian knew he had arrived when Frank took him there. The rule was that you didn't tell anyone about the Hole.

The department had been given the room by the grateful Chinese owner of the local movie theatre. Many years ago, his son was kidnapped by a Chinese gang and rescued, unharmed, by the NYPD. It was always used with discretion and care. It was a great place to use as a war room and a place from which to run investigations. The Pats had equipped it with all sorts of unimaginable whosits and whatsits. A conference table and a few chairs were installed. There was also a cot. There was a kitchenette with an up-to-date coffee machine and a refrigerator. Part of the deal was that the department would keep it clean, and they sent in a team to do that periodically. This was a perk no one wanted to lose. It came with two parking spaces in the sub-basement that could be entered from a gated entrance off of Canal Street controlled by a card key—priceless.

The chief of detectives considered the Bradford investigation significant and sensitive enough to direct that it be conducted from the Hole. He thought that the undercover aspects required that security. The chances of Bradford or his investigators seeing Bill Spence enter the Chinese movie theater for a meeting were remote. If, by some bucket full of bad luck, Spence was seen, his cover was that it was a great place to sleep. There was something about the Chinese movie music that calmed him.

The purpose of the meeting was to go over a touchy area of Bill's upcoming interview. Certain assumptions were made. They assumed that Jowls Jost would take part in the interview. He would be Bill's boss and have to approve him. If he wasn't at this interview because Bradford felt he wanted first whack at the process, then he would be at a later interview set up exclusively for Jost. At some point, Jost would be asking Bill questions and they all knew Jost was not shy about corruption. They further assumed that Bradford was not looking for Mr. Clean. He was running an illegal operation and, therefore, needed to surround himself with people who could take part in an illegal operation. He would want to get some sense of where Bill stood in that department, but he would have to be careful doing it. He might leave it to a separate meeting with Jost just to keep his own hands clean. But then again, he might not. It might be too important.

The only way they could avoid the topic was if Bradford and his team do such a thorough background check on Bill that they would be confident he was corrupt enough that they didn't have to worry about him. There was no such indication from everything LoMurko and Culkin could determine that had occurred. They were aware of some minor inquiries that were made. These were designed to confirm that Burns existed and once worked in the 20th Division. But nothing seemed to get down to the nitty gritty of "Will he look the other way if someone is committing a crime in front of him?" That was kind of a tough question to ask.

The group debated whether Bill should wear a wire for the meeting. There was always the outside chance that Bradford would tip his hand, that his boldness and bravado would get the best of him and he would say something incriminating. There was also the chance that Bradford would ask Bill to submit to a search. No matter how good the Pats were, no wire could survive a really good search. If a wire were found on Bill, this investigation was history. In the end, they decided not to do it. If something good was missed, there would be another, less dangerous opportunity to record it.

At the very least, the group assumed that Bradford would ask if Bill was aware of corrupt activity in the 20th. He should reply that it was common knowledge from the Frederick Commission. If asked about the present, he should appear offended and say, "If you're asking me if I was corrupt, I was not." If asked if he ever saw activity he wondered about, he would say he had been a cop for a long time and he had seen a lot of stuff he wondered about. No one would admit much more than that on a first interview. The game plan was to be very careful in this interview, no matter who conducted it. The group agreed that Bradford would want someone who was cautious and circumspect before they would want someone bragging that he could do anything the boss requested. It would be tricky for Bill, but it would be tricky for Bradford also. At the end of the meeting, it was clear to Ian that Bill was a pro. In this business you never knew what was going to happen, but they couldn't have a better guy going in there.

"Well, Detective Burns, thanks for sending me your impressive resume and for coming in to see me. Can I call you Sammy?"

"Certainly, Mr. Bradford. Thanks for seeing me so soon."

"Well, I'm certain that someone with your background will find many offers coming his way and I wanted to make sure I got a decent shot at you if this should be a fit. I'm afraid that my chief investigator Garner Jost was unable to make it today. So, if you and I are happy about today, you will have to suffer another interview with Garner at some future date."

"That's fine."

"Now I hope it isn't a deal breaker, but having been in the DA's office for as long as I was and having seen the things I've seen, I have to ask you if you would submit to a search. I hasten to add that the lot of a defense attorney is not an easy one. There are many competitors out there who, unfortunately, are not as scrupulous as I am and would go to any length to gain an edge. Of course, if you are wearing a wire, I would afford you the opportunity to graciously leave my office now and we will forget this whole thing."

"Well, it seems a little unusual to me that you would want to search a retiring New York City detective, but I am interested in this position and will submit to a search."

"That's great. If you end up working here, I think you will be glad we have this practice."

Bradford picked up the phone and asked an investigator to come in for the search. Bill was disappointed that it wasn't that thorough, but glad they had decided not to take the chance.

They talked at length about Sammy's career, his personal life and what he was looking for now that his time with the city was over. Sammy made it clear that he was leaving the department to be able to collect his pension and a healthy salary from a new employer. He tried to leave the impression that money was always a top priority, whatever he was doing.

"I would imagine that you have seen all sorts of things during your many years in the department?" was the closest Bradford got to the edge, and it was answered with a "Well, many things." It was clear that he was going to leave the rough stuff up to Jost. It just so happened that as the interview concluded, Bradford's phone rang. It was Jost and he was available. "Would you be able to meet with him now?" Imagine that!

Spence was given a ride over to Jost's office on Maiden Lane, which was a second-floor walkup. The building was kind of dumpy, but it was clear that Bradford spent some money making his investigators comfortable. The offices were spacious and well decorated. For those who had spent years in the detective squad rooms of precincts, this was plush stuff. Bill was impressed.

It was clear that Bradford had talked with Jowls. After the niceties and all the usual stuff about working in the department and who did what, Jowls got down to business.

"Let's do each other a favor and not bullshit each other. You may know that I barely avoided indictment after the Frederick Commission. I am not going to get into what I did and what I didn't do, and I don't expect you to either. I will say that I did some things I am not too proud of. How about you, in your twenty years, did you do anything you were not proud of?"

"I made some mistakes."

"Well some mistakes you can't avoid and other mistakes you can avoid. Did you ever make any mistakes you could have avoided?"

Bill smiled, but didn't answer for a moment. Then he said, "I think I did some things that I wish I hadn't done."

"What if you had the chance to do it over, would you still do it?"

"That's a good question."

"Thanks. What is the answer?"

"Well, since I did it in the first place, I guess I would do it again. But who knows? Life changes."

"How about doing some things that you knew you should not do, but, what the hell, you are dealing with the scum of the earth and who is going to care? Did you ever do any of that?"

Bill just smiled. He didn't say a word.

"Not going to give me an answer on that one?"

Bill smiled and shrugged his shoulders.

"Ok, I won't hold that against you. Let me ask you directly: you know what a pad is, don't you?"

"Of course."

"You know guys in your division were on the pad, right?"

"You mean in the past? Yes."

"How about now? Do you know guys in the 20th are on the pad now?"

"I don't know that for a fact."

"What kind of a detective are you? Were you on the pad?"

Bill smiled and shrugged his shoulders again.

Jost smiled also. "Loyalty. It's very important. But I want you to understand that working for an attorney, any attorney, is different from working for the NYPD. You are going to hear certain things and see certain things that might cause you some problems, but you have got to keep that to yourself. Your loyalty is to your employer, Mr. Bradford. Any problem with that?"

"None."

"And by the way, he can be a royal pain in the ass sometimes. He is in love with himself. He is smart and quick, but he isn't that smart and quick. Also be happy you aren't a female—I think he has a zipper problem."

"All I have heard is that he has an excellent reputation as a trial attorney. He really knows his way around the courtroom."

"That, my friend is an understatement. You have no idea what he knows about trials and about juries and jurors."

"Since you raised it, do we have any female investigators?"

"No, and I'm not sure I want to have to babysit one. But we do have a female associate; enough said about her. We have a receptionist, and I hear we have just hired a hot little paralegal. God only knows what he has in mind for her. When can you start work?"

"I've got some paperwork to do tomorrow on my retirement. How about Monday morning?"

"Be here at 8:00 AM Monday morning."

Bill Spence left Jost's office and walked to the Fulton Street subway station. He got on and off several trains before he felt confident that he was not being followed. He then went to his car and drove to the southwest corner of East Houston and Suffolk. He pulled over to the curb and waited. In a few seconds, Jeanne Dalton came out of a bodega and got into his car. They proceeded to the Chinese theater. Ian, Culkin and LoMurko were in the Hole anxious for a report.

29

Robbie was a half hour early for work. He waited in the super's locker room for his new boss to show up. Earlier in the morning, the Pats had done a great job concealing the wire on Robbie. They tested it and were satisfied with the reception. Smitty was hunkered down in his closet with his receiver and ear phones. He controlled a mike with which he could speak to two different squads of three detectives each. They were outside around the corner and would respond if Smitty ordered it. Smitty checked in with them so often that they were getting pissed. "Smitty we are here. We are not going anywhere unless you tell us to. Robbie will be fine." LoMurko arranged to be tapped into anything any of them said. He was pleased with Smitty's persistence.

Hal was supposed to start work at noon and the super expected him at about eleven fifty. "Don't be shocked if he has liquor on his breath. He usually does, but he seems to be able to function without acting tipsy. Sometimes he can be a little testy, depends on what kind of a mood he is in. I am going to have you guys rehabbing Apartment 3C. A bunch of hippies lived in there and it is a mess, but it should keep you busy for most of the day."

Hal came in as scheduled. He was in a shitty mood. Robbie didn't detect any alcohol on Hal's breath. After the introductions, Hal and Robbie went up to Apartment 3C. Hal unlocked the apartment door.

As soon as Robbie came in, Hal said to him, "I'm the boss here and I don't want any shit from you. You just do what I tell you to do and keep your mouth shut. I don't want no yakking. I can't stand fucking yakking. Now go in the bedroom and start getting that filthy shit out of there. Now go."

Not another word was spoken between the two men for the next two hours. All Smitty could hear was Robbie cursing under his breath. At seven fifty-five Hal told Robbie to go down and clean up. They were through for the day. The same thing happened for the next two days. Not a word was spoken.

"This isn't going too well." Robbie collapsed in Ian's office. "I am working my ass off trying to impress this guy, offering to get him a smoke or a soda, and nothing. He is a working fool. Are we sure we have the right guy?"

"Something is going on. Even the super says he has never seen Hal work so hard." LoMurko was puzzled. "But we gotta keep it up. We gotta see if he changes. Maybe Robbie should push him a little, you know, make him talk. Ask him questions."

"I don't know about that," said Robbie. "This guy is one big, tough, mean son of a bitch. I am not particularly thrilled about getting him pissed."

"No, let's not do that," pleaded Smitty. "But I have to admit this is painful. Nobody says nothing. It is hard listening to nothing."

"Stop bitching. You're sitting on your ass while I am working mine off. Anyway, let's see how it goes tomorrow."

That's all it took. One more day. The puzzle was solved. Hal came to work at ten to twelve and walked over to Robbie with a big grin on his face and said, "And how are you this fine morning, my working buddy? Are we ready to do our leader's bidding? I got to get to know you a little better. I tried that sobriety shit for three days and thought it was going to kill me. Please forgive me if I wasn't very sociable. I was feeling like shit. I took me a little pop this morning before I came to work and I am back to normal and raring to go. Yahoo and yippee, let's kick some ass." He threw his arm around Robbie's shoulder and marched him to the elevator.

After two hours of non-stop blah, blah they took their break. This time Hal pulled Robbie down to a closet off the basement hallway where he had a little cubby. He poured two drinks into paper cups from a bottle of Seagram's hidden in a shoebox. "Cheers, my man," he tapped Robbie's cup and threw the drink down. He poured another into his cup. "Come on my man, drink up. We can't be working in this dump unless we have a little warmth in our belly." He watched until Robbie downed his drink. As he started to pour another, Robbie put up his hand. "I got to take it a little slow. I'm not used to too much of this stuff."

"Oh shit, don't tell me they found me a teetotaler to work with. You ain't going to go square on me, are you?"

"No, no, I'm not a teetotaler. I got nothing against a good drink. I just got to take it a little slow. I been on some medicine," Robbie lied. The fact was that he wasn't much of drinker, but things were beginning to look up and Robbie didn't want to screw it up. He just hoped Hal didn't get mean when he drank.

"Well, we better get back upstairs before old lard ass has a hissey. We can have another pop at lunch." And pop they did.

This time Robbie didn't take a seat in Ian's office. "I don't know how much more of this I can take. My wife is getting a little nervous. I come home at the end of the day half smashed."

"But he is warming up to you." LoMurko was thrilled. "He is asking you about your life, your history. He is about to tell you his. Time to start getting philosophical with him."

"What do you mean?" Ian asked.

"I mean it is time to start talking about life and death, about good and evil, about the crazy things people do in their lives. You know!"

"I'll do anything to get him talking so that we can end this thing. I never want to see another bottle of Seagram's as long as I live."

"Speaking of which, I have a present for you." Jim went over to his bag and pulled out a fifth of Seagram's. "This ought to help your relationship."

Robbie grabbed the bottle and said, "To tomorrow," as he left Ian's room.

Early next morning, LoMurko stopped in and chatted with the super, Hal's and Robbie's boss. In the afternoon, at around twelve thirty, the super went to the apartment they were working in and spent about ten minutes chewing them out for the quality of their work. He ended with, "I better see improvement or you guys are history." That flipped Hal's switch. He spent the next hour bitching about the ungrateful super. At their break he slugged down a couple of extra shots. After work he insisted that Robbie join him in his cubby. Robbie took the opportunity to say, "Hal, you've had a tough day. I got a little gift for you because you have been so nice to me."

He gave Hal the fifth of Seagram's. Robbie was afraid Hal might cry. His mood shifted from maudlin, near weeping as he expressed his love for Robbie, to angry hatred toward the super for not respecting them. Back and forth he went as he threw down more shots until finally he said, "I'm going to kill that mother fucker."

"Easy Hal, you don't mean that. He is just busting our balls."

"We will see how many balls he busts when his head is bashed in."

"Stop talking that way. Neither you nor I could ever kill anyone."

"Speak for yourself. Killing doesn't bother me."

"Well, it bothers me. I have never killed anyone and I can't imagine any situation where I would."

"I have."

"You have what?"

"Killed. I have killed people."

"People. Like more than one. I'm not talking about like in a war or something where you are ordered to kill people."

"I'm not talking about war. I'm talking about everyday life. Sometimes you have to kill to survive."

"I don't believe you have ever killed anyone. You are too nice a guy."

Instead of insisting that he was a cold-blooded killer as Robbie hoped, Hal shifted back to the maudlin, weepy Hal. "Shit Robbie, you are such a good guy. I'm so lucky to have you to work with. Someday I'll tell you what a monster you are working with. Let's go home and call it a shitty day."

Smitty slammed his fist onto his equipment table.

They all agreed that Robbie had been right on the verge of getting Hal to spill his guts. The next morning the team went to their respective posts with high hope. Hal didn't show up for work.

Ian ran the meeting. "Let's not panic. We know where he lives. We have the place covered. The boss says he did this once before and he showed up the next day."

"I got to tell you something, Ian." LoMurko was very subdued. "When we got into this thing, after a couple of days, I called off the tail and we stopped taking him to and from his home. I did it because it looked like he was in a regular routine. We were just wasting manpower. As soon as he didn't show up for work today, I put some men on his home. They have not seen him or any sign of activity, but they are there. I'm feeling like a real jerk but that's what happened."

"Shit, Jim. Shit, Shit, Shit. If we have lost this guy, we are in deep doodoo."

"It's a little worse than that, Ian. If we have lost him, I am toast. I might as well put my papers in."

Smitty jumped in, "Stop the bullshit. We haven't lost him. He's an alcoholic. He's predictable. He will finish his bender and want to come back to work. He loves Robbie and knows he's letting him down. I'll bet he's back tomorrow."

He wasn't.

30

Ian needed a break. He picked up the phone and called Adele. They paged her, but said she was in surgery and would have to call back. Ian slammed the phone down and said to himself, "That's the way this day is going." If he couldn't talk to Adele, maybe Frank Carney was free.

"Come on in, I'm not doing anything important. I hear you got stuff jumping all over the place."

"Some good, some bad." Ian gave him a quick summary.

"Why am I not surprised. Isn't that the nature of this business?"

"Let me ask you a personal question, Frank. You got ten minutes to hear something that is bothering me?"

"Of course. I'll hold my calls." He fiddled with his phone. "Ok, shoot."

"Well you know me with girls. I have a date and then another and then they start to drive me crazy so I drop them. Right?"

"Right."

"Well, I got to tell you something strictly between us."

"Look Ian, if you are gay, you are gay. There is nothing to be ashamed of and no one is going to give a shit."

"I'm not gay."

"That's ok too." Frank was trying to be helpful.

Ian told him about Adele, her role in the Rusk trial and having dinner with her. "There is something different with her Frank, and there is something different with me and I'm a little worried."

"If you are worried because you feel differently about her than you have about any other girl, they have a word for that. If you are worried because you are trying her sister's killer, you should be. What's the immediate question?"

"I want to call her up and ask her out for dinner. Can I?"

"Oh, brother. Ian you have got to be careful about this. Let's start with the old O'Rielly rule. If two years from now, the Rusk case is on appeal and you're arguing the case before the Court of Appeals in Albany and one of the judges says to you 'Mr. MacDonald, what about this claim that, during this trial, you were dating the deceased's sister? Is there any truth to that?' Would you be uncomfortable? Would you have trouble answering the judge? Don't answer those questions yet. Then he asks, 'Mr. MacDonald, you agree, I'm sure, that a prosecutor is a quasi-judicial officer and, as such, he is to have no personal stake in the outcome of a case. Didn't your dating the sister put a personal touch to this case? I don't see how it could not.' The judge then sits back and says, 'Mr. MacDonald would not the better practice have been for your bureau chief to have recused you from this trial and assigned it to someone else in the bureau? Would not he want to avoid even the appearance of impropriety?' Now you can answer."

"What you're telling me Frank is that if O'Rielly were aware of this, he would take the Rusk case away from me and assign it to someone else in the bureau."

"You are a quick study, Ian. Now don't get me wrong on this. When I first met Dina, that was it. There was nothing that was going to keep me from going out with her; spending as much time as possible with her and marrying her. You may feel that way, and it is not the end of the earth to reassign this trial. We could give it to one of the senior guys and they would do a perfectly fine job on it. I could even try it myself if you wanted me to."

"I really don't want to have the case taken away. Not after the way the first trial ended. I really want to convict this guy."

"Is that because of your feelings for Adele, or is it because you know that Conti is guilty?"

"No Frank, it is because he is guilty. I better have a heart-to-heart talk with Adele."

When Ian got back to his office, there was a note that Adele had returned his call. The day was not getting any better.

Adele was again finishing up a shift and was pretty tired, but she wanted to see Ian anyway. Ian thought that it would be better if she got some sleep and they went for dinner the next day. It was not a discussion one should have when exhausted. Besides, Ian wasn't getting very good vibes about the day. Better to put things off until next day.

31

Next day started when Ian's phone rang at 2:10 AM. Ian fumbled around in the dark until he found it and managed to answer. It was Smitty. "We got Mr. Halyard Jackson located."

"Tell me it's the morgue."

"That would take all our fun away, so it is not the morgue. A couple of Port Authority detectives were checking out one of the shelters over on 8th Avenue looking for a robbery suspect. They heard that Hal was missing so when they saw him, they called us. We owe those guys. They say he is sleeping off a drunk on one of the cots. He isn't going anywhere, but they are keeping an eye on him anyway. We figured that we might as well let him sleep it off and see what happens."

"Why a shelter? Why didn't he just go home?"

"One of the guys who runs the place said he was really shitfaced when brought in by a couple of other drunks. You ok with that plan?"

"Yes. Let's see what he does. Maybe there is some way to make Robbie a hero so he loves him even more. Does Robbie know?"

"You know Robbie. As soon as he heard, he went over there to confirm it was our boy and to thank the Port Authority guys."

"Has LoMurko heard about this?"

"LoMurko is looking for some church that might be having a mass so he can appropriately thank the Good Lord."

Robbie figured he could stretch out on a cot in the shelter and catch a couple of hours of sleep. The backup team would wake him when Hal stirred. That all happened around 11:00 AM. Hal got up and started to work his way back to his apartment. Robbie made an end run and was waiting at his home when Hal appeared. Robbie approached him. "I was worried about you. I thought I would come over here and see if I could get you back to work. I am sure I can talk the boss into letting you come back."

When Robbie successfully got Hal's job back, Hal thought Robbie was God. They would have a drink tonight after work to celebrate.

Hal poured Robbie a shot. "Robbie, we got to get ourselves some extra money. This job is ok, but we could use some more money, don't you think?"

"Can always use some more money. Is there another job we should take?"

"Not another job, like you go to work job. One of my jobs. The ones I'm good at."

"What are those?"

"When I work some place, I observe things and make notes. Like I had a job delivering shit for this delivery service. Florists would have us deliver flowers. Stuff like that. I get to see where people live and a bit of how they live. You pick up on things when you look: what the people have on, how their apartments are decorated, how many people are there and lots of other information. When I'm done for the day, I make notes of what I have seen and what might be a potential target."

"A target for what?" Robbie paused for a few seconds, and then added, "You mean for a burglary or a robbery?"

"Now you're with me. Remember that apartment on the seventh floor we were in a couple of days ago? You were commenting on how nice it was. Remember?"

"I do. It was 7B, wasn't it?"

"Went right into my little book. Months from now when we are no longer working here, I will dig that apartment out of my little book and when I get a chance, slam, bam, I'm going to hit that place and make me some spending money. You always got to wait until you're no longer involved with the place. You got to be long gone so no one makes the connection. Got me?"

"I do."

"Smart, that is what I am. One of the reasons I drink. When I drink, I get smarter. Things make more sense to me when I drink. But I never drink when I'm looking to make some extra cash, when I'm on one of my jobs. Only after. So what do you think? You want to make some extra cash?"

Robbie didn't answer. He was thinking. Hal poured another drink for himself. He knew Robbie didn't want one.

"I don't know if I'm up to that sort of thing, Hal. I mean, what happens if you go in an apartment and there is someone there? Then what?"

"You use them. You smack them around a little bit. Nothing too serious, just let them know you mean business, then use them. Have them show you where the stuff is. Tie them up and get the hell out of there. But you got to be careful about the tying up part. One jerk I worked with wasn't so careful and there was trouble."

"But they see you."

"We wear stocking masks, dummy. They can't see a thing. Very little talking and masks. Works all the time. I have done about ten of these jobs. I got a record in my book, but I think it is about ten and I've never been caught. Now I've been arrested, mind you, for some minor shit over at the bus terminal, but never been arrested for any of these jobs. I actually think they are safer than the pickpocketing I do."

"What happened with the jerk you worked with who wasn't careful about the tying up?"

"We are in this rich guy's apartment filling pillow cases with all sorts of jewelry and shit. I smacked him and he was on the living room floor. I told this guy with me—who I think was a little nuts, but that's another story—I told him to tie the guy up and he did. Or at least I thought he did. We are getting ready to leave, we're halfway out the door and here comes this guy after us, yelling and cursing. I grab one of those hallway fire hoses and whack him to shut him up. Nutsy takes off. He doesn't even take his bag of stuff. He just takes off and starts running down the stairwell. I never saw the crazy son of a bitch again."

"Do you know what happened to the guy you hit?"

"When I left he was on the floor outside his apartment. I grabbed my bag of stuff and took off."

"Supposing someone came out of their apartment and saw you?"

"They didn't. But I got to be honest with you. I think I may have hit that guy a little too hard. And too often."

"Holy shit! You mean you killed him?"

"I told you I have killed. I think that was one of them."

"Now, you see I can't be doing anything like that. I can't be killing." Robbie was shaking his head and reached for another drink.

"Out of ten jobs, I only killed twice and there was nothing to it. Like that rich guy. He should have just stayed there on the living room floor. He didn't have to untie himself. And even if he did, why didn't he just lie there and let us leave? Why the fuck did he have to come after us and why all that yelling? He was just plain stupid. He deserved what he got. One less stupid bastard in New York. Same with the girl I killed out in Chicago. Whining was one thing, but then she started screaming. I couldn't let her do that. If she'd just kept whining, I wouldn't have hit her. I had to shut her up to stop the screaming. Had to." Robbie tried to get more details on the Chicago woman, but Hal was getting drunk again. It was time to end this. They had enough on the Freeman case.

"I'll think about your offer, Hal. I'm tired and going home. See you tomorrow."

"Yeah, Robbie. I think I'll just sit here and have one last pop before I leave."

32

Robbie left Hal's cubby and got out onto the street. LoMurko came up to him, gave him a hug and walked him over to his car. Ian got out of the back seat and said, "Congratulations, Robbie. You did a great job. Louie Balzo is back at the office drawing up a search warrant for Hal's apartment. Any reason we shouldn't lock him up now?"

"Did the whole thing get recorded?"

"Loud and clear. Smitty's bringing down the tapes."

"I'll wait for Smitty and catch a ride to the precinct with him."

The backup team went to Hal's cubby and arrested him. He was furious and became violent. It took three guys to subdue him. They cuffed him and took him to Manhattan South Homicide Headquarters where David Sean was waiting with the steno equipment. Ian gave him his Miranda warning, and Hal told everyone, "You could all, individually and collectively, go fuck yourselves. I'm not saying a word to anyone." As they took him to the cells, they passed an office where Robbie was sitting at a table, with his hands cuffed behind his back.

"You know that scum?" the escorting detective said to Hal.

Ian knew a prosecutor in the Cook County state attorney's office, which covered Chicago. He called her the next morning. He told her about Hal and arranged to send her the relevant part of the tape from the previous night. She told Ian that they would begin a search. Offhand she could think of three cases that might fit the description Hal gave of killing a woman. She was concerned about one in particular since someone else had already been convicted. She hoped that Hal might change his mind about talking and maybe she could come out and question him. Ian assured her she would be the first to know if that were to happen. They both agreed to keep in touch.

The search warrant for Hal's apartment was signed by a judge, and Robbie was going to go over there with the crime scene team.

Ian made several other calls. One was to Superintendent Mo up at Dannemora to give him the news. Bella, his secretary, wanted to chat, so Ian told her they had just arrested Handy's accomplice and he should tell her boss. She finally put him on. He left it to them whether they wanted to tell Handy and, if so, how. He asked that they let him know how Handy reacted. He told them that they would indict Handy for felony murder, but that it would be a separate indictment from Jackson's since Ian thought they probably would never be able to prosecute Handy.

Ian also called the people over at Oldmark to thank them for all their cooperation. He suggested they set up a meeting to discuss the best way to handle the upcoming publicity. Ian didn't want Oldmark to have a public relations disaster on their hands with their building owners.

His last call was to the chief of the Port Authority police to thank him for the great job they did. He promised he would make it up to them. The chief said, "Forget it. Come on over some time and I'll give you a bus ride."

Ian then went down to O'Rielley's office to brief him. They all knew the district attorney would be chomping at the bit to have a press conference and get his mug before the cameras. Ian was also prepared to hear the DA tell how he, the DA, had single-handedly captured the killer. Fortunately, O'Rielly and Carney would not go along with that.

After he got past the Mildred barrier and briefed his bosses, he made one thing clear: "The one guy who should get all the kudos in this affair is Detective Jackie. That guy not only put his life on the line with this killer, but he has suffered for the last week." When they heard the details, they all agreed but didn't have much hope for fairness at the DA's press conference. O'Rielly wanted Ian to accompany him up to the DA's office for the briefing. They stopped at Mildred's desk to get the draft press release they would take upstairs.

Th DA was there with his chief assistant and his assistant in charge of communications, in other words, press secretary, to whom O'Rielly handed the draft press release.

Most chief assistants worked their way up the ranks and knew the nuts and bolts of the office. This one was Harper's campaign manager. He had never set foot inside a courtroom. They all had broad smiles on their faces and heaped praise on O'Rielly and his Homicide Bureau.

Predictably, DA Harper couldn't wait to call a press conference and asked if the press release was ready. He was told by his PR guy that it needed considerable work.

Ian reminded everyone that things were still happening and they didn't have the whole story yet.

The DA's response was, "Good, then I will have more press conferences as more news develops."

Ian told the DA that he thought there was a good chance that Jackson might make a statement after he was arraigned later that morning. Once he was assigned a lawyer, Ian was confident that he could demonstrate to the attorney the strength of their case, and why Jackson should cooperate. Ian also explained the importance of getting Hal to talk about the Chicago killing. He suggested that the press conference be delayed. Harper shamelessly replied, "Screw Chicago. They don't vote for me. We are having a press conference. I might even handle the arraignment. It's been a while since I have been in court." With that remark, O'Rielly asked if he could see the DA privately and alone.

Ian returned to his office to await word on the results of the search and make sure everything was in order for the arraignment. A few minutes passed until O'Rielly came into his office and announced. "You, not the district attorney, will be handling the arraignment." He spun on his heels and marched out of Ian's office.

Louie Balzo put the file together for the arraignment, and the two assistants went down to felony court where those charged with serious crimes, the felonies, were arraigned. The law requires that those arrested and being held in custody be brought before a judge "without unnecessary delay." The purpose of the arraignment was to formally inform the defendant of his rights and, where appropriate, to set bail. On the last item, Ian was prepared to oppose any bail. Jackson had no roots in the community and would be out of New York in a heartbeat if he were released. Of most interest to Ian, at this point, was Jackson's attorney. Ian needed to talk to Jackson's attorney.

Because of Harper's press conference, the courtroom was packed. Jackson looked miserable. He was hungover and pissed. They kept his hands cuffed behind his back because every time they took them off he caused trouble. The court officers wanted him be arraigned in the holding cell instead of being brought into open court. The judge, knowing a good publicity opportunity when he saw it, insisted on Jackson's production in court. He permitted the cuffs to remain on.

The Legal Aid attorney was a raw rookie. She stood with Jackson for purposes of the arraignment. Hal was told he was being charged with the Freeman murder when he was arrested. He would not believe it. When he heard the charges being read in court, all his bravado disappeared. It was like someone took a long sharp pin and popped him. His shoulders collapsed and he leaned against the counsel table. Hearing the part about "you did, with your accomplice, Roger Handy, with malice aforethought . . ." seemed to do it. Did they actually have that nut who was with him?

The rookie Legal Aid asked Jackson, "You ok? You're not going to faint, are you?"

The judge asked Jackson if he had a lawyer. He didn't. He asked if he could afford a lawyer. He couldn't. The judge then appointed the Legal Aid Society to represent him. Ian was delighted. These guys were professionals, knew what they were doing and he could talk to them. As predicted, the rookie's request that some bail be set was denied and the case was adjourned to give the prosecutor an opportunity to present the case to the grand jury.

The rookie looked crestfallen. Louie Balzo leaned over to her and told her she gave it a good shot. She shouldn't feel bad. Ian thought that was nice of Louie. As soon as the case was adjourned and they took Jackson back to the holding pen, most of the spectators got up to leave. The judge tried to gavel the courtroom to order, but it was useless. He sat back and let the place empty out. Ian told the rookie to ask whoever got assigned the case in Legal Aid to give him a ring as soon as possible. She told Ian that she thought it was going to be Ralph Earlman. This was also good news.

When Ian got back to his office, he called Jimmie Vacco and told him Legal Aid had been assigned the case. Jimmie already knew that. He confirmed that he'd put Earlman on it. Ian said it was important that they talk, and Jimmie asked if he could come along. "That would be perfect." They planned to meet within the next thirty minutes. Earlman was in the holding pens talking to Jackson then.

Ian made coffee for Ralph Earlman. He had never seen the man outside the courtroom, without a cup of coffee. Vacco was a beer man, but that would have to wait. Ian had David set up a recorder so they could play the tape of Robbie and Hal. Both Jimmie and Ralph had poker faces as they listened. Ian gave a brief summary of the investigation starting with Handy's letter, and ended with the fact that the search warrant had produced Jackson's notebook with all sorts of information in it and a box of very suspicious looking jewelry.

"I would obviously love to take a Q and A from him, but I don't really need it. What I am more concerned about is the Chicago case. The best of all worlds would see the Chicago prosecutor flying in here ASAP and finding out whatever she can about that killing. She told me there are several possible cases, but she is most concerned about one where they have already convicted a guy. He could be the wrong man."

Not unexpectedly, Ralph asked what Ian could do for Jackson if he were to cooperate. "Let's say hypothetically he tells you everything you want to know. I don't see what you can do for him. This is too heavy a case for any plea bargain. Harper would never allow that."

"You're right, Ralph. Obviously, we would bring his cooperation to the attention of the sentencing judge, but that isn't going to help him much. Maybe we can appeal to his sense of humanity. Maybe he has an interest in seeing that an innocent man in Chicago doesn't spend time in jail? I don't know. But now you know what we have and where we stand. Maybe it will help when you talk to him. I sure can't see us going to trial on this case."

"You never know Ian. You never know. I'll call you."

Later in the afternoon Ralph called. "We talked and you may have some leverage. He seems to be concerned that you guys have arrested a guy who worked with him? Some guy named Robbie? No one mentioned that another person other than the guy in Dannemora was involved. Jackson seems to say that this Robbie guy didn't do anything and shouldn't be arrested."

Ian told Ralph about Robbie, but asked him to hold off saying anything to Jackson. "Will he consent to coming to my office with you?"

"Yeah, I can arrange that, but it's going to have to wait 'til Monday."

"That's ok, Ralph. Now listen to me. Be careful with this guy. He is not a nice person."

33

Ian was dreading his conversation with Adele. He really thought that it might mean the end of their relationship, and he didn't want that to happen. He had no idea how she was going to react and he was petrified. He was even a little amazed at himself that he was so nervous. He considered himself to be a pretty calm, rational person. When he got to the lobby of the dorm, Adele's roommates Megan and Peggy were there, but there was no sign of Adele.

"She has gone up to get her glasses," Peggy explained. "So, you can tell us all about the Apartment Killer. That is what the press is calling him. What's he like?"

"I don't know him very well. I asked him one question and he told me to go F myself."

"How exciting is that, and the man didn't even use the F word."

Adele was excited to see Ian and ran over to him after she got off the dorm elevator.

"This man didn't even use the F word."

"Leave him alone or you'll hear the F word from me. Come on, let's get away from these doctors. They're dangerous." She was wearing her glasses. She grabbed his hand and asked, "Didn't you have something to do with that case that is making all the news today?"

"Come on. Let's go to Jimmie's. I'll tell you all about it on the way over."

Ian told her the story as they were walking to the restaurant, and by the time they got there, she hated the DA. "He is a typical egotistical politician. He doesn't give you guys the credit you deserve. Robbie is the real hero in this one, not that jerk. Besides, you should be the DA."

"Don't say that. Don't even think it. Harper will fire me."

Jimmie gave them a table by themselves in the back room.

"We have to talk."

"Ok." Adele suddenly looked ill.

When Ian told her of his conversation with Carney, a tear started to run down Adele's left cheek. "Now I've made you cry."

"I'm not crying. You just said something very nice about me."

"You make tears when someone says something nice about you?"

"Yes."

"I'll try to be more careful."

"Please. I think you just said that you told Frank Carney that you have special feelings for me. Is that what you told him?" Another tear rolled down her cheek.

"That is what I told him."

"And isn't he kind of like your second father?" Now both her cheeks were covered in tears.

"Yes, he is, but you have got to stop this crying stuff. You're upsetting me."

"There you go again. You just said something nice about me again."

"What? What did I say? I'm trying to be more careful."

"That it upsets you when I cry. That's nice. Do you have a hankie by any chance?"

"Adele, I'm having trouble with all this because I don't like the idea that we have to be careful about seeing each other. Doesn't that bother you? Here. Take my handkerchief. Men don't carry hankies."

"It will work out. If it is meant to work out, it will work out."

"Now you sound like your father."

"Well, don't you think that if we are meant to be together, we will be together? I do. If we aren't meant to be together, we won't. I kept worrying that you were going to call me up and tell me we couldn't see each other again and use the case as an excuse, and all you're doing is saying that you want to see me." She was really crying now. Ian's handkerchief was a mess, so he handed her a napkin from the next table.

"So let me get this straight. You are not crying because we may have to be real careful?"

"No. I think it might be kind of fun. We can see how clever we are. There are all sorts of things spies use. Like they have drop spots where they leave notes under rocks. We can get burner phones. Besides, you are going to start the retrial sometime soon, and this trial isn't going to go on forever. Then we can GP."

"What are burner phones? What's GP?"

"Burner phones are throw-away phones. No one will be able to trace our calls. I'll get us a couple. GP is 'go public.'"

Ian looked around the back room of Jimmie's. There was no one there. Jimmie even drew the little curtain that separated the busy front room from their back room. He got up from his chair and walked over to Adele's side of the table, took her face in his two hands and bent down to give her a long kiss. "You are the best."

"Honest?"

"Honest."

34

It was late Sunday afternoon. Both Bill and Jeanne were going to work at Bradford's first thing Monday morning. They were all on their way to the Hole to prepare. To Ian, this was a big step.

Jim LoMurko picked up Culkin and Ian, but they agreed to hold off discussion of the case until they were all together. Instead, their conversation centered around Hal Jackson.

Bill Spence picked up Jeanne, and they were having coffee in the Hole when the others arrived.

Ian led the meeting. "Let's start with what our goals are. I think it is pretty easy to agree on those. Number one goal, as far as I am concerned, is establishing probable cause that the Bradford firm is committing crimes, that Peters' information was accurate and reliable and that, if we were to bug their offices, or tap their phones, we would gain further evidence of the crimes. The number two goal is to find evidence that they fixed 11, paid him and killed him. Of course, we are not sure if Bradford did the paying and or killing, or if someone in the Conti camp did, but that is what we should find out. Any additions or corrections to those goals?" They looked at each other and agreed.

LoMurko chimed in, "So I guess we can all go home."

"Right! Now all we have to do is figure out how we go about it", concluded Ian. "Bill, tomorrow is your first day. Should we anticipate any problems?"

"I think I'll have a pretty good idea right off the bat if they suspect anything. I'll take it slow in the beginning and just do what they ask me to."

Culkin said, "I want you wearing the same kind of panic button Jeanne has. I see you have a cross on a chain around your neck. We can give you a cross with an almost invisible button. They will never find it. If there is a problem, you hit that button and we will be in there in thirty seconds. It also has a homing gizmo so that we know where you are, or more precisely we know where your cross is. I also want you to hit the button twice if something is up, if you are on the move or if we should try to make contact. This will be an alert to the backup team, and they will be looking to see where you are going. We can't be too careful with these guys. They are not choir boys."

"That will work. But I think I need a day or two of just doing my job, keeping my eyes and ears open, before I can make any suggestions on proactive stuff. Is that all right?"

"Sure it is. That makes perfect sense," said Ian. "What about you Jeanne? You've spent a day there."

"Well, the biggest problem is that there is no organization. His files are a mess and all over the place. I was going to give him several suggestions tomorrow. He needs a New Case Sheet that sets forth all the particulars about the client and the case. He needs a Conflicts Memo that tells everyone in the office who is involved in the case. That way they can spot any conflict. Is there a client or witness that raises a problem with some other client? Bradford probably wouldn't care, but he can't object to the form and it will help us. Then we should get to work on where the files are kept. We need an alphabetical filing system. We need chronological and alphabetical correspondence files. That ought to give us a start, and it sure as hell will help us look for stuff."

"Holy shit, Jeanne, where did you learn all this stuff? This is great," LoMurko was impressed.

"From the junkies on the street."

Ian felt that they were covered for the next day and offered to buy everyone a drink.

"What about dinner also?" LoMurko asked. "Didn't the DA give you a big bonus after that case we just cracked? By the way, the chief is really happy with me. He might make me God."

35

Monday was a busy day. Bill Spence was starting work. Jeanne Dalton was reorganizing Bradford's office. Backup teams were sitting in cars monitoring panic gadgets. Ralph Earlman was coming to Ian's office with Halyard Jackson. Smitty was checking and rechecking Hal's handcuffs. A Chicago prosecutor was anxiously sitting by her telephone.

Ian decided that Robbie should stay in the closet for the time being. He also requested two more detectives from the squad to accompany Smitty when he went to the tombs to pick up Jackson. He did not trust Jackson. At ten in the morning, Ralph arrived and fixed his coffee. Five minutes later, Vacco arrived and then in came Smitty, the two squad guys and Jackson.

Jackson asked that the handcuffs be taken off. Ian refused. Ralph asked that they be loosened. They were. Jackson remained cuffed behind his back. The two squad guys said they would be upstairs in the squad any time they were needed.

"What have you done with Robbie? Why have you arrested him? He has done nothing wrong. I will tell you what I did and what Robbie did and then you'll have to let him go."

"I don't care what you did or Robbie did here in New York. I want to know what you did in Chicago."

"Why should I talk about that? What's that going to get me?"

"It will help Robbie if you tell us about Chicago." This was sort of the truth even if Ian didn't mean it the way he was sure Jackson took it. At any rate, Ralph Earlman didn't complain. "Do you want to talk to your lawyer before we go any further?" He did. Smitty handcuffed him to a part of Ian's desk and Ian took Ralph outside. "Do not go near this guy. If he gets his hands on you, I don't know what will happen."

"I'll be careful."

Ian was hoping that Ralph might succeed in getting Jackson to open up. After a few minutes, Ralph came to the door and said he will talk to Ian about Chicago. He wanted Robbie "unarrested."

The Chicago murder had occurred three years ago, a week before Christmas, in an apartment off of Michigan Avenue. In keeping with Jackson's MO, it was a wealthy woman in a fancy apartment.

A call to the state attorney's office confirmed that there was a tremendous amount of pressure on the Chicago authorities to solve the case. A man had been arrested, tried and convicted.

The Chicago prosecutor could be in New York in three hours, a two-hour flight on a plane that was leaving in about an hour. Everyone decided that it would be best to keep Jackson in the DA's office, rather than sending him back to the tombs. They could use the holding cells upstairs. In the meantime, Jackson was told that if he continued to cooperate, Robbie would probably spend the night with his family. Hal was greatly relieved.

Denis Sean came down to Ian's office and set up his equipment. Ian took a Q and A with Ralph Earlman present. Earlman was not about to be criticized for his representation of Jackson, and he wanted the record clear that Jackson was talking because he wanted to talk. The notebook was identified by Jackson, as was some of the jewelry, and the jobs they came from. There was a significant amount of follow-up work for the police to do from the information in the notebook. The chief of detectives decided to assign a group to check on each entry. They didn't want any undiscovered bodies lying around.

They arranged to get Jackson a decent lunch. He was taking some medications to help him with his withdrawal from alcohol. All in all, he was in pretty good shape at four in the afternoon when the state attorney from Chicago started to question him. She was convinced he was the killer. She called her office and spoke to her boss about preparing the necessary papers to have the man convicted prepared for release. She thought the state attorney would want to call District Attorney Harper to thank him for all the cooperation the New York authorities had given Chicago. Ian convinced her to hold off on that idea. She understood.

Earlier in the day, Ian had checked in with Louie Balzo to make sure that there were no problems with Spence and Dalton. Everything seemed under control, and there were no emergencies. They had decided to let everything ride for three days without any special meetings. Unless there was a problem, they would not go to the Hole until close of business on Wednesday.

Everyone was in the Hole by six thirty on Wednesday evening. Ian knew they had suffered long days and didn't waste any time getting down to business. "The first thing I want to know is whether any of you are getting any bad vibes or feeling unsafe."

Jeanne started, "I feel safe, but I got two problems. Barbara Banner, the associate, does not like me. I suspect that is because of the second problem. Bradford never stops looking at my boobs. He clearly considers himself God's gift to women and he will at some point make a move on me. I hasten to add that I can take care of myself, but I would like to do it in a way that I don't get fired. I am sure that Barbara is stabbing me in the back every chance she gets. She would like to get me out of there."

"So what do we do?"

"Well, the changes in office operation I have suggested are going to work. Bradford is going to like them and will not be interested in firing me for that. I thought, if you don't mind, I might cozy up to Barbara and give her the idea that I might be gay and more interested in her than in Bradford. Any problem with that?"

"How is she going to react to that?"

"Who knows, but it could accomplish two things. It might ease the jealousy factor, and she might tell Bradford he is wasting his time. That will get him away from my pants."

"I think you should try it. What about you, Bill?"

"There were no problems. It's a small group. There's Smitty's friend Steve Upper. Then there's a guy named Isaac Team. I can't figure out why he's there. We should do a background check on him and maybe we'll find out. The DEA guy is Pete Fusco. I guess he is the federal connection and I guess, being narcotics, he knows what dirt is and how to handle it."

"Let's run another background check on him," added Culkin. "I'll call our contacts over at DEA. They'll be helpful."

"For the most part, they've been trying to figure me out. Lots of questions about the 20th Division, but no problems. I think it's gone pretty well because they seem to be more comfortable with me. There's been nothing yet that has concerned me, but they also have not said anything around me that's been the least bit interesting. I've been given no investigative assignment yet. More significantly, none of us seems to be doing anything along those lines. I don't know if it's because Bradford has nothing going on or because they don't want me to see what's going on. It's early in this project. I think we have to be patient and just keep going."

When Ian got home that night, there was a package that had been delivered for him. Inside was a cell phone and a note from Adele that read, "Call me and I'll explain how we will use this. Love. 007"

36

Frank Carney came into Ian's office and asked, "Got a minute?" Ian said he did and Carney closed the door. "I had a drink with Bernie Dickerson last night."

"Would that be Judge Dickerson?"

"Yes, that would be Judge Dickerson. His full name is Bernard I. Dickerson. Anyway, he talked to me about the DA thing and he also told me that he talked to you. He was very pleased to learn that you didn't mention it to me, but I must say, I wish you had. Maybe I could have stopped him before he did anything."

"Why would you want to do that? We are assuming in all this that Harper is no longer the DA. I know you, and I know you wouldn't do anything to challenge him if he were still DA. You are much too loyal a guy. Besides, we could both get fired for having this conversation if we weren't making that assumption."

"That was a large part of the discussion with the judge. It seems that there are many who are unhappy with Harper and that these malcontents have been scheming his demise for some time. They're convinced he will politicize the office even more than he already has and, if he has his way, he will set it back into the dark ages. They say he is just using it as a stepping stone for higher office and he will use every chance he can to gain publicity. Often, they fear, at the expense of justice. They are really serious and concerned about this. The movement has a full head of steam. I'm not sure I want to be a part of it."

"Look Frank, this conversation is between you and me. It is not going anywhere, so let's be frank about this situation. Don't you agree that these so-called malcontents are right? Do you think he is a good DA?"

"I do and I don't."

"That will teach me not to ask two questions at once."

"I think the criticisms of him are accurate and fair, and I don't think he is a particularly good DA. I'm not sure how bad he is, but he certainly does not measure up to his predecessors."

"So then assuming that his successor would be to your and my liking, why should we not be supportive of the thought or concept of him leaving?" Frank was silent and he looked out the window. Ian continued, "Do we know if anyone has spoken to him and if he would be willing to change?"

"We know the answer to that question. There was a meeting recently between Harper and the Dickersons that didn't go well. He was obstinate and said he would run the office any way he wanted to. It was pointed out to him that he was DA by dint of a gubernatorial appointment, that he was elected and that the party might very well run a candidate of their own choosing against him. He became outraged. It was further pointed out to him that the governor didn't even select someone from within the office, someone who was a part of the tradition of the office. He basically told everyone at the meeting that he would fight them all. Judge Dickerson thinks that is just bravado and that Harper knows he can't have any political success in either New

York city or the state if he bucks the party. The judge is convinced he would take a judgeship if offered one."

"Well that, it seems, is dispositive of the issue. If he said 'Gee whiz, I didn't realize I was being such a jerk. I will do everything in my power to change. Please help me do a better job,' I might feel differently, but that certainly is not the case. Don't you agree? Let me ask you, where is Dina in all this?"

"Supportive."

"Dina is supportive of what?"

"Dina thinks I should be the district attorney."

"Yes," Ian jumped up from his chair and pumped the air. "Good for Dina. So what is your problem?"

"I'm not sure I could do the job."

"Frank, forgive me, I know you too well so I know you are sincere, but that is just dead wrong. You have been in this office for twelve years. You came here right out of the service. You went through all the junior bureaus and you were put in the Supreme Court Bureau where you tried every conceivable type of felony. You tried them with such distinction that they grabbed you and put you in the Homicide Bureau, not because they wanted just another trial assistant here, they wanted the best here. There is no one in this office who would oppose your opportunity to be the district attorney. That includes some of the assistants here who are senior to you. You may not know it, but you are universally admired, not only in the office, but by the police department, which is very important, and by the defense bar including the Legal Aid Society. This is a no-brainer."

"So I tell the judge I'll do it?"

"I think you have to be careful. They will have to assure you that you will have the party backing if someone decides to challenge you in the primary and that you will have the party backing for the general election. Party backing is spelled M-O-N-E-Y. You need to have these guarantees. Otherwise you're getting yourself in a big political mess. This all assumes that the judge is reading his party correctly and that he knows what he is talking about. If you have any question about that, you'd better pause."

"You are right about all of this. I want to have another talk with Bernie and I would very much appreciate it if you would be with me when I do that. Would you do that for me?"

"Yes, but you have to stop calling him Bernie. He is Judge Dickerson."

"Where did you get all this political savvy?"

"From my father. All ministers are part politicians."

Judge Dickerson stood as they approached his table in the dining room of the Yale Club. There was a big smile on his face. "You would not have brought your attorney if you were turning me down. I am a very happy man."

"Let's talk," Carney said.

Dickerson explained that the governor was on board. The governor acknowledged that he had made a mistake in appointing Harper, that he let Harper talk him into the appointment and that the New York county district attorney's office was unique and special. It was too important to be involved in politics. He wanted to make amends. This was one of the reasons he was a good governor.

There was a vacancy on the Appellate Division Bench, which would give Harper a little more pizzazz and therefore more incentive. The governor would talk personally to Harper about how he, Harper, would be doing the governor a personal favor to fill this important position. In the event that Harper resisted, the governor was prepared to roll in all sorts of nasty artillery.

He was also prepared to appoint Frank Carney as the interim DA and to give him his considerable support. The governor would work to prevent anyone from running against him in the primary. He also would work to elect Frank in the general election. Of course, no one could assure that there would not be a maverick entering the primary. Nor could anyone control what the Republicans would do in the general election. History had shown, however, that having the undivided support of the Democratic organization in New York county was tantamount to having a victory.

Carney made it clear that, while he wasn't shy, and he knew how to deliver a speech, he was not enthusiastic about having to campaign. He hoped that activity could be kept to a minimum.

The judge pointed out that one of the reasons for all this was to get the office out of politics. That should be part of his campaign. He would have to show his face at each of the Democratic clubs in Manhattan and ask for their support. He would have to tell them that only with their hard work could he keep in the background, could he keep the office out of politics. Unless he ran into significant opposition from a powerful opponent, there should be little campaigning.

They spent a moment on who they thought might possibly run against Frank, and could not come up with anyone. That could always change. They agreed that the sooner this could happen, the better it would be for Frank and for the office.

Ian and Frank grabbed a cab back to the office. It was dawning on Frank that things were moving fast and his life was about to change.

Ian said, "Frank, you have got to start thinking about what nasty things can come out. Is there any reason why you should not do this? Is there anything that could embarrass you? Are there any skeletons in your closet? How does this affect your two kids and their schooling? Are there any political enemies out there from any of your cases, or your career or from any connections your extended family might have? Thinking about things like that are unpleasant, but necessary. Sit down with Dina tonight, because from the way the judge was talking, you've got about two days before all this starts to happen. Once the governor picks up that phone and tells Harper he needs to see him, that is it."

"I know. I am starting to have second thoughts about all this."

"I think you are starting to have first thoughts about some of it, but this is going to be good for you, good for the office and good for the people of Manhattan. It is all good, Mr. Carney. It is all good."

When Ian got back to the office, there was a note to call Dina Carney. Ian called her and she asked if there was some way they could meet. Ian had a million things going, but knew it was important that Dina be on board. If she had reservations about any of this, now was the time to get it out in the open. They agreed to meet at a coffee shop in about an hour.

"I just don't want him to be hurt. He is such a good guy and I love him so much, I just don't want him to get hurt by any of this."

"Do you agree that he should be DA and that he would make a great DA and that it would be good for him, for the office and for the community?"

"Yes, but I don't want him getting hurt."

"No one wants to see him get hurt. That is our job. You have got to have a heart-to-heart with him tonight and try to figure out if there is anything out there that might embarrass you or cause any problem. If there is, we should talk about it. Maybe it can be handled. Maybe it can't and Frank shouldn't do this."

The next morning Frank came into Ian's office and closed the door. "The only thing we could think of was that we smoked pot a couple of times together when we were in college."

"That's it?"

"That's all we could think of."

"Get out of here."

37

Jeanne Dalton was combing her hair in a peculiar way.

"What's with the hair? You look kind of shitty," her husband said.

"That's what's with the hair."

"Huh?"

"I'm trying to look a little shitty. I'm trying to send a signal to Bradford that I am not interested in him. Maybe it will cool him off a little."

"I trust you told him that, if he touched you, Deputy Inspector Dalton would break every bone in his body."

"I thought about telling him that, and then it occurred to me that such talk might put a damper on my undercover activity. I thought combing my hair might send a more subtle message."

"Seriously, you are safe over there, aren't you?"

"You see my charm bracelet? What do you think happens if I squeeze this little apple?"

"Some help comes?"

"Most of Manhattan South."

As soon as Bradford's receptionist, Rita, saw Jeanne step into the office, she couldn't help herself. "Jeanne, I noticed your new hairstyle. Honestly, it doesn't do that much for you."

"Really, I'm disappointed. Let's give it a couple of days and see if it grows on you. Do you know when Barbara's coming in this morning?"

"She should be in soon. She doesn't have any appointments on her calendar that she told me about. I think she will probably like your hair."

"Let me know when she arrives. I need to talk to her. How are we coming on the case files?"

"I'm almost done. Things are much more organized and all the files are easier to find."

Jeanne went back to her workspace, and in ten minutes her intercom told her Barbara was in.

"Oh my God, what the fuck have you done to your hair?"

"We need to talk. Have you got a minute? I have a problem."

"Sure, let me get a cup of coffee." Barbara Banner got her coffee and sat across from Jeanne. "What's up?"

"Well, I'd appreciate it if this could be confidential because it involves the boss. I don't know if you've noticed, but he never takes his eyes off my boobs."

"I certainly have noticed. He wants to get into your pants."

"I am not interested in him getting into my pants. The fact is, I am not interested in any man getting into my pants. Do you know what I'm saying?"

There was silence. A smile started to creep across Barbara's face.

"Holy shit! Are you telling me you're gay?" Jeanne was silent. "You're gay, aren't you? And to think that ever since you got here, I've been pissed because I thought you were moving in on my territory. You're gay, aren't you?"

"Look, I can tell you don't like me, but I don't want to lose this job and I sure would appreciate any support you could give me to help keep it. Yes, I'm gay. Frankly, you interest me more than Bradford does, but don't worry, I'll keep my hands to myself."

"Well, that certainly does put a different spin on things. Don't you worry about a thing. All your innovations have been super. The office is running much more smoothly. Now that I don't have to worry about you and Barry, you and I won't have any problems."

"How do I handle it with the boss?"

"I guess the hair might be a good start, although I don't think I can stand it. I think it will handle itself. If it doesn't, I ought to be able to help. By the way, you better keep your eyes on Rita Receptionist. I think she might be interested in your proclivities. Get my drift?"

Jeanne hadn't counted on that one. She gave Rita a close look as she went back to her workspace. They were down to the last two files and then they would be finished with alphabetizing. Jeanne thought that she would see how the rest of the morning went and then she might start to do some serious snooping.

Jowls asked that the meeting start at ten and that gave Spence three minutes to get some coffee, a pad and a pencil. Everyone was on time. "We have an assignment. We have been retained by an attorney to give him as much information as we can about the makeup of a jury. It is a drug case being tried in Part 51 of Kings County Supreme Court. It involves the possession of a large quantity of heroin. The defendant is Rickey Richardson. The main jury has already been picked, but because it promises to be a lengthy trial, the judge has ordered that four alternates be picked as well. They are to start at around eleven this morning. I would like Isaac and Sammy to go over to the court. Steve and Pete will stay here in the office to receive any information that comes in from Brooklyn and to start work on the information the boss has got for us already. Sammy, this is your first case with us so it is time you understand what we do. We get paid a lot of money to be able to get juror information to the trial lawyer. This is all legal and all above board. The more information the trial lawyer has about the jurors, the happier he is. He wants to know what sympathies to play to, what prejudice to take advantage of, what pitfalls should be avoided. We have the transcript of the voir dire conducted by the prosecutor and the defense attorney. We will be going over that here in the office while you guys are in court. Do you know what a voir dire is, Sammy?"

"I do, Garner. I was involved in several trials while on the job."

"Call me Jowls; everyone else does. Ok. Come back here when court adjourns for the day. Don't bother returning here for lunch. You might as well stay in Brooklyn. Call us if there are any interesting developments that we should know about.

"You will probably see Bradford in the courtroom. If you do, act as if you have never seen him before. He likes to observe the jury selection process and get a feel for the jurors. He prides himself on never having made a mistake in any juror he ever picked."

The meeting broke up, and as they started to go their respective offices, Isaac announced to Sammy that he would be getting his briefcase and they would meet downstairs and get a cab to Brooklyn. It turned out that Isaac Team was Jowls' son-in-law. He had married

Jowls' daughter about a year ago. The background check didn't turn up any further information on Isaac that Spence was aware of. He wished he knew more, but would have to go with the little there was at the moment. The most immediate problem was getting the news of these developments to Ian and the team as soon as possible without raising any suspicions. Spence went into the men's room and called Culkin on his cell.

This was the first time Spence was alone with Isaac. As soon as they got into the back seat of the cab, Isaac said, "I hate this frigging job. We have to spend the entire frigging day listening to those frigging lawyers ask their frigging questions and then taking notes on the frigging answers those stupid frigging jurors give. They never tell the frigging truth anyway. Why would you frigging want to do this for a frigging living? Was it that you couldn't find any other frigging job, or was it that you didn't know what you were getting into?"

"A little of both. I just retired and I didn't like the idea of having nothing to do. I thought I might get another job in law enforcement, with the feds maybe. Then I thought of PI, you know private investigator, work. I thought I was signing up for traditional private detective kind of stuff. You know, like following adulterers to motels and taking pictures."

"Yeah, well, lots of frigging luck. This is what we frigging do all the frigging time. Don't frigging get me wrong; I'm grateful to frigging Daddy Jowls for giving me a job, but I know he frigging did it so I could frigging support his daughter. As soon as I can find another frigging job, I am frigging out of here whether Daddy Jowls likes it or frigging not."

"Can I ask you a question? What's with all the friggings?"

"The friggings used to be fuckings, but Daddy Jowls said I use the word too much and should try to say something else, like frigging, so that I wasn't saying fucking so much. If Daddy Jowls wants frigging, he will get frigging. That's another frigging reason I want another frigging job, so I can go back to frigging talking frigging normally."

"How about using neither frigging or fucking?"

"I found I couldn't speak."

The cab driver couldn't hold it in any longer. "Oh man."

"Just frigging drive. Listen, Sammy, when we get to frigging court, we split up and sit on opposite sides of the frigging courtroom. If this frigging judge has the selected jurors present and in the box, your job is to frigging watch them and see if you pick up any frigging reactions to the frigging answers that are given. Like frowns are very important and any frigging smiles. Do the selected frigging jurors smile at anything? Bradford is frigging big on that. We will meet at the frigging bar across the frigging street after the court breaks for the day. If you see me leave frigging early, don't worry. I have gone across the frigging street for a drink because I frigging can't stand this anymore. But Bradford will probably be in the courtroom so I gotta make sure he doesn't frigging see me leave."

The cab pulled up to the courthouse, and they went their separate ways. Spence was never happier to leave anyone. He watched Isaac leave the courtroom five minutes after they got there. The attorneys were just beginning their questioning. Bradford took a seat pretty close to the jury box.

Spence decided to stay and do as instructed. He was afraid that Isaac might be setting him up. Maybe he wanted to see what Spence would do when he left the courtroom.

Spence saw someone he recognized enter the courtroom. It was one of the backup team, and he took a seat in the back. They made eye contact.

It didn't take long to pick the alternates. The judge announced that the trial would go over until the next day when they would have opening statements.

Spence then walked over to the bar and found Isaac. He looked a little drunk. They grabbed a cab back to Maiden Lane.

Jowls called a meeting and almost immediately asked Isaac what he thought of juror number 6. Isaac said, "Nothing unusual."

"Did he appear attentive or like he didn't give a shit?"

"He didn't appear frigging anything to me. He just sat there."

"Did anyone laugh at anything?" Jowls clearly was addressing the question to Isaac, but Spence jumped in, "I noticed number 9 laughing quite frequently. I'm not sure Isaac could see him from where he was sitting, but the guy was kind of in front of me. A couple of times I wondered what he was laughing at. There didn't seem to me to be anything that funny going on."

"Ok, that's it for today. See you tomorrow. Sammy, could I see you for a minute?"

Everyone left Jowls' office except Spence who remained in his seat. "Sammy, you know what's bothering me, don't you?"

"The fact that juror number 6 was a she and not a he."

"Was that stupid son-in-law of mine even in the courtroom, or did he go across the street and go drinking?"

"He was in the courtroom. Why are you putting this on me?"

"He was in the courtroom for what, for five minutes before he left?"

"That's about right, but I would rather not be in the middle of this."

"I know you wouldn't, and I appreciate your honesty and also the fact that you're trying to not get that stupid shit in trouble. What am I going to do with him?"

"Get him another job. He doesn't like this one. Let him be someone else's headache, but please don't let him know I gave him up."

"I won't and you really didn't give him up. Upper was watching. I think I know someone who will do me a favor and hire Isaac."

"That would be good."

"There is another guy looking to work here. Do you know Leslie Collins? He spent most of his time in Bronx narcotics? He just got a little jammed up and put his papers in. I think he might fit in and then I can replace Isaac."

"No Jowls, I don't know him. But if there is anything I can do, let me know." *Thank God*, thought Spence, *no more frigging.*

They met at the Hole. Spence briefed everyone on his day, including the possibility of Leslie Collins coming on board. The background checks on Isaac Team and Pete Fusco were finished. Isaac was a screw-up who had gotten Jowls' daughter pregnant. He married her. He barely got out of high school and had two minor arrests for driving under the influence and possession of pot. Fusco had been disciplined for messing up an operation down at the Mexican border. He got pissed off with the way the DEA treated him, and quit. He apparently possessed a bit of a temper. He discharged his weapon more than once under questionable circumstances.

Ian's biggest concern was whether to tell the Brooklyn DA that Bradford might be doing something with one of his cases. Everyone concluded that they didn't know enough yet and bringing in Brooklyn would be a big deal.

Jeanne said she would try to find out what, if any, paperwork there was on the Brooklyn case. She wanted to know who the client was, who was paying the bills and what lawyers were involved. If there wasn't paperwork, she wanted to know why.

Culkin would check into Leslie Collins.

Ian reminded all of them that, so far, there was not a scintilla of evidence of a crime. Everything Bradford was doing was legal. There was no chance of a bug.

Jeanne handed Barry Bradford several pieces of paper. "I want you to fill these forms out as soon as possible."

"I'm not filling anything out until you fix your hair. What are these forms anyway?"

"They are forms for you to apply to become a member of the Criminal Committee of the City Bar Association. It would be good for you and for the firm, if you were on that committee. It is filled with a bunch of movers and shakers in the criminal defense field. You should be one of them. Here is list of the present members. I'll bet you know them all." Jeanne handed Bradford the association year book, opened to the Criminal Committee. He took it and started to read the list.

"This is an impressive group. I know most of these guys. Sort of a snooty bunch."

"That is why you should be on it."

"But we have a different kind of practice. We specialize in jury stuff."

"Almost all these guys try either federal or state jury trials. They need your kind of expertise. The more you hob knob with them, the more likely they are to retain you. It will be good. Most of the application form is boilerplate stuff and I can fill it out with Rita. What we need from you is the list of cases you have been involved with. Look at page three."

Bradford looked. "Holy shit, they want the kitchen sink. 'List all cases you have had anything to do with during the past five years.' I have only been in private practice for four years, so I will have to list some cases I prosecuted. 'List name of case, type of case, what your role was in case, name of adversary, where tried, name of judge, result of trial, any relevant comments. If you have had any matters with present members of committee please give details . . .' on and on. This is going to take forever."

"No, it's not, and you are going to be president of the association someday so you might as well get started now when it can help you get business." Jeanne knew he couldn't resist flattery.

"Ok, I'll get on it, but I'll need your help pulling the information together."

"You got it. Let's start with the most recent cases and work backward. I should think the most recent cases are the most important anyway. Who cares what you did five years ago? Let's start with the last three cases you handled. You can work on the rest of the list while I dig up the stuff on those three."

Jeanne was proud of herself. She had thought of the Bar Association and its committees the other night when she couldn't sleep. Her husband, the deputy inspector, had given a speech before one of them last year. She had gone over to the association and got the forms. This was a great way to find out about Bradford's cases and to start digging through his files. Proud, she was very proud. Right at the top of the list was People of the State of New York vs. Guido Conti.

38

Barry Bradford was no dope. He knew that anyone who wanted to fix a jury trial was not the kind of person you would normally want to be dealing with. He thought about precautions and decided to consult with a law school classmate who was smart, a friend and pretty much a trust-and-estates kind of guy. This was an area of the law that Bradford stayed as far away from as possible while in law school. Now that he was starting to make good money, he needed some assistance.

"I want to retain you as my trust and estate attorney. I know we are friends, but that doesn't matter. I want to pay your regular fees. I can afford you. So are we straight about that?"

"Yeah Barry, but—"

"There are no buts. Will you first draw up a will for me? I want something fancy with all sorts of ways to keep those assholes in Washington from getting my money. I'm not married. I have no kids. I don't give a shit about my brother or sister, but I do want to take care of my parents. If something happens to me, I want them to get everything. If there is some way to keep my parents from giving my money to my brother or sister, that would be great. If that can't be, then fine. I still want my parents to get whatever I have if I die. Are we clear so far?"

"We are clear."

"Good. Now here's the tricky part. I have some shitty clients. They are not nice people. Some of them are connected. Do you know what that means?"

"That they are, you know, in the mob?"

"That's right. They are in the mob."

"Holy shit, Barry, the last thing I knew you were in the DA's office."

"I was. I learned what I went there to learn. I fulfilled my commitment of four years, and I got out of there. Now I am making money."

"Just keep in mind that everyone is entitled to a lawyer. Whether he is a cardinal in the church or a mobster makes no difference. If he wants to hire a lawyer and he can pay for a lawyer, then he is entitled to a lawyer. It doesn't mean the lawyer is committing a crime if he represents a mobster. Nor does it mean that he has to commit a crime in order to properly represent him."

"What if the mobster wants you to help him commit perjury or to do something illegal?"

"I can refuse. I can tell him to go find another lawyer. If someone asks me to do something illegal, I can say I don't do that shit, go somewhere else. I will further tell him not to worry about me telling anyone what he wanted me to do because he is protected by the attorney-client privilege. No one can ever make me tell what it was a client asked me to do. I have that conversation with potential clients all the time."

"And you don't worry?"

"That's another reason I'm here, because I do worry, but let me continue. Besides having some clients who are connected, I might have some clients who are in illegal businesses. Like they might be drug dealers. They might run prostitution rings, whorehouses. They might be bookies. They might commit white collar crimes on Wall Street. There are all sorts of people out there who make money doing all sorts of things. My lifeblood is greed, arrogance and stupidity. Nothing better than a client who is greedy and arrogant enough to think he can get away with it. What I don't like is a killer, particularly a killer of me."

"I can understand that."

"Good. So here is what I want to do. I want to give you an envelope. I don't want you to open the envelope; I just want you to hold it in your safe for me. The envelope will have an address and a stamp on it. If you hear that I have been killed or I am missing, I want you to mail the envelope. That is all you have to do. You don't have to look at who it's addressed to. Just give it to your secretary or the mail boy or whomever you use in the firm and let it be gone. Is there any problem with this so far? I'm not asking you to do anything you shouldn't do, am I? There is nothing illegal or unethical, is there?"

"No. Nothing wrong that I can think of. If I come up with something, I'll call you. I'm ok so far. I just hate to think that you are in this kind of position."

"As I said, everyone is entitled to a lawyer. They pay their bills better than most clients. The deterrent is that they know the letter exists and that it will be mailed. They will be told that the letter is with a lawyer, but they will not have your name or know anything about you. It may not stop them from killing me, but maybe it will cause them to pause. There may be more than one letter. If there is, I want you to mail whatever you have."

"Just please keep my name and my firm's name out of this."

"I will. It does me no good to have anyone know that information."

Gus Conti fumbled for his ringing phone. "Well, Barry Bradford, long time no speak."

"Hi Gus, you're right; we haven't talked in a while and we need to."

"It costs me lots of money every time we talk. And I don't have any money left after the last time."

"I'm glad you told me that now, before I did any more work for you. So you will no longer be using my firm's services?"

"No, I think I can afford one more fling. You know I don't leave the Bronx. When do you want to come up here?"

"I thought I might drop in on the way home this afternoon. Maybe get to your place around three and then get home in time to play nine holes of golf at the club."

"If that's the case, I don't have to pay door to door. You are driving home. Correct?"

"Ok, I'll give you a pass this time, Gus."

Bradford pulled up to the warehouse garage door off of Arthur Avenue, and before he could hit his horn, the door started up. He drove in as the door was closing, and was met by one of Gus' men as he got out of his car. He took the elevator up to the office, and after the usual pleasantries, Bradford got down to business. "Gus, there is a nasty little rumor going around the courthouse that the juror from your son's case is missing. No one has seen him since the trial and there is speculation that he might be dead."

"I heard the same rumor, only I heard that he was shot during the course of a robbery down at some ritzy resort in the Caribbean.

How on earth would either you or I have anything to do with that, with either the rumor or with the possibility of his death?"

"Those are good questions, and I am not suggesting that either you or I did have anything to do with any of that. I am not even suggesting that it is anything more than a rumor. I am simply stating that there is this kind of talk going around. It got me thinking and I wanted to talk to you about what I have in mind."

"Barry, let's back up here a minute. You were hired to find a juror that could be fixed and you did that and you did a great job. You found him and you prepared him and it worked wonderfully, just as we planned. You specifically told him that he was going to get a boatload of money after this was over and that you didn't care what he did or where he went after he did his job. Am I correct?"

"You are correct."

"You didn't tell me I had to do anything other than pay your bills and provide the money to pay off the juror. You didn't tell me to do anything else, nor did you tell me not to do anything else. That was not part of our business relationship. Am I correct?"

"You are correct."

"So, hypothetically, if I decided to hire this guy and put him on my payroll, which I haven't done, I could do that and it would be none of your business. And if, hypothetically, I decided to kill this guy, which I have not done, it would be none of your business. Am I correct?"

"You are correct."

"So why are we having this conversation? I don't like it."

"I'm sorry you don't like it, Gus, and I don't expect you to like what you are about to hear, but that is not my job. My job is to keep your son from being convicted of murder and, so far, I have done my job very successfully. So just hear me out.

"I need a little insurance policy and maybe a little protection. So I have written a letter and I have given it to someone. I am going to give you a copy of the letter. If something happens to me, the person who has this letter is going to mail it. The person who has this letter is one of my lawyers. You don't need to know his name and I will not give you his name. He is a smart lawyer. If I end up dead, or I am even missing, he will conduct an investigation. If he finds that I have died of natural causes, there is no problem. The letter gets destroyed. If he finds that I have been shot in the head, there is a problem and the letter gets mailed. Is this all making sense to you? Do you understand the insurance? Do you understand the protection?"

"I'm no idiot. Of course, I understand. But let me ask you some questions. You have just spoken of two relatively simple, clear-cut situations. On the one hand, death by natural causes, and on the other hand, shot in the head, black and white. Don't you think there could be a lot of middle ground situations, grey situations, where it isn't so clear? Suppose, hypothetically, you are crossing the street and you get hit by a car. Does your lawyer friend know whether someone intentionally ran you down or if it was a traffic accident that happens several times a day in the city of New York? Don't answer yet.

"Now, furthermore, I suspect that you are a busy, talented lawyer. Mine is not the only matter you have handled. Supposing, again hypothetically, that one of your other clients decides to put a bullet in your head. Your lawyer is going to have a letter covering your relationship with that client and a letter covering your relationship with me. Which letter does he send? Don't answer yet.

"Now let us further assume that, without even seeing this letter, I can tell you I don't like it. I don't want to have this sort of thing involved with our attorney-client relationship. It was never mentioned when we had our discussions about whether you should be retained, and if it had been mentioned, I can assure you I would not have retained you. I assume that the letter says something like 'If I, Bradford, am ever found dead, go after Gus Conti because he is the one who killed me and he did it to keep me from talking about how I fixed a juror in his son's case. He has killed that juror and he has killed me.' You will agree with me, will you not, that such a letter violates all of your ethics as an attorney? It violates the attorney-client privilege. It is unfair because you have no knowledge of whether I killed the juror or if he is even dead. It is unfair because maybe one of your other clients decided to kill you, not me. Now you may answer."

"Gus, you didn't get where you are today by being stupid or by being a nice guy. I have watched you operate, and I have admired what I have seen. You don't play by the rules of society. You play by your own rules and the rules of the society within which you operate. I am sure it's not always been pleasant and it's not always been fair. I am sure that mistakes have been made and people have been hurt who didn't deserve to be hurt. Or people were hurt because they put themselves in a position where they risked being hurt. It was a risk they took in order to accomplish the goals they sought.

"You have raised some very fair questions. They are questions which, in the normal world, I would have trouble answering. But I don't have trouble answering them in your world and my world. We live in a different world, a world of evil, a world of unfairness. I want you to worry about how I cross the street. I want you to worry about whether some other client might kill me. I want you to protect me. This is a risk you run because you got me involved in fixing your son's case. And it is a risk you will continue to run because you are going to want me to fix your son's next case.

"I also am not an idiot. I knew you were not going to be happy about this. In fact, I know that, as you are sitting there in your big, overstuffed chair, you are thinking, 'I am going to kill this little prick,' so I didn't come here without taking a precaution. This letter, which I will show you, is not here for you to proofread. It is here because I have already given it to my lawyer. If I don't come out of this meeting, it gets mailed. He is waiting to be convinced that all is well with me and that the letter he already has can stay in his safe.

"You are correct when you say it is unethical. So what? You are correct when you say it violates attorney-client privileges. So what?

"You are correct when you say you might be unjustly accused. So what? You, above all others, know that life isn't fair. Things are not what you always would like them to be. You may be correct when you say that had we talked about this when I was first retained, you would not have hired me. So what? That is why I didn't raise it. You hired me. You had me fix your son's case.

"It is like the cop on the beat who takes the first free apple from the grocer. He is hooked. The grocer sees the cop a few days later and says, 'Here're some tomatoes. Take them home to the Mrs.' That goes on for a while and then the grocer says to the cop, 'I just got a summons from the health inspector for some mouse droppings near my beets. Can you do anything about it for me?' What is the cop going to say? No? Of course not. He is hooked. It all started with the first apple. The next thing you know the cop's family is eating fresh vegetables and the health inspector is getting nothing cleaned up. Then the cop says to the grocer, 'Hey Jimmy, I hear you are taking book on the ponies, could that be?' 'Aw Patty, you're not going to rat on me, are you? It's just a few bets. Here have some more tomatoes.'

"So, make sure I look both ways when I cross the street, and tell anyone, who asks, that you don't want anything happening to me. You, Gus, are my insurance and my protection."

"Barry, when the word gets out, that this is what you are doing, you are not going to get any more cases. Your business will dry up. You will be ruined."

"I'll take that chance, Gus. I'm good at what I do and it's not like there are many people around who are willing to do what I do. There are those who want the results and are willing to pay the price, be they legal fees or keeping me alive. I'm sure that the district attorney will start Guido's trial soon. It is only a matter of time. Do you want me to do my thing or not?"

Gus Conti looked at Bradford for a long time. Bradford knew this was it. He might not get out of this meeting alive. He said nothing more. He looked back at Gus. Finally Gus said, "I want you to do your thing. I'd offer you a drink, but I don't want anything to happen to you on the way home."

39

Just before opening statements in the Brooklyn narcotics case, the defendant took a plea and the case was over. Bradford looked disgusted as he walked out of the courtroom without acknowledging his investigators. "Well, I guess that is a few billable hours down the drain," Spence said to Collins. "Let's grab a cab back to our office. I'll call Jowls and let him know what's happened."

Nails Ballen was really pissed. "Oh Shit. Shit. Shit. This is terrible. What do you mean you're going to move the case for trial? I thought we were going to put it off for another month or so."

"Nope. I think that you've had enough time to get your practice back in shape. And you promised you weren't going to use that vile language in front of Bunny. Right Bunny?"

"You're right, Mr. MacDonald. Nails, you have to stop using the S word in my presence."

"What the fuck are you talking about Bunny? You use the S word more than I do."

Ian jumped in, "Now you're even using the F word and in a courthouse, no less."

A couple of weeks ago the Conti trial had been adjourned until today. Judge Hastings had been champing at the bit to start the case again. He was just waiting for Ian's signal.

Nails started to walk away when he suddenly turned to Ian and said, "I hate to put this on a personal basis, but it's what I've got to do. I've got to plead with you. It comes down to this: I have tickets for a cruise for me and my Dolores. Ian, she will kill me if we have to put this trip off. If I go home and tell her we can't go, I don't know what she will do to me. Oh God, she is liable to get her father after me. I'm a dead man. Please Ian, I'm begging you; give me a week to go on this cruise."

"Nails, did it ever occur to you that some of the rest of us have lives also? Maybe I want to get this case off my docket and move on to some other cases. It has consumed me for the past year."

"I'm sure it has. I promise you I will never ask for another adjournment in any case you and I have together in the future. Never."

"Bunny, I want that in writing. When is your cruise?"

Nails saw a sliver of hope. "We are scheduled to leave tomorrow and to be gone for a week. I could be here in court a week from the day after tomorrow and ready to go."

"That would be the fifteenth. You would be ready to start picking the jury on the fifteenth? How can you go away and enjoy yourself knowing you have to try a case as soon as you get back? When are you going to prepare?"

"What prepare? You have to put in your case. I already know your case. I know what witnesses you're going to call, when you are going to call them and what they are going to say. What's to prepare? I told you to make me a plea offer. I know your entire case."

"I may have some surprises for you, Nails."

"So surprise me. Just don't do it until the fifteenth. I am begging you."

"Ok, Nails, we will tell Hastings we have an agreement. There will be none of your pretrial bullshit motions. We will start jury selection on the fifteenth."

Nails dropped his briefcase and threw his arms around Ian. "I love you Ian. You are the best human being in the world. I will never, ever, ever bust your balls again. Bunny, write a memo when we get back to the office not to bust Mr. MacDonald's balls ever again."

40

When Ian arrived back in his office, Smitty was waiting for him. "We should probably meet at the Hole later today. It looks like there're some developments." He paused as Robbie came in with some coffees. "Looks like things are beginning to fall into place."

"Not a moment too soon. We probably will be starting jury selection on the fifteenth. Try to get word to both Bill and Jeanne to be on high alert today because Bradford's office may be getting a call. I also want you to run down our witness list and confirm that everyone is going to be around for the next three or four weeks."

Smitty said with a smile, "I think you should be the one to notify Adele. She might consider it a little strange to be hearing from me."

"You're right; I'll call her. I'll also see if we can get everyone together this evening on such short notice."

Bill Spence was excited and his enthusiasm was contagious. He greeted his inspector when he came to the Hole, "We had a good day today, boss. Jowls is warming up to me. I think encouraging him to get rid of his dopey son-in-law has gained his confidence. It also looks like this Collins guy is going to be a help."

"Well, we know why he's with Jowls," Culkin interjected. "They worked together and the same flaking suspicions that dogged Jowls, dogged Collins. Jowls should be very comfortable with him."

"He is, and here's what happened. I got a call from Jowls to come into his office this morning, just before lunch, and he introduced me to Collins. They have worked together for years and Jowls is feeling all warm and fuzzy because he says he has gotten rid of a stone and has picked up a diamond. Collins said he heard good things about me when I was in the 20th Division. That makes Jowls warmer and fuzzier. Then Jowls tells us that Bradford has gotten the news that one of his top clients will be needing him again. Jowls emphasizes the 'again' part. He then says that he is going to tell us some highly confidential stuff and he trusts both of us.

"I am now starting to wish I was wearing a wire because I got a feeling that I know what he is about to tell us. Sure enough he starts to talk about the first Conti trial, about screening the jurors as they were selected, about targeting the eleventh juror and about running the background check on him. He goes into some detail about how labor intensive all of this work is and how we are all going to have to work our asses off."

Ian jumped in, "Bill, I'm sorry to interrupt, but you didn't have a wire on so I want the next best thing. I want you to go into the next room and write down everything each one of you said when the three of you were in that room together. I want you to do it now before any more time goes by. Do it like you are writing a stenographic recording of the session. Identify each person and then what they said and do it to the very best of your ability. Your conversation corroborates all that Peters told us and we probably now have enough to get an eavesdropping warrant."

"I'll get on it right away. I thought you might also like to know that while we were meeting, Bradford called and said that he just spoke to old man Conti on the phone. Bradford wants to meet with Jowls tomorrow morning."

"Perfect!"

"Well shit, that sure steals my thunder," a dejected Jeanne Dalton cried. "I thought I had some goodies for you, but this is nothing compared to what Bill's got."

"Every little bit helps. Talk, Jeanne."

"I got my hands on the Conti file and made copies of each and every page. There is no proof of a crime that I can see, but it sure shows that Mr. Conti has been a good client of the firm. It ought to let us get all the billing records if we ever execute a search warrant."

"Excellent! Great work, Jeanne," Ian encouraged.

Ian called Louie Balzo and told him to meet with Bill Spence and to start drafting the eavesdropping order early next morning before Bill went to work. "Bill, call Jowls and leave a message with him that you got a dental emergency and you have been able to get an appointment with your dentist first thing tomorrow morning. You are going to be a bit late for work. This will give you some time to work with Louie. He's got to draft an affidavit for your signature. The sooner we can get all this approved the better."

Culkin was seated at the other side of the Hole placing a call to the Pats.

41

The diagram of Bradford's office was back up on the easel in Ian's office. Spence, who had been working with Louie Balzo on the warrant since seven that morning, was now huddled with the office artist. They were working on a draft diagram of Jowls' Maiden Lane complex. This was going to be a bit trickier than Bradford's office. The Pats were standing at Ian's desk.

Ian asked, "How will you be able to know if they have any bug detecting stuff around? How about alarms and stuff to know if you guys are breaking in? What happens if they use some kind of sweeping device that tells them something's up?" Ian was a nervous wreck.

"Ian, relax, this isn't the first time we've done this. All of your questions and concerns are legitimate ones, but we will take care of them." Patricia was trying to put a calm, motherly spin on the whole operation. "We'll take our time and manage."

"You know of course, that if this gets discovered, the entire investigation goes in the crapper. We are screwed. How can you be so calm about all this?"

Inspector Culkin thought it was time for him to put in his two cents. "Ian, this stuff is never easy, but you've got the two best people in the whole country doing this. If you don't want to do it, or you don't think the time is right yet, we don't have to do it. We can put it off. It's your call."

"That's what's bothering me. It is my call. Ok so let's review where we are. We've got a solid warrant. I am not worried about having Hastings sign it. We have a pretty good idea of the setup in Bradford's office. We know where to put the bugs. We don't know shit about Maiden Lane, do we?"

"We will after tonight," Pat declared.

"What happens tonight?"

"We will take a look at the place. See what is there. We'll take a little inventory. See if they have things protected and, if so, what we will do about it. We'll take some measurements and see where we can hide stuff. Then we'll be more comfortable going in and planting the stuff."

"You aren't telling me that you are going to break in there twice, are you?"

"Sure. No big deal."

"That means there is twice as much chance that you get caught."

"Ian, as I said before, this is not the first time we have done this."

Ian got up from behind his desk. "I got to go to the bathroom."

42

Collins knocked on Spence's door. "I want to take you to lunch. Get to know you a little better. You free?"

"Sure. I was a little late getting in this morning. Had a dentist appointment. Let me finish this report I'm doing for Jowls and I'll be right over to pick you up."

They went down Maiden Lane to an Irish bar that made good hamburgers and found a booth in the back where there wasn't much noise. They ordered beers and cheeseburgers. Collins wanted his cooked to death, and Spence wanted his almost raw. They agreed that neither of them would get what they ordered.

Collins asked, "What was it like working in the 20th Division?"

"What do you mean, what was it like? What was it like working in Bronx narcotics? Aren't they all part of the job?"

"Of course they are. My bad. I just have heard so much about the divisions and particularly the 20th, I guess I was a little curious."

"Do you want to tell me what you heard about the 20th?"

"Sure. I heard that it was tough. You never knew where anyone stood. You didn't know which bosses were straight and which weren't. That there was a lot of turnover. That you no sooner got to know your team when, bam, they got transferred and new people came in. I also heard that the guys always wondered if there were rat bastards working there." Collins paused as the waiter delivered the cheeseburgers. They were done perfectly to order: one raw, the other stewed. Collins asked for two more beers.

"What do you mean by a rat bastard?" Spence asked as he took a chunk out of his food.

"Oh, come on Sammy, don't play with me. You know what I mean. We had the same deal in Bronx narcotics. Ever since the Fredericks Commission, you didn't know if your partner was for real or some rat bastard out of the Internal Affairs Division who had been planted there. The two places hit the hardest were the narc squads all over the city and the divisions. You know that."

"Let me ask you a question Les. Did you ever find one IAD undercover in Bronx narcotics? I'm not talking about some guy you suspected or some guy you thought was fishy. I'm talking about actually finding an IAD guy in Bronx narcotics. Did you?"

"No. I think if we did, he would have been killed."

"Look, I know what you meant by rat bastards. I suspected they were planted in the 20th. But so what? After the Fredericks Commission, anyone who wasn't careful about what they did and who they did it with deserved whatever they got. They were just plain stupid, and they made life hell for the rest of us. There are too many know-it-all wise guys on the job, arrogant guys who think they are supermen. They are all jerks. Stupid jerks who piss me off. I don't want to talk about it."

"Whoa Sammy, I didn't mean to get you pissed. I know exactly what you're talking about. Exactly. I just would have thought that it would have been tough to work in the 20th because of all that went on there."

"You know what you are doing, Les? You're pumping. You're looking for information from me, and I don' t like it."

"No, I'm not Sammy. I'm just having a conversation with you."

"That's bullshit, and I'll tell you why. It's bullshit because the only reason it would have been tough for me to work in the 20th would be if I was doing something. So you are trying to find out if I was doing something. And I'm not going to talk about what I was doing or wasn't doing. And I'm not talking about what the other guys in the 20th were doing. I don't trust anyone in this town. The statute of limitations has not run on several of my years in the 20th. How do I know you aren't some IAD plant who right now is trying to get me to say something that you could use against me? Just because I left the job doesn't mean that, if I committed a crime while I was a cop, I couldn't be arrested for that crime. Well, I didn't commit any crimes and you are not going to get me to talk about what I did or what the guys did, so go pump someone else. Lunch is over." Spence threw a twenty-dollar bill on the table, and walked out as fast as he could. He thought he heard Collins call after him, but he never stopped. He went back to his office and closed the door and waited.

Something had to happen. It did. In about thirty minutes Spence's phone rang. Jowls wanted him in his office.

Spence took a deep breath. He hoped that his reaction had had an effect on Collins. He wanted both Collins and Jowls to know that he didn't appreciate either of them suspecting him. He'd decided it wouldn't hurt to act a little pissed. He knocked on Jowls' door and was invited in.

"Collins tells me we have a little problem."

"Maybe we should have him in here if this is about what just happened at lunch."

"It is. But let's you and me talk first. Then we can bring him in. What happened?"

"I'm sure he has given you his version and that's why I'm here. Who the hell is this guy anyway? I'm beginning to think he is with Internal Affairs."

Jowls laughed. "I'll have to tell him that one. That's the first time anyone ever accused old flakes of being in IAD. I have known him for about twenty years. I was in narcotics with him from time to time. He is a very suspicious guy. The reason he is so suspicious is that he can't believe that everyone wasn't as bad as he was. Flakes got that nickname because he deserved it. He was forever planting drugs on guys. When the pushers saw him coming down the street, they ran for their lives. They knew, if he caught them, they would end up with either a possession charge or they would have to hand over a fistful of money to keep from being charged. Leslie 'Flakes' Collins is one of the most solidly corrupt cops I have ever known. He just figures that everyone else must also be corrupt and he wants to hear about it."

"Well, tell him it's none of his fucking business. I thought you made it quite clear when I interviewed with you that I didn't have to go into chapter and verse about what I did or didn't do when I was on the job. Did you put him up to asking me those questions?"

"I did not."

"Do you have any question about my loyalty or where I'm coming from?"

"I do not."

"If you do, speak up and I will be out of here in a heartbeat. I don't need anyone snooping around me."

"You don't need to go anywhere." Jowls picked up his phone and told Collins to come in. Collins slowly opened the door and peeked in. "I'm not going to get shot, am I?"

"Come in here, asshole, and apologize. Sammy doesn't like all your questions and neither do I."

"Sammy, I am really sorry. It will not happen again. I promise you. I guess I was up to so much shit when I was on the job, I think everyone else must have been also. There is something comforting to me about hearing others talk about what they did."

"Well, my job isn't to comfort you or worry about you. My job is to do what Jowls wants done. I accept your apology, but I am not the least bit interested in hearing about anything you were involved in when you were a cop. Nor am I interested in any of your extracurricular activities. I don't want to be involved in any of that shit. Is that clear?"

"It is, Sammy, and again, I'm sorry."

"Is everything square with you, Jowls?"

"It is, Sammy."

As they left Jowls' office, Collins had a funny feeling in his stomach about Burns.

43

The Pats were not completely forthcoming with Ian. They knew more about Maiden Lane than they let on. With Culkin's help, they obtained some records from the building department. When Bradford rented the space, he got a work order and was permitted to have certain physical changes made to the space as part of his rental deal. This required plans to be filed with the building department. The Pats had those plans. They were very helpful in that they showed where much of the wiring was installed. They gave the plans to the office artist, and he was able to incorporate them into his drawings of the Maiden Lane facility.

The Pats also did some late-night scouting. They had a pretty good feel for the amount of foot and vehicle traffic that occurred during the early morning hours. It was negligible. About once a night, a patrol car went down the block to make sure there were no problems. That schedule would be obtained.

There was no night watchman. The main entrance to the building was in between two retail stores. It appeared that the door to the lobby was locked at around seven at night and unlocked at around seven in the morning by some sort of super type guy. He was seen occasionally during the day emptying garbage and doing general cleanup.

In addition to a rickety elevator, there was a stairway going both up to the four floors above the retail stores and down to the basement where there were some utility and furnace rooms. The main phone lines for the tenants all came into a box in the basement, and could be discreetly tapped from down there should that need ever arise.

The Pats knew that, besides Jowls' complex on the second floor, there was some sort of garment import business on the third floor and a mail order travel company on the fourth floor. Both of those places only employed about four people each and emptied out by six at the latest. Usually, everyone was gone by five thirty in the evening. Neither of them was going to be a problem in the middle of the night.

What the Pats still didn't know was what kind of security system, if any, Jowls had installed. They purposely kept away from the second-floor premises to avoid any problems. They wanted to wait until the eavesdropping order was signed to give them some cover and authority. They didn't explain any of this to Ian, but they didn't think Maiden Lane was going to be the problem. They thought it better to let Ian stew about the entire operation. Stewing kept him on his toes. Ian was good all the time, but great when he was on his toes.

The Woolworth Building was another matter. It had first-class security, night watchmen, lots of late-night activity—the whole nine yards. There was an all-night security sign-in desk in the lobby. The Woolworth Building was a challenge. A challenge was what they loved.

In many of the buildings in Manhattan, security was run by one of several large security companies. Culkin knew them all. Most of the buildings that had their own security people employed former police officials to run them. Culkin also knew all of them.

There were a few buildings that had security teams with no NYPD connection. The Woolworth Building was one of them. Culkin kept looking for a hook with their outfit, but could find none. He discussed with the Pats the possibility of sitting down with the security team, showing them the eavesdropping warrant and getting their assistance in gaining the Pats access to Bradford's office. The Pats asked him to hold off on that until they could first see what they could accomplish on their own. The fewer people who knew what they were up to the better.

"What are you going to do if it turns out that the chief of Woolworth security was Bradford's college roommate and got him his office space?" Pat asked Culkin. Culkin, with Ian's consent, agreed to see what could be learned without involving anyone else.

44

The mailroom courier plunked the envelope down on Ian's desk. It contained several pages. It appeared to be a list of all the tenants in the Woolworth Building, with the location of their office and the dates of their present lease. Ian figured this was the product of Culkin's labors.

He got Louie to run off enough copies for all the people who were aware of the Bradford investigation, still under twenty. Ian's idea was to distribute the list to those in the know and ask them if they had any knowledge of any of the tenants. It was his hope that they might come up with someone who might be of assistance in helping the Pats get by security. Amazingly, there were four possibilities.

Culkin came into Ian's office unannounced. "There is a guy on this list I think we know."

"I just saw him. You're referring to Ed Purns, the former assistant."

"Right," replied Dick. "Didn't he have to leave because of a death in his family? Wasn't he an all around good guy?"

Purns came from a wealthy family and now occupied an office on the sixty-first floor of the Woolworth Building from which he managed his family's fortune. After clearing it with LoMurko, Ian and Culkin called Purns. They asked him if they could take him to lunch.

Purns insisted on meeting them at his club. When Ian asked when he might be available, Purns replied, "Always, I do nothing but count money." They agreed to meet a little after noon. Ian wanted to see how receptive Purns might be to their plan as soon as possible. It was only about a six-block walk.

"I loved every minute of my time in the DA's office. I would still be there if Dad hadn't become ill. I owed it to my family to take care of things after he died. It is still my dream to get this damn money in such great shape that I can go back there to my old job. The trouble is there is never enough money. No matter how much you make, someone always wants more.

"God, it's good to see you guys. How have you been? How is the office? What are you up to? I got all afternoon and can't think of anything I would rather do than bullshit with you. We just had twins, by the way."

Ian somehow thought that this wasn't going to be a heavy lift. Having Inspector Culkiin there added some gravitas to the whole scene, and Ian wasn't going to waste any time.

"We will spend all the time you want, but let me first get right to our problem. Let me ask you a hypothetical, Ed. Supposing there were a really bad guy in the Woolworth Building who was doing some really bad things. And supposing that you could help us by saying that a couple of our people were doing some work for you. You would say it was essential that they be able to get into your office, let's say, all night. Let's say they are accountants who are doing an annual review of your books and you don't want them around during the day when you are working on things. Let's say that I know these people because they are NYPD detectives working for me. You don't have anything to worry about as far as the security of your office is concerned. Do you think you might be able to do that?"

Purns looked like he was about to enjoy a banana split. "Are you kidding me? That is my office. I can do anything I want with it. I have plenty of room. If you want to run World War III out of that office you could do it. How soon do you need to do this?"

"Probably pretty soon. It is very confidential and you really can't tell anyone what you are doing. Is that ok? Do you need to know what it's about?"

"I don't need to know. I sure as hell am dying of curiosity, but I don't need to know."

"I'll tell you chapter and verse as soon as I can, but no one will have to know about your involvement in this, and I think it would be better for you if you didn't know right now what is going on."

"Let's do it."

45

They gathered at the Hole at 6:00 PM. Ian told them about the development with Purns. Pat high-fived Pat. "Now, here's the bad news." Ian picked up a statute book and read. "The eavesdropping order shall be signed by either the district attorney of the county or his designee if he has designated someone to sign in his stead." Ian looked around the room. Eyes rolled. Everyone understood what this meant.

"And you are going to tell us that Harper has not designated anyone to sign eavesdropping warrants so you have to go to him to get it signed," LoMurko stated dejectedly. "So much for the confidentiality of the Bradford investigation. Should we reconsider this?"

"Believe me," said Ian, "I have given that serious thought. I am going to go up to Harper's office with at least O'Rielly, but maybe Carney and Schooner also. We have to impress upon him the importance of confidentiality. He will be told that police officers' lives are at stake. We have two undercover officers who could get killed if they are exposed. This is not a publicity opportunity.

"I honestly do not think he will blow this one. He could be severely criticized. At any rate, it is my judgement that we have come too far with this to back down now. So I'm expecting that by the end of tomorrow, we will have a warrant and you will be able to do your thing, Pats, starting tomorrow night."

Patrick asked, "Is there any chance we could go over to Purns' office this evening and he could introduce us to the security crew? Or maybe even get us passes so that they would be accustomed to us going in and out at all hours of the night."

"I'll call and see if Ed is still there. He has new twins and he may be using the office for peace and quiet." Ian tried calling Purns, but got a voice message. He'd left for the day. Ian left a message for Purns to call.

"Is there anything else I should know?" Ian asked.

Jeanne jumped up like a little school girl. "I have something, bossman. I think I may have found another hung jury Bradford was involved in. I asked him to fill out an application for a Bar Association committee which required him to list his latest trials. One of them ended in a hung jury. It was in the Bronx. I told Louie Balzo about this, and he is going to see what he can dig up. It may all be nothing, but it could be something.

"They have also filled out a new case form for Conti. They are calling it Conti II. If I can see the time sheets, I'll know who has been doing what."

Ian asked, "What do you mean by time sheets?"

"You get paid a salary every two weeks, Ian. Like I do. You don't have to show how you have spent your day. When you are in private practice, you are supposed to break down each hour of your day into fifteen-minute segments. At the end of the day, everyone submits a time sheet for that day. It shows what cases each individual was working on and for how long. Rita allocates the various times to the various clients from the time sheets. Then, depending on what rate that individual's time is billed at, the bills for the client get calculated. So if, for example, I spend an hour putting a file together to start a new case up, my time is billed at $45 per hour to that new client. Jowls' time is at $100 per hour. Spence is billed at $80. The time sheet usually says what the individual did during the time like 'checked background of juror.' Some of it can be pretty illuminating. Most of it is vague. But it helps."

"What does Bradford get for an hour?"

"$350."

"You're kidding! I've got to go into private practice."

"Nah, you're a public service type. So if I volunteer to do some of the time sheet stuff, take some of that work load off of Rita the receptionist, she will be happy and I will be able to see who is spending time on what. Win, win."

Ian's phone rang. It was Purns returning Ian's call. Ian got him up to date, and Purns told him he would be down at the lobby of the Woolworth Building in thirty minutes, would introduce the Pats to security and show them around the office. Ian said it could wait until tomorrow. Purns said, "Nonsense. The recently fed twins are asleep. I'd would like to get out for a bit." The Pats were on their way.

46

"I really have given serious consideration to forgetting this eavesdropping warrant, but I think we should do it."

O'Rielly took over, "Ian, I think Carney and Schooner should come with us when we see Harper. I think we should tell him that this is a highly confidential matter involving a former member of this office and that we want to see him alone. You have done a hell of a job keeping the number of people who are aware of the investigation to a minimum, and he should not do anything to change that. Having said that, I would be amazed if he didn't have his two aides there. Maybe it's just as well if they are there. We can tell them to their faces that police officers' lives are at stake in this and we know we are dealing with people who kill. I just can't believe he isn't going to use his head about this."

Schooner said, "I wish I were as confident as you. I don't trust the bastard. Give us your thoughts, Frank."

Frank Carney was silent for a few seconds. He was thinking. "We should have a plan B. I can't believe he would screw this investigation, but I don't know about the people around him. What do we do if this investigation gets leaked?"

Ian spoke up, "We immediately pull out Spence and Dalton. We immediately hit Bradford's office and Joust's office with search warrants and seize everything we can. We haul Smitty's friend in and try to break him. We haul Barbara Banner in and try to break her, then the investigators and then Bradford. Old man Conti is the *carrot*. We tell Bradford that giving up Conti is his way to help himself. We threaten him with a murder charge on either a conspiracy theory or a felony murder theory. My problem is that Bradford is the bad guy in all this. He is corrupting the system and he is a lawyer. Old man Conti is just trying to save his son. He may have committed murder, but at least he has a better motive than just plain old money."

Vince O'Rielly called Harper's office and asked for a private meeting with the DA. He was told to come up in half an hour. O'Rielly explained that the purpose of the meeting was to have the DA sign an eavesdropping warrant. He made it clear that this was a very confidential matter. He got no indication about who would be attending the meeting.

That issue was answered when Harper's chief assistant came out to the waiting room and asked the assistants to come in. O'Rielly was right up front. "Mr. District Attorney, this is a highly confidential matter that involves the lives of police officers. Could we meet with you alone on this?"

"When you are meeting with my chief and my communications assistant, you are meeting with me."

"Could you, at a minimum, first privately hear what this is about with the understanding that you can always call them in if you think it necessary?"

"Jesus Vince, you'd think we were launching atom bombs here with all your secrecy. This is a law office. We are prosecuting people.

We aren't launching bombs. Tell me what's going on so we can move on. I am a busy man. I don't have time for all this secrecy shit."

"Very well. We have been conducting a highly confidential investigation of a former ADA from this office who has been engaged in fixing jurors. We believe we have developed the requisite probable cause to apply for warrants to bug this attorney's offices. We further believe that if we do this, we will obtain evidence that the attorney and his staff will be attempting to identify and bribe a juror in a murder case this office will be trying in about a week. As you know, the law requires that the application for the warrant be made by and signed by the district attorney of the county where the warrant is to be executed. That would be New York county and, therefore, you are the applicant. We need your signature on the application so that we can take it to the judge."

There was silence. Harper looked to his two aides. They appeared to be in shock. Neither of them said a word.

"Why am I only learning about this now?"

"We have worked very hard to keep the number of people who know about this to an absolute minimum both within this office and within the police department. That is the reason we asked to see you alone. We believe that the people involved in this conspiracy have killed at least one person and are capable of killing others. There are two New York City police officers, both first grade detectives and both experienced undercover officers, who have infiltrated the attorney's operation. We have no doubt that if this investigation were to surface, their lives would be in danger and we would have to extract them if we could. Before entering this room, there were five ADAs who knew about this investigation: two bureau chiefs, a deputy bureau chief, the trial assistant whose prosecution was derailed by a fixed juror and his rookie assistant. From the department there were eight: your squad commander, a captain of the NYPD, the two undercover officers and four other detectives. That is the extent of those who were aware of this investigation. That is how we were able to keep the investigation confidential. Now, there are three more. Would you please sign the application so that we can get it to the judge? Time is of the essence."

The PR guy spoke up. "God damnit Ferris, this is why I'm saying you are not getting enough information about what is happening in your own office. How am I supposed to prepare for something like this if I don't know it is going on?"

"Excuse me," O'Rielly interrupted, "no disrespect intended, but there is absolutely no reason at all for you to know about it now, or to have known about it previously. This cannot possibly end up in the public domain until after this investigation is concluded, the undercover officers are extracted, and arrests have been made. You will have plenty of time to be briefed on all aspects of the case at that time. That is when you can prepare for it, not before. It would be a monumental disaster for any of this to be leaked prior to all arrests having been made."

"You don't seem to understand that we have a political campaign on our hands here."

"You don't seem to understand," O'Rielly continued, "that you are going to have to put that campaign aside until we do the job we have been placed here to do. Right now, that is to get this order signed and to go about this investigation without anything happening to it. Mr. District Attorney, will you please sign this application so we can take it to the judge."

"Leave it on my desk. I'll call you."

"I can assure you it is in order. Could we wait in the waiting room while you read it and then we can take it to the judge?"

"No, I'll call you."

The four assistants silently walked to the elevator and took it to the sixth floor. Without saying a word to each other, they got off the elevator and walked all the way to the north end of the hallway to the Homicide Bureau, about a city block away. The first words spoken were when O'Rielly asked them all to come into his office. When they were seated, he shut the door and said, "Can you believe what just happened? I can't believe this. Can you believe this?

"I'll bet that is the first time since before Dewey that a bureau chief has gone to the district attorney to ask him to sign *anything*, not just a warrant, but *anything*," he was shouting, "and not had him sign it. I am really offended."

Lem Schooner said, "Don't take it personally, Vince. We are dealing with a whole different DA here. I don't think he is even his own boss. I just want to say that I am damn proud to have been in that room and to have seen how you handled yourself. You have nothing to be ashamed of. You were direct and to the point. You were fantastic and you should be very pleased with yourself." The others agreed.

"I didn't get the warrant application signed. Thank God there was no one from the police department with us. They would be wondering if we had all lost our marbles. So now what?"

Ian had remained silent throughout this entire trip up to the eighth floor. When no one said anything, he spoke up, "Vince, thanks so much for all your efforts. I really appreciate all you did and the way you handled everything. I have never been prouder to be in this bureau than I was today. For what it's worth, I think the phone will ring in a few minutes and you will be told that he has signed the application. The only question I have is whether he will let someone come up and get it or if the three of them want you to come up so they can beat you up. If they call for you, I would like to go with you."

Everyone left for their own offices except Frank Carney. As he and Ian walked to Ian's office, he asked, "Are you ok?"

"I don't know. I think I'm ok. Now how do you feel about Ferris Harper getting a judgeship?"

Before Carney could answer, Ian's phone range. Ian could go up to Harper's office. His secretary had the signed application.

47

A Homicide Bureau meeting led by Vince O'Rielly was held every Friday at 2:00 PM. No one missed it. You were either on trial in a courtroom, or dying in a hospital bed, or at the meeting. In addition to general bureau matters, cases caught by the junior members of the bureau on the duty chart were presented to the entire bureau. If they were in the nascent stage, there might be suggestions as to the investigative steps to be taken. If the investigating assistant had some issues as to whether he should take certain steps, he could get advice. If the investigation was completed, the presenting assistant would ask the rest of the bureau for a vote: indictment or no indictment? The presenting assistant would be subjected to a rigorous examination by the senior trial assistants. You did not go into these meetings unprepared. It was a terrific learning experience.

As the assistants gathered for this Friday's meeting, they noticed that neither O'Rielly or Carney were present. Their concern ended when, at quarter past two, both men entered the room and took their places. Vince sat behind his desk and asked for everyone's attention. Carney sat in a large leather chair to the side of the chief's desk. That chair had been occupied by the deputy bureau chief for years. Something was up. Both men seemed unusually tense.

"I have some news. Frank and I have just had lunch on the eighth floor with the other bureau chiefs." "The eighth floor" was short talk for Harper's office. "It seems that the DA, the chief assistant and the assistant in charge of communications think that they are not being kept advised of the various investigations that are underway in many of the bureaus. They would like to have more vigorous reporting to the eighth floor. They would like to be aware of any investigation at an earlier stage. They would also like to have more frequent progress reports."

There was a collective groan from all the assistants. "To state the obvious, he is the district attorney and he is entitled to know what is going on in his office. He is entitled to know what his assistants are doing. We work for him. He bears the ultimate responsibility for what goes on in his office. So it is pretty hard to argue with him." Vince paused to take a sip from his coffee cup, and glanced at Carney who was staring at his feet.

"As you can imagine, there are some highly sensitive and confidential investigations underway in this office. As you can also imagine, this is nothing new. The chiefs were quick to point this out. I thought that Scopo was going to have a stroke." Arthur Scopo was the chief of the Rackets Bureau, the repository of several highly confidential investigations. "Frank and I knew we could let Scopo do the talking. So we did. Scopo pointed out that in the past, when an investigation ripened to a certain stage, the bureau chief always met privately with the district attorney to brief him and find out what the DA wanted to have done. On some rare occasions, the chief assistant would attend those meetings, but everything usually was kept on a need-to-know basis. More significantly, Scopo told Harper, the press was never involved until an arrest was accomplished.

"Harper acknowledged that he was aware of that history and said that he was changing it. He was putting his chief assistant and his assistant in charge of communications 'under the cone.' Those were his words, and he took the time to explain what that meant. It meant that what he knew, they knew. He made no bones about the fact that he was in a political position, that he was running for office and that it was important for him to have his two top political advisors, his chief and his PR man know what was going on. He said, 'Talking to me is talking to them and talking to them is talking to me.' He used those phrases several times.

"I don't have to tell you how this news was greeted by the chiefs. Please don't ask me 'Did you ask him this' and 'Did you ask him that.' We did. That is why Frank and I got here late. We put things in hypothetical terms and tried to show how this policy could put him in an untenable position. His answer to that was 'Is there anything about this policy that you don't understand? I expect to be kept aware of all investigations in this office. I expect to know about them from the beginning. I expect to be advised of any significant developments, and when I say I, that will mean the three of us.' He then said, 'I would like to know if any of you think you will have a problem following this policy. If you do, then come see me and we will discuss whether you should continue in your present position.' Scopo, God bless him, told Harper he had to think about it. So that is the news. Any questions?"

Several hands went up. Vince went by seniority. "Al, you've been here a hundred and six years; you go first."

"It has only been a hundred and five. Won't be a hundred and six until next April 2. As you know, we've had situations where close personal friends of the sitting district attorney were suspected of shenanigans. We have always conducted a discrete, thorough investigation to establish whether there was any substance to the allegation before we brought it to the DA's attention. Some of these allegations have been bullshit and didn't get to first base. Some of them were blatant outright crimes. Surely Harper doesn't want early notification of that kind of case, does he?"

"That is exactly one of the hypotheticals we presented to him, and he made it clear that not only does he want to know, he wants to know as soon as we know, and he wants his chief and his press guy to know. It was clear to Frank and me that he wants to be able to have an early assessment of the political ramifications—benefits and liabilities— of what is going on. Does that answer your question, Al?"

"I don't see how we can continue to run a professional, non-political office under those conditions."

"You might be correct." Vince surveyed the room. "Pete, you're next."

"This is all hitting us kind of sudden as I'm sure it hit you and Frank. It goes to the very foundation of all of our principles, and I am sure we all want to think about what it means and what we should do about it. That is assuming there is anything we can do about it. I'm wondering how the press is going to react to this new policy when they hear about it. I'm sure they will hear about it. Will they like it, because they see it benefiting them? They will have more knowledge of what we are doing. Or will they see it for what it is—dragging the office back into the political dark ages?"

"I never have been able to figure out what the press will do. Fred?"

Fred said, "Let's call this as it is. We all know that his chief assistant is his chief campaign manager. We all know that his so-called assistant in charge of communications is his PR man and his deputy campaign manager. He is telling us that we have to bring them in on every investigation in this office so that they can assess the political worth or detriment of each investigation. If it is worth it, he will give it to the press to make himself look better. If it hurts, he will bury it or, God forbid, maybe even obstruct justice so that it doesn't hurt him. I'll be damned if I am going to give him any information on an investigation I think he might impede."

"Fred, I love you like a brother. We have come into this office and greeted each other every morning for the past ten years. I don't want to see anything happen to you, or to any of the rest of you. I don't want to see anything happen to this office which has remained the gold standard of prosecutors' offices since Tom Dewey. But you have to be careful about what you say and do. We all know each other, and we all trust each other. We have been through hell together, and we have celebrated victories together. I don't want to lose any of you. Please be careful what you say and to whom you say it. It is Friday. We are going to hear the week's cases. Then we are going to have the weekend to cool off and reflect about where we are. Let's promise each other to take things slowly and not do anything rashly without considering the consequences. I am here to support you, and I will support you. We will take one issue at a time.

"Now enough of that stuff. Let's get down to business. Which of you rookies wants to start with the first case?"

"I do." It was Louie Balzo. Ian's stomach did a flip. Louie was his man. This was his first presentation.

"We have ourselves a virgin," said the usually staid, proper and prim Vincent O'Rielly who was obviously relishing this opportunity to cheer up his depressed bureau. "Get out your knives."

"Wait a minute, Louie, I've had you running all over the place. You sure you're ready for this? Should you maybe go next week?" asked Ian.

"Boo, boo, boooo" was the chorus from the peanut gallery. "Ian's a party pooper," "Ian's protecting his little girlie" were some of the cries from the assistants.

Louie stood up and walked to the side of O'Rielly's desk. "I am ready and I am going, and you can't touch me."

A sudden silence fell over the room. That was a reckless thing to say to a roomful of seasoned trial lawyers. Ian lowered his head and covered his eyes with his left hand.

Chief O'Rielly said, "You may proceed."

"Last Monday afternoon, at approximately 3:36 PM, one Martha Ray Jocobi walked into the law offices of an attorney named Peter Valenti, located here in the county of New York at 345 Baxter Street. She pulled a meat cleaver from her purse and proceeded to chop Peter's head off..." Louie went nonstop for about fifteen minutes before even coming up for air. His presentation was flawless, a tour de force rarely seen in the history of the Homicide Bureau. There were four witnesses, the expedited medical examiner's report and a forty-three-page Q and A that Louie took Monday night at the Wall Street precinct. In her statement, she explained how she had been planning this for a solid month, that she knew exactly what she was doing and, lest anyone thought she was nuts, she understood the consequences of her action. She was looking forward to spending a long time at Bedford Prison for women. At the end of his presentation, he asked if there were any questions and then said, "Hearing none, I propose that you approve an indictment for murder."

Then it started. It wasn't a good idea to challenge fifteen seasoned trial lawyers who have been attending Homicide Bureau presentations for years. They asked him how this case squared with the Hopkins case, which Louie had never heard of. They asked him questions that called for him to know what the deceased was thinking, which Louie could not possibly know. They questioned Martha Ray's motive and questioned its plausibility. What searches of Martha's home did he conduct? Did he talk to her coworkers? Maybe there were diagrams of the lawyer's office in her office desk. Did he know where and when the meat cleaver was bought? Did he seize the clothes she was wearing? Why not? Reynolds wanted to know how this would affect the Poolman Statute that was presently before the assembly in Albany.

O'Rielly took Louie out of his misery by asking, "Is there a motion?"

One of the most senior trial men said, "I move we have more thorough preparation and a better investigation."

"Second," someone shouted.

"All in favor", asked O'Rielly.

"Aye," they unanimously roared.

Louie returned to his chair, and O'Rielly quickly called for the next case. Ian thought Louie was going to cry, but said nothing to him. There were two more presentations before the meeting was over.

Ian then went down to Louie's office. "What have we learned today?"

"Why did I say that? Why did I say you can't touch me? Am I nuts? Wasn't that the stupidest thing you have ever seen anyone do?"

"I have a suggestion if you would like to hear it."

"Please, Ian. I feel like I should ask for a transfer to another bureau."

"Pick up the phone, call Vince and ask him if you can see him. Then go down and apologize. Don't tell him you want to apologize when you call. Just tell him you want to see him."

Louie called Vince, and Mable told him to come down in five minutes.

Ian walked down to O'Rielly's office with Louie. The door between Mable's office and O'Rielly's was shut. Mable told him, "You can go in. He's expecting you."

Louie plucked up his courage and opened the door. The entire bureau was there.

Vince raised a glass of wine and shouted, "To the virgin. He lost his cherry. Great job, kid. We decided to vote an indictment."

They all raised their glasses, "To the virgin." They got Louie a drink.

48

It was time for the Pats to do their thing. It was a Friday night, and the city had emptied out for the weekend. Spence hung around with Jowls until everyone was gone, and then they left the office. He watched Jowls lock the door, but didn't see him trigger any alarm system. They went for a beer, and then Spence went to the Hole. The Pats were there looking over the eavesdropping warrant and waiting for Jeanne.

Jeanne had asked Rita to work with her so that they could get some filing done before they went home. Bradford and Barbara were leaving together.

"Will you have to come in this weekend Barry, or can you stay away from the office for a couple of days?" Jeanne asked Bradford in a solicitous manner. "It would be good for you to take some time off. You work too hard."

"Not sure, may have to come in. Hope not. Anyway, taking the night off. Taking Barbara to Broadway tonight. Right, Babs?"

"Can't wait. A show and dinner and who knows what." Barbara gave Jeanne a knowing smile and nodded toward Rita who was over by the filing cabinet. Jeanne gave a quick thumbs up.

Bradford and Banner wished everyone a good weekend and left.

Jeanne said to Rita, "I can finish up these two files if you want to go home. Is there anything special you do to lock up? Any alarms or things I set."

"That would be great. I got a kind of date tonight and would love to get out of here. Let me show you the alarm system under my desk. You just pull this little lever here," she said pulling it. "It's alarmed or set or whatever." She flipped it back. "It's off. Got it?"

"That's simple enough. What about the door lock?"

"Just push in this thing and pull the door shut. Give the door a little wiggle to make sure it's locked."

"Ok, I got it. You go on. I'll finish up."

Rita said her goodbyes and left without even a hug. Jeanne was relieved, but thought she was losing her touch. Jeanne went to her phone and dialed Patricia to report that she was locking up and would be on her way.

Once everyone was at the Hole, Ian took over. The plan was to see how things looked and, if all was well, install everything they could tonight. Plan B was to come back tomorrow night if they needed more time. They would do the Woolworth Building first starting around eleven. Security was used to seeing them come in around that time. They would go over to Maiden Lane after that.

Ian was trying to look cool, but was a nervous wreck. Culkin was doing his best to be helpful. "Ian, if it does you any good, I'll bet, as head of Rackets, Scopo has supervised over a thousand wire-tap and bug installations, and he never got used to it."

"No wonder he looks so old."

"He has seen it all. Some great successes and some real screw-ups."

"You're not helping, inspector. Now listen you two, I want to be called and kept up to date as often as possible. You have my cell number. For obvious reasons, I will not call you, but please call me."

"Ian, you know nothing's happening until after eleven. No point in Patricia and me going in any earlier. Why don't you have a date or go to a movie? You are going to drive yourself nuts. We really have this under control."

"I don't have to drive myself nuts. I already am nuts."

Jeanne asked, "Would you like to come over to our house for dinner? It would help pass the time."

"No thanks, Jeanne, but that's real nice of you. Dick, are you heading back to the office or heading home?"

Dick said he would take Ian back to his office.

49

When Ian got back to his office, he collapsed in his chair, picked up his burner and dialed Adele. She answered on the third ring. "Hi," she tried to sound cheery, but it was obvious she had been asleep.

"Damnit, I woke you up, didn't I? I'm so sorry. Go back to sleep."

"Hey, hey, hey wait a minute. Not so fast. I got off at two and have been asleep since three. That's four hours. I'm ready for dinner. Can't we take a flight someplace where no one will see us? How about the shuttle to DC?"

"Would you really be available? There is some stuff I got to tell you, so it could be a legitimate meeting. I could have you down here, but you are a doctor and you should be near the hospital."

"I will be in your office in half an hour. Quick shower. I'm naked already and have the water almost on. There, it's on. I will grab a cab and see you in a few minutes."

"Fantastic. Just come to the main door. I'll tell Tommy, the lobby cop, to expect you. This is really neat. Oh boy."

"Ian, you sound like a third grader."

Adele looked down the long empty hall of the sixth floor. "This place is creepy at night, Ian. There's no one here."

"There are some assistants here. Guys who are on trial or running investigations. I'll take you up to the ninth floor if you would like. That is where the squad is. There will be plenty going on up there."

"What are they doing?"

"It's sort of like any police squad in the city, only they are working on just our stuff. But our stuff goes on all hours of the day and night. Come on down to my office." He took Adele's hand in his and kissed it. "I can't tell you how happy I am you came down here tonight. Let me tell you what is going on, and then we can go have dinner."

First, Ian told her about the trial starting up on the fifteenth and he asked her to be in charge of explaining that to her family. She agreed that that would be a good idea. He told her Louie Balzo or Robby would be calling to set up dates for trial prep. It was understood that Adele was the main and perhaps the only family witness to testify. Ian wanted to prepare the others in case Nails called them. He didn't think Nails would.

Ian then got real serious. "I shouldn't be telling you this, but it is killing me so I've got to. I have to swear you to secrecy. Is that ok?"

"What is it? Is there a problem? Have they found something about Mary? Oh God—"

"No," Ian cut in sensing her anxiety. "Take it easy. It's nothing like that. Everything is ok." Ian then told her about what was going on tonight. Adele sat on the edge of her seat. She couldn't believe that she was hearing this. "How can you stand it?"

"I can't. That's another reason I'm so happy you are here. Let's go to dinner. There is a great Italian restaurant up the street. It's my version of Jimmie's."

As they walked toward the elevator, Adele asked to see the squad. They took the elevator up to the ninth floor, and Ian asked if the inspector was around. Culkin came out and Ian introduced Adele. "Inspector, this is Adele Rusk. You know the Rusk case. This is Mary Rusk's sister. She is down here for trial preparation. We may be starting the trial soon."

Ian could see why Dick held the plush job of the DA's squad commander. He was Mr. Charm. He took Adele by the arm and led her into his office and showed her a seat. The squad was alive with activity. Detectives were all over the place. There was even a well-dressed guy in a suit sitting in one of the two cells that were in the squad room. Culkin explained that he was a banker who had been arrested for embezzlement. Adele thought he looked sick. Over in a corner were the Pats, getting ready, talking to their backup teams. Ian thanked Culkin for his time and told him they were going to dinner.

At dinner, they talked about how long Ian thought it would be before the case would be over and they could go public. They discussed how different things would be if events didn't turn out tonight as planned. "If we get caught tonight, all hell will break loose."

"That isn't going to happen. You've got too many professionals doing their job. Everything is going to be fine." Ian just stared at Adele. "You're staring."

"I can't help it. You're so beautiful."

Just then they heard a familiar voice. "Well, look who's here. He actually comes out of the courthouse. And he is with Adele Rusk no less." It was Bunny, Nails' Bunny.

Ian explained to Bunny that Adele was here for trial preparation and, after a long day, he offered to take her to dinner. Ian then quickly

covered the universe: "How are you? What do you hear from Nails?" .
. . "Looking forward to the trial." . . . "Have Nails call me when he gets
back." . . . "Enjoy your dinner." . . . "Sorry you have to work so late." . .
. "Goodbye."

She went over to a booth to join a guy for dinner.

"Oh shit," Adele said. "Do you think she'll tell Nails? Have we
screwed up?"

"Relax. Just be happy it happened down here and not up at
Jimmie's. She knows we have witnesses in all the time and at all hours of
the day and night. There are at least two other assistants having dinner
here tonight. I have no idea who they have with them. I wouldn't be
surprised if she told Nails, but I'm not worried about this. Do you want
to go for a walk or should I get you home or what?"

A smile came over Adele's face. "I think we should go back to
your office for some more trial prep."

50

At eleven on the dot, the Pats strolled into the lobby of the Woolworth Building and approached the security desk. The bags they had with them were larger than usual. "Getting down to the good books and records now," they explained to Ben, the night security man, whom they had gotten to know. Ben signed them in, and they went to the elevator for the trip up to Purns' office.

Knowing the routine of night watchmen was an essential part of the Pats' business. They knew that he would knock on their door and pop his head in around eleven thirty. They should be in Purns' office, working on the books, when he did that. He would be off the sixty-first floor by eleven thirty-five, and he would work his way down floor by floor. He would be past Bradford's floor in ten minutes and would not be back until sometime after three in the morning. That was their window: 11:45 PM to 3:00 AM. The security guys were used to them leaving the building shortly after three, and with any kind of luck, the Pats wouldn't disappoint them tonight.

At eleven twenty-nine the watchman knocked, opened the door, said good evening and left. At eleven fifty, they gathered all their equipment, gave each other a hug and a kiss and walked to the stairwell to take the stairs down to Bradford's floor. Patrick cautiously opened the door to the floor and confirmed that there was no one around. They went to Bradford's door and checked it. Jeanne had pulled it tightly shut and made sure it was locked.

As Patrick kept watch, Patricia took out her lock set and had the door open in about fifteen seconds. Patrick went directly to Rita's desk and disabled the alarm system, easily within the required time, to keep it from going off. They made sure that the door was locked and secure. They reengaged the alarm system and took a few moments to let their eyes adjust to the dark.

The only light in the office came from the small flashlights they were holding in their mouths that sent off a narrow direct beam, much like a laser light. They went into Bradford's office, then Banner's office, then the conference room and expertly hid the miniature microphones that would clearly pick up any conversation in each of the rooms. Patricia tested them all by having Patrick whisper while she listened with earphones. The bugs were working. They sent a signal to the backup teams and got a reply. Recordings could begin when needed.

They took a careful inventory of all their equipment so that they were sure they were not leaving anything behind. As Patrick prepared to open the door to the common hallway, he was startled by a loud female voice shouting, "Yahoo! The mile high club. Let's do it." And then, "Babs, for Christ's sake keep your voice down. You are going to wake the dead."

The Pats looked at each other, turned off their flashlights, grabbed all their equipment and crammed themselves into the utility closet, which was off the reception area. There was barely enough room. They were pressed against each other. Pat could feel Pat's heart beating.

They heard the door being opened and a male saying, "Slow down, slow down, you are going to rip my shirt." It was Bradford, and it sounded like they were moving into a back room, probably Bradford's office where the couch was.

Patricia made sure the utility closet door was tightly closed, turned on her flashlight and put it in her mouth. Patrick resisted the impulse to say anything. She always knew what she was doing. She silently fumbled in her bag until she found the earphones and put them on. She listened for a moment, and a satisfied smile came across her face. Patrick watched her as she closed her eyes and listened. She sent a signal to the backup team. She figured they had never heard a copulating jury fixer before.

She took off the earphones and put them on Patrick. The moans and grunts were coming through with perfect clarity. Patrick smiled and put his hand on Patricia's ass. She quietly smacked his face. Soon they heard a loud scream from Banner and then silence.

They heard Banner say she was going to the bathroom and then heard her leave the office. Bradford started talking to himself as he was walking around the office. "I am something else. I really am something else."

The Pats knew this was crunch time. If Bradford was going to start looking around, now was when he would do it. Patrick shimmied himself around so that, if Bradford opened the utility closet, Patrick could clobber him before he knew what hit him. This might work if Banner was still out of the room. They waited. It sounded like Bradford was staying in his office, patting himself on the back. Patricia kept listening with the earphones.

Barbara came back from the bathroom and said, "That was the best. How about another fling on the couch?" Patrick held his breath. He didn't think he could last another fling in the cramped closet.

"Come on, let's get out of here. There are more comfortable places than that couch."

The Pats collectively let out a sigh of relief.

Once the copulating couple left, the Pats waited until there was silence and then slowly opened the utility closet door. They got out of the closet, and Patricia said, "Let's go back there Patrick. I want to see what that couch is all about." Patricia then called the backup team. "Did you hear that ok?"

"Yeah, the reception is perfect. What were we listening to? It sounded like—"

Patricia interrupted, "A copulating jury fixer."

"That sounds like the name of a bird."

"We had a slight interruption, but all is well."

Next Patrick dialed Ian's cell. "We are done in Bradford's office. I have called the backup teams and they are hearing everything perfectly . . . "No, it was uneventful. Could not have been easier. We will get something to eat and then go to Maiden Lane . . . "Because we are hungry, Ian. Talk to you later. Goodbye."

Patricia asked, "How's he doing?"

"He wants to know how we can eat."

Ian noticed that Adele was fading. He called Tommy and asked him to get them a cab. He rode with her up to the dorm. His arm was around her and her head was nestled against his shoulder. She was sound asleep. At the dorm he told the cabbie to wait and he walked her inside. She asked, "What are you going to do?"

"I'm taking the cab back to my apartment and get some sleep."

"Can I come with you?"

"In a couple of weeks."

"Honest?"

"Honest."

The Pats stopped at one of their favorite all-night diners. In their line of work, they did a lot of all-night diner eating, and tonight was just another night. They finished eating, and drove over to a spot they knew they could park their car. They grabbed their equipment and walked over to Jowls' building.

Downtown Manhattan was deserted. They didn't see one other person on their way over. They walked past the entrance and got to the end of the block. They turned around, and Patricia went into the alcove between the two shops where she could get at the lock on the entrance door. She checked carefully for alarm equipment, found none and soon they were inside. They made sure the door was locked and took the stairs up to Jowls' office.

Another check for alarms and she found one. The installer had done a great job, but he was up against a master. She was quite sure it was a Balendorffer and would probably be controlled by a switch in the boss' office. They traditionally have at least a one-minute delay time to give the property owner time to get to his controls and deactivate the system before it goes off. She knew if she didn't find the controls in time, she could use Plan B, but that would take a little time to repair the damage Plan B would cause. Of course, she could be wrong about the delay time; some controls are in proximity of the entrance door and therefore of shorter duration. She was confident that, if that were the case, they would find it fast.

Patrick was ready to start his stopwatch as soon as she got the door open. That took a little longer than usual, and Patricia was beginning to admire Jowls' taste for security. When the lock popped, Patrick hit the stop watch.

They were in. Patricia found the wiring that led to Jowls' office, and then found the control switch down by the right knee area. It was flipped, as was the stopwatch, and the whole deal took eighteen seconds. They checked for some sort of backup system, but didn't find one. They waited a minute to see if anything went off. All was quiet, so they started planting the bugs.

It took them almost an hour to finish. They took special care to hide everything. They ran their tests and called the backup teams to make sure there was good reception. The backup team asked them to call Culkin; he was waiting to hear how things went. They called the inspector and reported, and then Dick said, "Hang on. Ian's here. He wants to talk to you."

Patrick gave Ian a rundown, and then listened carefully while Ian told him how proud he was of the Pats. Ian also said he was grateful for all their work. Pat ended the call, hugged Patricia and remarked that it was terrific working with those two guys. "It is three thirty in the morning and they were waiting in the office to hear from us."

51

Monitoring a bug is an expensive, labor-intensive job. Listening in on a person's conversation is an invasion of privacy, and the law requires that such an invasion be kept to a minimum. So, for example, eavesdropping warrants don't go on forever. There is a beginning date and an ending date. Whatever listening that is done must be done within those dates.

Subject matter is also limited. The listeners, the DA's Squad in this case, were not allowed to listen to conversations Bradford might have with other clients, unless those conversations were about fixing juries. In order to know what they were listening to, they had to listen, thus requiring manpower to do the listening. The conversations were to be constantly monitored. If they were not about jury fixing, they couldn't listen. They had to keep turning the thing on, listen and then switch it off if the speakers were not talking about jury fixing. This could go on for as long as the warrant allowed. Culkin had to man the backup teams.

The chief of detectives had promised all the manpower needed. He hated what Bradford was doing and spared nothing and nobody. They had to keep meticulous records of what was being recorded, because Bradford, being a lawyer, was sure to challenge every aspect of the eavesdropping.

The teams were hoping to have the rest of the weekend off as any action would not start until Monday. Monday was the fourteenth. Jury selection was to begin on the fifteenth.

Adele had called her mom on Saturday. She had to tell her family about the new trial date. She told her mom the she wanted to come over for church and Sunday dinner, and her mother was thrilled. Brian was off someplace, but the other three went to church without him.

Adele took them to lunch at Grandma Rosey's Turkey House. They served the best roast turkey and mashed potatoes. The church, the Rusks' home and Rosey's formed the three points of an equilateral triangle. All were easy to get to. Pete Rusk loved Maggie's cooking, but always opted for Rosey's whenever the opportunity presented itself.

Adele broke the news about the new trial starting. She knew it would not be a happy thought, but she had to get it out of the way. Predictably, Maggie once again raised the possibility of a guilty plea so they would not have to live through Mary's death again. That didn't get very far since Pete was wishing the state still had the death penalty. Since it didn't, the only satisfactory alternative would be that Conti would die in prison. Adele wanted the trial to be over, but kept her counsel. She really wanted to be able to "go public."

When they got home, Adele used the excuse that she needed to look for something she thought she packed in the basement. She went downstairs and was relieved to see that Pete's pistol was still in its hiding place.

Pete went into the bedroom to take a nap, and Adele used the opportunity to have a heart-to-heart with her mother. "I think I am in love. He makes me happy. I have never felt anything like this before."

Maggie Rusk sat and listened, and then a small smile came across her face. "Are you supposed to be dating the man who is prosecuting your sister's killer?"

"Oh, God no, Mom, that is the problem. It could be disastrous if this got out. Ian and I are trying to be very careful so that no one knows about it. You can't mention this to Dad or Brian. We are acting like we are a couple of spies in the CIA."

"What will you do if someone finds out and asks you about all this when you are testifying under oath?"

Adele was a little frightened about telling her mom the truth. "What would the CIA spy do?"

"He would lie?"

"Maybe I would also."

"Your father is going to want to know if Ian's a catholic."

Pete Rusk put his feet up on the bed to take his afternoon nap, but he couldn't sleep. All he could think about was the news. The retrial was going to start on the fifteenth. It was time to put his plan into effect. He'd thought about this for too long not do it. Later that night after Maggie went to bed, he would go downstairs and get his gun. He had bought some cleaning material and some oil. He wanted to make sure it was in perfect working order and fully loaded.

52

Louie Balzo was certain he'd located Bradford's Bronx case. It was a pretty heavy narcotics case involving the sale of a large quantity of crack cocaine. The defendant was clearly a major dealer, and it looked like a solid case involving a sale to an undercover detective. The trial ended in a hung jury after four days. The facts were simple, but the juror maintained he didn't believe the police officers and thought they were framing the defendant. Despite significant pressure put on him from the trial judge, he was not going to change his mind. Toward the end of the deliberations, the juror accused the judge of being part of the police conspiracy because the judge was putting so much pressure on the juror to change his vote. The judge figured he better back off and declared a mistrial.

All this had happened about two years ago. The assistant had left the Bronx DA's office in disgust and was now in private practice. Louie asked the former assistant if he could come down to his office. The assistant came down in a couple of days.

Ian, Louie, Smitty and Culkin met with him and got as much information as possible. They didn't tell the former assistant what was up, but promised that they would brief him if the investigation went anywhere. The former assistant was still pissed that the juror held out for an acquittal.

Ian ordered a discreet investigation to try and locate the Bronx juror. They got a name and home address that the jury clerk had used to summon him, but the juror had sold his home and moved shortly after the mistrial. Culkin contacted some connections in Bronx narcotics to see what could be discovered. The neighbors thought that a wealthy relative died and left the juror a bunch of money. The rumor was that he had bought a place in Port Saint Lucie, Florida. Within days, Culkin located his new home. The decision was made to find out whatever they could about him, but leave him alone until things developed with Bradford.

53

Culkin told Bill Spence that the police commissioner wanted to see him. Culkin had explained Spence's situation to the commissioner so had arranged to meet with Spence, out by the Verrazano Bridge, in the ass end of Brooklyn, at an elementary school that was closed on Saturdays.

Spence asked Dick what was going on. Dick was no help. He even wondered if Spence could have a problem. Spence laughed. He could think of nothing.

At 11:00 AM the next morning, Saturday, Spence pulled up to the school. He saw the usual array of vehicles that accompanied the commissioner wherever he went. When he got inside, his wife Deborah, their three daughters and their husbands were there. Bill was shocked.

Culkin and Ian, along with several colleagues from the DA's Squad, were gathered at the back of the classroom. The commissioner was smiling and used a teacher's desk for a podium. Once he got everyone's attention, he started.

"How do you celebrate the work of a police officer who has spent his entire career as an undercover officer? His incalculable value is because of his anonymity. The fact that he is a police officer is never known.

"Bill came to the department right from the Navy Seals. He has done nothing but outstanding undercover work. He was assigned to the district attorney's squad to serve in that capacity after only one year on the job. This was an unheard-of assignment for such a rookie. In investigation after investigation, he has distinguished himself. I have letters from two district attorneys and seven bureau chiefs praising Bill's work. Most of them asked, 'How do we honor him?'

"Bill, none of us can measure what you have done and continue to do for this department. We have to celebrate your accomplishments. But we can't celebrate them out loud because, so to speak, you are an undercover cop. No one is supposed to know you are a cop.

"You are already a first grade detective. You can go no higher unless you take exams and become a boss. We all know what you think of exams and what you think of being a boss. None of that is going to happen. So, I decided to create a new position, that of Master Detective. You are the first Master Detective in the history of the New York City Police Department. You are the only Master Detective. Who knows if there will ever be another one?

"I'm sure you will be sorry to hear that you will go into a higher tax bracket because with the title goes a hefty raise. I was so happy that we were able to get your wife, your three daughters and their husbands to come out here today. Two of those husbands, I might add, are members of this great department, so it wasn't so hard to get them out here. The grandkids are going to have to be a little older before they learn that Grandpa isn't a produce salesman.

"Master Detective Spence, we are honoring you the only way we can, by an anonymous ceremony. We can't tell the world, or the press, but we can tell you. We can tell you how grateful we are for your outstanding work. Please come up here and hand in your badge. I have a new one for you."

The commissioner pinned a specially designed badge on Spence, shook his hand and stepped back to let him speak.

"Wow, this sure is a surprise. I thought I had done something wrong and was getting fired." Spence took a few minutes to thank everyone. He looked at Ian and smiled, but he couldn't say anything about what they were doing. He talked about the difficulties of the 20th Division investigation that had lasted for five years. He concluded by explaining how his wife and daughters had helped him over the years. "They deserve all the credit." He went down and hugged and kissed each of them. There wasn't a dry eye in the place.

He realized with this raise they could get their place in the country, as his wife had always wanted. He was a rock-solid citizen. He was a saver. He put his three daughters through college. He was now helping to put his youngest son-in-law through law school. He never was able to tell anyone what he did. When anyone asked, he would say he was in the produce business. He went over to Ian and thanked him for coming.

Ian said, "I would not have missed it for the world. I'm just so happy nothing interfered with the morning. The commissioner has been trying to figure out where and when to do this for weeks. I'm afraid things are going to get a little hectic for the next few days."

"Yeah, I've been told to be at work early on Monday."

54

On Monday morning, as Sammy Burns was reporting to work early, Vince O'Rielly was looking at a phone message on his desk. "The DA would like an update on the eavesdropping case!" He asked Mabel to request that Ian, Frank Carney, Lem Schooner and Inspector Culkin be in his office at ten.

"So what are we going to do about this?" O'Rielly was waving the phone message. "Ian, let's begin with a brief update from you."

Ian took a deep breath and told himself to relax, but he could feel his blood pressure rising. He looked at Frank who was seated across from him in the deputy bureau chief's overstuffed chair. "Ian, let me remind you that, in this room, you are among friends," O'Rielly added.

"I know I am. It is just that we are right at the cusp of this thing. We have the bugs in place. They are working perfectly. We have already picked up some good stuff, and if we let this play out, it is going to get much better.

"We are to start jury selection tomorrow. This is when Bradford will start to do his thing. As jurors are seated, he has to make a decision as to whom he will approach. We will hear those deliberations. The hope is—no, let me change that—the expectation is that we will know when he decides to pick someone. We will know who that someone is. We will be able to cover the approach.

"Once money changes hands, we will make an arrest. We want to do it quietly for two reasons. First, so that we can substitute an alternate and keep the trial going. That is what Hastings is going to want. But, more importantly, we want to get Gus Conti and lock him up for the murder of juror number 11. It is absolutely essential that none of this becomes public until we have done all we can. I am just afraid that the DA will not be able to resist the opportunity to gain publicity, and that is going to screw up everything."

"I'm afraid your fears are well founded," added Vince. "So what do we do? We can tell him the truth or we can give him some bullshit. We can't ignore him. Actually, I honestly think we could ignore the DA, but we will never get around his two minions. They're the ones who want to be able to use this."

Frank Carney jumped in, "We have no alternative. We have to tell him the truth and we have to persuade him to wait before having any kind of press conference. If we show him how things can get fucked up, maybe he'll listen and agree."

Schooner added, "Frank's right, but this isn't going to be easy. Who's going upstairs?"

O'Rielly ruled, "We all are. The more of us there, the more it emphasizes the importance of the situation. Also, the more of us there, the more witnesses there are to whatever the DA does."

There were no surprises. Harper's two aides were there and they were not caring about the integrity of the investigation. Harper said, "I hope this is clear to you all. I not only want to know when an arrest is made, I want to know if an arrest is imminent."

O'Rielly saw that Ian was about to say something and wanted to save him, "Well, if you want to know if an arrest is imminent, we are telling you an arrest is imminent. Once Ian starts picking a jury, we anticipate Bradford is going to select one of the seated jurors to be his mark. When Bradford makes his pitch to the juror, he is going to be arrested."

The PR man said, "That's nonsense. Why do you have to wait for all that to happen? You could grab him this morning and we could have a press conference this afternoon. I think you are deliberately stalling."

That was it for Ian. He got up and walked out.

"He has been having some indigestion problem," O'Rielly quickly added. "We are not stalling. We are running an efficient and, so far, very successful investigation that goes not only to the heart of our jury system but includes murder. We are going to do it the right way, not the publicity way."

Harper concluded the meeting with, "I have told you what I want. I am the district attorney. I expect you to follow my orders. This meeting is over."

Ian actually had gone into the men's room to get control of himself. Now he knew he had to face his bosses and was trying to think of some reasonable excuse. "I just figured if I stayed in that meeting, I was going to say something that wouldn't make any of you happy so I got up and left."

"What if we had all gotten up and left?" asked Carney. "Sometimes you just have to sit there and take that shit."

"I know. I apologize."

"Forget it," said O'Rielly. "You've been working very hard on this investigation. You are trying a case. You're carrying a lot of baggage. Here is what we are going to do. Ian, you run your investigation. You keep me advised of whatever you think I should know and you should assume I am informing the DA. I'm the bureau chief and that is my responsibility, not yours. Let me know if and when arrests are made. I don't need to know the details of what you are doing and when you are doing it.

"Frank, speak to Judge Dickerson. Let him know what is going on with Harper. This does not leave this room, but the sooner the governor does something about this, the better.

"Lem, go run the Supreme Court Bureau. I'm sorry we got you involved in this. You don't need this headache."

Ian called Judge Hastings' chambers and asked if he could come and brief him. Hastings told him to come right up.

"Judge, I'm afraid we have a problem." Ian told Hastings about the meeting with Harper and how he was afraid that everyone's desire to not have a mistrial would be outweighed by Harper's desire for publicity.

"Why don't I call him up here and read him the riot act? I could tell him that if he has a press conference, I'll hold him in contempt. Maybe that'll slow him down."

"I don't think you should, judge. I guess you could try it, but I don't think he will give a judge's order the dignity it deserves. He comes from a different bunch of lawyers."

"To tell you the truth, Ian, I'm more concerned about Gus Conti taking off when he hears about this than I am about the mistrial. We can always start the trial over again. But if Conti gets away, there's no telling when you'll find him."

"All this seems so obvious to both of us. I can't understand the DA's thinking."

"He's a politician."

Jowls met with his staff at seven thirty Monday morning and told them what their assignment would be the next day, the fifteenth, when jury selection would begin. He then excused himself to go over to Bradford's office and meet with the boss. He told everyone to be available when he got back in case there were any changes in what he expected them to do.

Jeanne was busy in her cubby getting more papers together on the Bronx case when Jowls came through the main door. "Good morning, everybody. The boss in?"

"He's in his office. Go on in," Rita replied. Jowls went in the back and greeted Bradford.

Bradford opened with, "This meeting is just going to be between the two of us. I don't mind telling you that old man Conti gives me the creeps. I think we will have our hands full if we don't get another hung jury."

"He hasn't threatened you, has he?"

"No. But that guy is a killer. I told him about a letter I gave to a friend that sets forth everything that we did for him in Conti I. That letter goes to the cops if anything happens to me."

"Do you want us to do something about him?"

"Just stay alert. We don't know who his men are. My recollection is that the old man spent almost every day in court and I suppose he'll do that again. We are going to have to use the same routine we have used in the past. I'll be there to make the ultimate decision, but you have to have your guys ready to do the leg work. I have never been wrong on a juror."

"I wish you'd stop saying that."

"Well, I haven't. I'm good."

"I know you are, boss. I just wish you would stop talking about it. So, if we find our mark early on, will you approach him?"

"Or her. As soon as we feel we are sure."

"You wouldn't pick a woman, would you?"

"I will if she is the right woman. Anyway, you use your same routine. I'll have Barbara with me in the courtroom and she will call you with any requests."

"Barbara makes me nervous. I wish you could leave her in the office. I think you would be better off taking that Jeanne kid with you. She is a sharpie."

"Jeanne's too new. Barbara will be ok. She does everything I tell her. She likes the sex."

Back at the squad, Ian and Culkin were listening with the backup teams. Culkin said, "We have enough to make an arrest."

"Not yet. I want to catch them in the act."

55

"So how do I look? Am I all bronzed and beautiful? My Doloris says I am bronzed and beautiful."

"You are, Nails. I am going to have trouble keeping my hands off you," Ian responded.

"I bet I'll drive the women jurors crazy."

"Undoubtedly, Nails."

"Before we go into the courtroom, I want to know something."

"What's that, Nails?"

"I assume you are putting Mary Rusk's sister, Adele Rusk, on the stand like you did last time."

Ian's heart jumped into his throat, sort of, right at the base of his tongue. He actually sounded a little horse when he said, "Is that a question or an order? You know I don't discuss who my witnesses will be."

"You got a thing for her?"

"Nails, have you gone nuts? Of course not."

"That's not what Bunny says. Bunny says she saw the two of you together, and Bunny says you got a thing for Adele."

"Oh, for God's sake, Nails. Ms. Rusk was down here for trial preparation. She was down later in the day because of her duties at the hospital. We were working late and we went out for a bite to eat and ran into Bunny. We all said hello, ate our dinner and Miss Rusk and I went back to work." Ian's heart left the vicinity of his tongue.

Nails said, "You're talking better."

"There is nothing wrong with the way I'm talking. I just got a little frog in my throat, a Louis Armstrong thing."

"I don't know, Ian. Bunny seems to know about these things. Supposing when I cross-examine Adele, I ask her, 'Have you ever had a date with the assistant district attorney who is prosecuting this case, that man sitting over there, Assistant District Attorney Ian MacDonald?' as I walk over pointing a finger at you. What will she say?"

"She will have taken an oath to tell the truth and she will tell the truth." Ian was pleased with his answer. Nails stood there with a smile on his face. He said nothing. Ian stared at him.

"Don't you worry, Ian. You can put her on the stand. I won't ask those questions. I won't go near that subject. I'm not a shit." Nails pushed open the swinging doors and started walking into the court-room. He stopped and turned, "But I know you got a thing for that girl and you know what? You're smart. She is a good girl." He left Ian standing in the hallway.

Davey Garr called the case, and Judge Hastings asked if the attorneys were ready for trial.

"The People are ready, your honor."

"The Defense is ready."

"Then let's get to it. Bring down the jury panel, Davey."

"They are on their way, judge."

Hastings left the bench for his robing room. A panel of about fifty prospective jurors would be working their way down from the central jury room on the fifteenth floor. Davey would have to call the roll to make sure no one got lost, and then he would pull twelve names from a wheel where all the jury slips were placed. As each prospective juror's name was called, he or she would take a seat in the jury box.

Bradford and Banner were out in the main hallway by the entrance to the courtroom so that they could watch the panel get off the elevator and work their way to the courtroom. No observation was insignificant to Bradford. Who got off the elevator first? Who stepped aside to let another person pass? Who held the door for another? Who went to the front of the courtroom and took a seat in the front row? Who was wearing what? Anyone chewing gum? Anyone dumb enough to try and bring food or coffee into the courtroom? He trained Banner to look for these things. He told her they all meant something.

Banner told Bradford to check out the guy wearing the red flannel vest. He looked "Mamby Pambyish. Maybe you can push him around."

The first name drawn from the wheel was Millicent Marion. She was a well-dressed woman in her fifties. She looked like she might be a housewife. Bradford immediately ordered, "Give her the big X." This was not the type that Bradford would be trying to fix. If selected she would be the foreperson.

Ian was fascinated. He kept saying to himself, *Thank God we have those bugs in place.* He couldn't imagine what Bradford was thinking.

He leaned over to Louie Balzo and said, "Louie, try not to stare at Bradford. You are a little too intense."

"Shit, I'm sorry, Ian," Louie whispered. "I'm just trying to figure out what he's thinking."

"Pay attention to my questions in the first round, because I may have you conduct the second round."

"You didn't tell me we would be doing that."

"I wanted you to get some sleep last night."

Louie suddenly looked a little flushed. He grabbed his pad and started taking notes.

It was too simple. Pete Rusk had taped the gun to the inside of the morning paper. He entered the courthouse, but instead of getting in the screening line where the scanners were, he went over to the blind guy who ran the candy kiosk and bought a pack of Marlboros. He opened the pack, walked over to the trash can, threw the cigarette wrapper and the morning paper in the trash and then went through the screening line. Once he was cleared, he approached the candy counter from the cleared side and bought a Hershey bar from the blind guy. He tore open the wrapper, walked to the trash can from the cleared side, threw the wrapper in the trash, picked out his morning paper that he tucked halfway into his backpack and walked over to the elevators that took everyone up to the courtrooms. He had just passed the only part of his day that could have caused him problems, and he had done it without so much as a twitch.

The case would be tried in Judge Hastings' courtroom on the twelfth floor down at the south end of the hall. Rusk knew from the first trial that, once the court sessions ended around five, the place emptied out like there was a bomb scare and there would be no one on the floor until the cleaning crew came in much later. That would give him plenty of time to hide the gun.

He went into the nearest courtroom and took a seat in the next to last row. The attorneys were finishing up a round of challenges, and then the judge would adjourn court for the day. That's what happened at 5:05 PM. By 5:10 PM, everyone—the judge, lawyers, court officers, clerks, stenographers, jurors who had been selected, potential jurors, everyone —had left. The doors to the courtroom were locked. Lights were out.

Rusk left the courtroom with the others, but peeled off to the men's room as everyone else headed for the elevators. He went down to the furthest stall where he knew there was a vent grate. He pulled out a dime and used the edge to unscrew one side of the grate. He gave the gun one final check. It was fully loaded, cleaned and oiled. He then securely taped his gun to the back side of the vent shaft. It would never happen, but even if someone looked in the shaft, they wouldn't see it. He refastened the grate and went to one of several basins where he washed his hands, combed his hair and went out to catch an elevator down to the lobby.

This time, if the jury didn't take care of Conti, he would.

"Ladies and gentlemen of the panel, I am Judge Hastings. I will be presiding over this trial. I have been doing this for twenty years, so I operate under the delusion that I know what I'm doing. We are about to pick a jury." Hastings gave a terrific one-minute history of trial by jury and its importance.

"Now let me tell you who some of the people in the courtroom are. At that table closest to the jury box are prosecutor's Assistant

District Attorney Ian . . ." Hastings introduced Ian, Louie, Nails and Bunny.

He went on with the introductory remarks that he had given hundreds of times before. He was unhurried. He was clear. He was the judge, but he was the benevolent, kind, Solomonic judge. The panel liked him. They started to enjoy being on jury duty.

"Now, we have filled the jury box with twelve of you. I am going to ask you some questions. They are important questions. You are going to be sworn to tell the truth by Mr. Garr, our preeminent court clerk. You must tell the truth. After I ask you questions, then either Mr. MacDonald or Mr. Balzo will ask you questions."

Louie couldn't believe his ears. For the second time, the judge had said his name in open court. Where was his mother?

"Then Mr. Ballen or Ms. Bloxy may ask you questions. The trick here is for us not to be redundant. Let's not keep asking the same questions over and over again. That will not please me. The other trick is for us not to be stupid. Let's not ask dumb or embarrassing or improper questions. Now here is a little bit about this case and some of the people I am told may be called as witnesses. If any of these names are known to you or you have any independent knowledge of this case, you have got to tell us."

Hastings gave a concise summary of the facts of Mary Rusk's death. He named the witnesses Ian gave him. Nails gave no names, but reserved the right to change his mind. The judge could do nothing about that.

He then started to ask the jurors questions about themselves. At the end of his questioning, he asked each prospective juror if they had any reason why they could not be a fair and impartial juror. He knew that this was when those who were looking to get excused would use the opportunity to come up with some reason, but he encouraged them to come forward. He even told them he would hear their problem at the bench or in his robing room to give them privacy. He would rather hear about it now than later.

Two of the jurors raised their hands and asked to approach the bench. The first was Millicent Marion, the woman in the foreperson's chair. She very discreetly removed a packet from her purse and handed it to the judge. It contained a State Department shield. "I'm supposed to go to South Korea for the secretary of state." Hastings excused her. The second was a man dressed in work clothes. He told the judge and the lawyers at the bench that his job was too important. He could not waste time to sit on the jury. He was a crane operator. The judge told him to get back in his seat and serve.

The morning proceeded with the first round of questions from Ian and Nails. After they finished, Hastings declared that there would be a fifteen-minute recess to allow the lawyers to consider their challenges.

Ian asked Louie, "Well, Mr. Trial Lawyer, who're you keeping?"

"I hate them all."

"Wrong attitude. You love them all. They all love you. They believe everything you say and will do whatever you ask them to do. Besides, if you challenge them all, you are going to run out of challenges."

"Which ones do you think Nails will challenge?"

"Wrong again. You can't count on him challenging for you. That's the way you end up with surprises. Maybe toward the end, when you are low on challenges, you have to roll the dice, but not now. So who are you going to challenge or are you now keeping them all?"

"I think I would challenge that crane operator. He is just going to be pissed through the entire case."

"Ok, but pissed at whom? Does he hate the defendant more than the government? I'm also wondering if this is the kind of guy Bradford would make his mark."

"What do you say, Ian? This is your case."

"You represent the People of the State of New York, Louie. Kind of a big deal, isn't it?"

Louie just looked at his pad and said, "4, 5, 7 and 9."

Ian smiled and handed Louie a folded piece of paper. Louie took it and unfolded it. Written on the paper were the numbers "4, 5, 7." Ian said, "Tell me what's wrong with 9."

"There is something about the way she is looking at us. She is giving me the creeps."

Hastings came out of the robing room. The court officer smacked his hand against the courtroom wall and shouted, "All rise."

"Will the attorneys please approach the bench?"

When they got up there, Hastings said, "You first, Mr. MacDonald."

"4, 5, 7, and 9, judge." Hastings made a note, and then said, "Mr. Ballen?"

"I'll add 3 and 12."

Hastings ordered the lawyers to step back and announced, "The following jurors are excused with the thanks of the court. Jurors 3, 4,

5, 7, 9 and 12. You may return to the central jury room. The remaining jurors will please move up to the now-unoccupied seats and be sworn in as jurors."

Juror number 7, the crane operator, beat a hasty retreat. Bradford separated some of his notes and told Banner to take them back to the office and shred them. He then asked her to call Jowls with the information on the six remaining jurors and said, "This is not such a great bunch."

Adele talked Maggie into staying home until the trial actually began. Pete Rusk, however, attended all the jury selection proceedings. One reason for doing so was to keep his son Brian away. Brian needed to work. He couldn't miss time from his job. Pete promised to give Brian daily reports on the jurors that were picked. It did no good having Brian around. He didn't know what he was talking about, and he was annoying. It was better this way.

The real reason Pete attended every court session was so that he could watch Conti. If Conti was in that courtroom, Pete was going to be in that courtroom. Pete actually studied Conti. He mentally recorded how he sat, what direction he was most accustomed to facing, whether he leaned forward or not. If he had to, Pete was going to shoot Conti. He wanted to give himself his best chance to kill him.

He didn't want to think about what he would do after he fired the shots. Probably he would throw the gun down on the floor and put his hands up in the air. He didn't care what they did to him. He couldn't think of Maggie. He just knew that Adele would take care of her. Maybe he could plead insanity. That was it. That Conti bastard made him nuts.

By the end of the day, they only picked two more jurors for a total of eight. Louie was having a fit over their challenge situation, but

Ian only wanted to get up to the squad to hear what was going on with the bugs. He asked Louie if he wanted to come up to the squad with him. Louie declined. He was too preoccupied with the jury selection.

Ian sat down in Culkin's office. The inspector called in his lieutenant who was running the bug operation and asked for a summary.

"Well, the chatter in the investigators' offices is pretty routine and frankly, if you didn't know what was ultimately going on, fairly innocent. It is the kind of stuff you would expect from any legitimate jury consulting type firm. They have been running verifications of jobs, family life, social background and the like. Some of the jurors have taken some liberties with the truth. It will be interesting to see what Bradford and Jowls do with those situations. We are really waiting for the meeting in Bradford's office to start. Jowls is on his way over there now. That could be interesting. The guys will buzz us."

"Everything alright with Spence?"

"Yea, Sammy Burns is a pisser. He keeps harping on the little liberties the jurors take with their histories. He keeps calling them 'prevaricators' and gives them a rating. Juror number 10, for example, is a 'number 7 pre.' We haven't figured out yet whether the higher number is better or worse."

A voice from the other room yelled, "Hey lieutenant, you better get in here." They all went into the monitoring room.

56

Jowls sat down in front of Bradford's desk. Bradford's feet were up on his desk. He poured a Dewar's over some ice. Jowls was happy that Banner was not in the room. He was there to hear if his boss wanted to make any changes in their approach.

"No. I don't see any reason to do anything differently from what we did in Conti I. We were pretty damn successful in that trial, and we'll do the same thing in this one. I am not thrilled with today's batch, and I think we could be in trouble if we don't get better prospects tomorrow."

"We will, boss. There is always going to be someone who doesn't have any respect for trial by jury. Someone who considers jury duty, 'Not my job. Let someone else do it.' That crane operator would have been great."

"Probably, but if MacDonald hadn't challenged him, Nails would have. I could tell he was scaring the shit out of Nails. He thought the guy was going to come down to Conti, grab him by the neck and strangle him to death for making him miss a day of work."

"I just wanted to make sure nothing has changed. So let's see what my investigators dig up. We may still find someone who is on the balls of his ass and would be happy to accept a bushel basket of money for keeping his mouth shut. You and I both know, there are a ton of greedy people in this town."

"How are the new guys Burns and Collins working out? Any problems?"

"Nah. I've known Collins for years. They don't come any rottener. Burns is still a bit of a mystery, but he is sharp. He's waiting for me to get back to my shop. I think he has a few questions about what I want him to do. I'm so grateful to the guy for helping me get rid of my dopey son-in-law that he can do no wrong."

Spence saw Jowls return to his office and asked if it was a good time. Jowls told him to come in and close the door.

"What's the problem?"

"I want to know what I'm looking for. There is too much beating around the bush here. We are checking on the background of the jurors, and we are finding that some of them are not quite truthful. So what? We can't be spending all this time on just that. What specifically do we want?"

"Specifically? Specifically, we want someone who is going to take money to hang up the jury. How is that for being specific? So we want someone who doesn't give a shit about the sacredness of a jury by your peers or whatever the wording is in the constitution. Someone who thinks this is all a waste of time, who hates being down in court and wants to get out of there."

"Unfortunately, Jowls, that describes a lot of citizens. Even some pretty upstanding citizens who would never think of fixing a jury."

"You're correct. So we are looking for someone who is going to be persuaded by money, a lot of money, a ton of money. Everyone has their price, even some of those upstanding citizens you're talking about. But some people can be gotten cheaper than others. Money is not a problem. The client has plenty of it, and he is willing to spend it. It is his son's life that is on the line. A son who is a good-for-nothing bum. But it is his son. The client is convinced that if he gets another hung jury, the DA will bargain his son's case down and he will not spend the rest of his life in prison. So we want the juror who is going to listen to the opportunity to make a bundle of money and keep his mouth shut. Now do you have it?"

"Absolutely. We have to be careful, but this is certainly doable. I'll get back to work." Spence figured all that must have sounded pretty good back at the squad.

57

When Ethel, Smitty's wife, wasn't in the kitchen cooking, she was at the parish hall playing Bingo. She always sat with Hazel Monte. They were best friends.

This afternoon, Hazel was not herself. "Something has gotten into my Marvin. He insisted I tell you that he has to talk to your Smitty about that case Smitty has been on forever. You know, the Rusk case? He says it's important. It has something to do with the father, Pete Rusk. My Marvin works with Pete Rusk, and there is a problem."

At Ethel's insistence, Smitty reluctantly called Marvin Monte. Smitty knew Marvin and didn't like him. He was a busy body who was always sticking his nose into other people's business. Whenever there was a parish social event, Smitty avoided him. Marvin talked Smitty into meeting him at Patsy's Pub down the street.

"Don't ask me how I know or why I know any of that stuff you cops ask. Just take my word for it. I work with Pete Rusk. I like Pete Rusk. The murder of his daughter has been hell for him. He has to be forgiven for anything he might do. I don't want him to get in any trouble. I just think—"

"God Almighty Marvin, get to the point. What is it?"

Marvin said nothing. Smitty couldn't believe he saw tears welling up in Marvin's eyes.

"Smitty, there are times when you have to think like a human and not like a cop. Can you think like a human?"

"Yes, Marvin. I can think like a human. What is it?"

"Pete Rusk has a gun and he is going to kill that kid."

"What kid? What the hell are you talking about?"

"The kid you are trying for murdering Pete's daughter. He is going to kill that kid."

"What? How do you know that, Marvin? Pete Rusk is one of the most religious men I have ever met. He isn't going to kill anyone."

"There you go, Smitty, asking me how I know. I told you not to ask me how I know. I know. Pete Rusk is going to shoot that kid."

There was something about how Marvin was acting. Smitty didn't know if it was the tears, his tone of voice or his nervousness, but this wasn't the usual busy body Marvin. Smitty was worried.

"Ok Marvin. I'll take care of it. Don't say another word about this to anyone. Can you do that?"

"I haven't even told my Hazel."

Smitty asked Ian if he had a minute to talk. He was very apologetic because he knew how busy Ian was. Ian always had time for Smitty.

"I know you are going to think I am losing it, Ian, but I got to talk to you about something." Smitty told Ian about his conversation with Marvin. "There was something about the way he was telling me. I think there may be something to it."

That same thing was happening to Ian's heart. It was back up behind his tongue. He started to talk funny again.

"I got to tell you, I find it hard to believe that Pete Rusk would do anything like this."

"You got a cold, Ian? You're talking funny."

"I'm ok. Just got a frog in my throat. So, Pete Rusk kills Conti. Pete Rusk goes to prison after his daughter is murdered. What's that going to do to that family? Never mind murder, even if Pete Rusk was charged with possession of a weapon, it would be tragic."

"Terrible. I can't imagine it. Something has got to be done."

"I agree, Smitty. Why don't you see what you can find out? Maybe you'll be able to get to the bottom of this."

Please God, Ian thought, *help Smitty figure this out.*

58

It was six thirty in the morning when Ian's phone rang and woke him. He groped for the phone and answered.

"Got bad news, Ian." It was Jim LoMurko, "Bill Spence has been shot."

"What? Jim, is that you? What did you say?"

"I said Bill Spence's been shot. They've taken him to Bellevue, but it's not looking good. They're rushing him into surgery. It's touch and go. I think he's lost a lot of blood."

"Shit, shit, shit. This is awful. What happened? Where are you? Can you get me a ride to Bellevue?"

"I am leaving for your place now. Throw on some clothes and come downstairs. I should be in front of your place in a few minutes."

Ian got downstairs just as LoMurko's car came around the corner. The back door opened, and Ian jumped in. He was afraid he was going to lose it when he saw LoMurko. Danny Washington was driving. He turned on the red flasher and hit the siren as soon as Ian was in the car.

"We don't know yet what happened, but it looks like Bill parked his car in a lot he uses around the corner from Jowls' office. He was going to work early. He was walking toward the office and had just turned onto Maiden Lane when he was shot. He was able to hit his alert button before he passed out. There was a pedestrian about half a block away who ran to Bill's aid and called 911. The backup team was there in about a minute and an ambulance about a minute after that. We have the pedestrian and that is about it. We have put the undercover protocol into effect."

The undercover protocol was a standard operating procedure used when an undercover police officer was injured. It essentially meant that only those who had to know the victim was a cop were told. The hope was that the victim would eventually recover and his status as an undercover would not have been blown. He or she would be able to return to undercover duties when recovered.

"How many shots?"

"Looks like one, up close, to the chest."

"This is fucking unbelievable. Has Jeanne been called?"

"Yes, I spoke to her. I told her what happened and told her to call in sick. She wanted to go into work and see if she can learn anything. I told her to meet us at the hospital."

The car pulled into the Bellevue emergency entrance. Ian and Jim jumped out and ran inside. They were told Spence was still alive, in surgery and needed blood. Ian was O positive, a universal donor, and they took him into a donor area. LoMurko was negative and wasn't going to be a match, but he went in also, saying, "Maybe someone else can use mine some other time."

By the time they were finished, the emergency room was filling up with other officers. The word was out. A cop needed blood. The donors had arrived.

Bill's wife, Debbie, came in with Culkin. She was taken over to one of the doctors and they spoke. It was going to take some time. A major vessel had been damaged and he had lost a ton of blood. The doctors thought they had that under control. There were few places like Bellevue for trauma.

Deborah Spence came over to Ian. They had met at the elementary school ceremony for Bill. "Ian, I'm just going to say this once. No matter what happens, Bill loves his job. He loves this particular assignment. He believes he has never done anything more important than what he is doing right now. He loves working with you and Jeanne and all the bosses. There is going to be no blame here if things don't work out. Is that clear?"

Ian could hardly talk, "Yes, Mrs. Spence."

"I've been his wife for a long time. We have talked about this sort of thing a million times. Everything is going to be all right." She approached Culkin and took his hand. They walked over to a faux leather couch and sat next to each other. Ian went outside.

Ian found a pay phone and dialed Adele's number. They paged her, and she got on the phone. She was at the hospital in the middle of another shift. He told her what happened. He wanted to make sure she was all right.

She was understandably upset, but ok. He asked her if Spence stood a chance, and she was fairly reassuring. "He is in the best place in the world for this kind of thing. They see it all the time. Frankly, it is going to depend on how strong the rest of his body is. He is no spring chicken from what you have told me. All his other organs have got to hold up, but the immediate trauma they can control. Let me ask you, are you all right? You haven't been crying, have you? You sound like you have been crying."

"I'm ok. It was just a little tough talking to Bill's wife. She is a remarkable woman."

"Do you want me to try and get free to come down there?"

"No, there is nothing for you to do. I have to go to the office soon anyway. There are a million things going on. It helped talking to you."

"Ian?"

"Yes?"

"I love you."

"I love you too, Adele."

Robby and Smitty drove up. After Ian briefed them, they went back inside and they were given the latest report from an OR head nurse. Spence was critical, but stable. The bleeding had been stopped and the other damage was being repaired. He would not be out of the OR for a while, and there was nothing anyone else could do except say a prayer. They were overwhelmed with blood donors and couldn't keep up with all the officers coming in.

Ian went into the waiting area where LoMurko was on the phone barking out all sorts of orders. "Make sure you get Bill's clothes from the nurses. And where is the God damned bullet? Was it still in him? Have we cordoned off the crime scene? If I hear that that slug is missing, someone is going to pay. I want to know if anyone is living in that part of town. Who goes to work early?"

LoMurko thought there might be a good chance that Spence saw his shooter. "If Bill survives. maybe he can ID the son of a bitch."

The police commissioner arrived and immediately went over to Mrs. Spence. He took her hand and they talked privately. He then stopped to chat with the other officers.

Ian spoke to Culkin about security around Bill. Someone wanted him dead, and sooner or later the shooter was going to realize he hadn't done such a great job the first time. He might try again. The commissioner told his aide to take care of the security problem. He was reminded that the undercover protocol was in effect.

There was another problem. It paled by comparison to Spence's survival, but it was a problem that needed to be discussed. Ian, LoMurko and Culkin walked down to the end of the emergency room hallway.

Ian asked, "What do we do about the investigation? Do we pull the plug? Do we end it? Shouldn't we be getting Jeanne out of there?"

"Let's slow down for a second. Maybe we don't have to pull the plug," suggested LoMurko. "Supposing we put out the word that Sammy Burns has been shot and taken to Beekman Downtown Hospital. He is in the OR. Then he'll be in intensive care. He'll not be seeing visitors. He's in critical condition. We can arrange all this with the administrators at Beekman. We essentially have a phony patient. This accomplishes two things. First of all, if the shooter is looking to complete his job, he goes to Beekman and looks for Burns. This takes a little pressure off of protecting Spence up here at Bellevue. Secondly, if we do this, we can keep the ruse going."

Ian was impressed. It sounded like it might work.

"What is the latest?" Jeanne Dalton came running down the hall. They filled her in on Spence's condition and told her it looked like he might make it. "Thanks be to God," Jeanne said.

Then they explained the Beekman Downtown plan.

"I love it!" Jeanne exclaimed. "Send some detectives to Joust's office and to Bradford's office. The usual stuff. They are investigating the shooting of a former NYPD detective. They knew he took a new job with Bradford. He's at Beekman. Critical condition. No visitors. They think it may be connected with his work in the 20th Division. Dirty Division. The whole nine yards. Perfect. Let me go. Get all the teams on the bugs. Let's hear what they think happened. Whether they suspect anything. Who knows maybe one of them did it?" Jeanne was breathless.

"Easy, Jeanne. You got to come up for air. We are not so sure we want you going in there. Did you call in sick?" asked Culkin.

"I told them it was that time of month. If I could make it in, I would be a little late. I've got to get in there and hear the talk." Jeanne started to walk away.

"Hold it kid." It was Culkin. "We have the bugs being monitored. Let's see what they say for an hour or so before you go in. Joust and Bradford aren't even at work yet. More importantly, we got to get to the press. We want the story to be that the victim hasn't been identified yet. He is at Beekman in critical. Once we hear what they are saying, we can make the decision whether to send you to work. Jim, would you handle the press angle and talk to Tim MyGott at the Wall Street squad about what is going on? We are going to have to bring him in on the Bradford investigation, but maybe the squad detectives don't have to know. This is going to require some dipsy doodle, but there is nothing we can do for Spence at this point so we might as well see if we can save the investigation. Is all this ok with you Ian? This is your investigation and you are at a critical point in jury selection. You have to be in court in a couple of hours."

"Absolutely. I really don't want Jeanne going in until we get some sense of what they are saying. Let's see what we get away with."

59

Culkin took charge. After he left Bellevue emergency, he swung into action as soon as he got back to the squad, which was about fifteen minutes from the hospital. He told the eavesdropping monitoring teams about all that had happened. He put them on high alert. He got his lieutenant and two sergeants into his office, briefed them and set up teams. Within minutes, the story about an unknown white male being shot and taken to Beekman Downtown Hospital was given to the press.

The emergency medical technicians who had responded to the scene were instructed to change their reports to reflect that the victim was taken to Beekman, not Bellevue. "Just do it and don't ask any questions. Everything will be explained later."

The Beekman biggies were alerted, and Sammy Burns, the gunshot victim, was "admitted" to the OR. If he survived the surgery, he would be in intensive care until further notice. There would be no visitors. A bodyguard would be placed by his bed.

Word went out that no more blood was needed at Bellevue and everyone should resume their normal duties. The commissioner was told of the efforts to try and save the investigation, and he returned to his office. The sea of blue stopped flowing into Bellevue.

The captain of the Wall Street detective squad, Tim MyGott, was summoned to Culkin's office and briefed on the Bradford investigation. He understood the critical nature of the investigation, and volunteered to put together a team of detectives to investigate the shooting. The story line was that Burns had enough ID on him to make it clear he was a retired NYPD detective. The pension people's records showed his recent hiring by Bradford. The detectives would naturally go to Joust to find out what he was doing in his new job.

If it appeared safe for Jeanne Dalton to go to her office, she would.

Ian, Culkin and his men looked at each other and tried to figure out what they might have missed.

The good news was that Bill Spence survived the surgery. He was moved to intensive care. He was in critical condition, but his vital signs were good and the doctors thought he would make it. They were keeping him sedated, and it would be some time before he would be conscious and able to talk. The bullet had been recovered in his back muscle. It had just missed his heart.

60

Around 9:30 AM, Joust and his people started to arrive at their office. The only mention of anything unusual was that the guy at the news stand down by the Maiden Lane entrance to their building heard that there had been a shooting somewhere in the neighborhood earlier in the morning. No one seemed to have any of the details.

Jeanne wanted to leave for her office, but Culkin insisted that she stay with them until the Wall Street detectives had arrived and asked their questions. That happened a little before ten.

The detectives spoke to Joust first. He seemed genuinely shocked. He told them about his background with the NYPD and that he and his people worked for Bradford. He asked if they wanted to talk to each of his guys individually or together, and they took each one individually. After about an hour, they left and Joust called his men into the conference room.

"All right, let's get right to it. Is there anything I should know?" Jowls looked around the room. No one said anything. "I am about to call the boss and tell him the cops are on the way. If there is something I should know, God damnit, speak up so I can give Bradford a heads up."

"I think we are all as shocked by this as you are, Jowls." It was Collins who spoke. "I'll bet my pension that it has something to do with his time in the division. That place was a cesspool, and he was there for a long time. No way you can do that without having something happen. I'll bet that's it. That's what I told the detectives, and they agreed that they were pursuing that angle."

Jowls picked up the phone and dialed Bradford's private line. He told Bradford the news, and that none of them thought it was related to his present job. Jowls ended the conversation by telling Bradford that Burns was in Beekman Downtown and not expected to survive. Bradford was going to court to continue covering the jury selection. Jowls would call him if he heard anything new. He hung up the phone and told everyone but Collins to get back to work.

"Leslie, go out and find out what you can about this. It's making me nervous. I know you have always wondered about this guy. See what you can find out."

Back in the monitoring room, everyone looked at each other, but said nothing until Ian asked, "Did that sound to you like, so far, we have pulled this off?" They all agreed they had. "Now, if they just can get Spence through this."

After everyone left, Culkin called one of his sergeants in and said, "Get the U-Group on Collins. I want to see who he goes to talk to in order to find out about Burns. I am going to try and keep him in the office while you get the group down there before he leaves." Culkin called the Maiden Lane office and asked for Collins. When he got on, Culkin said, "I have some information for you on the Burns' shooting."

"Who is this?" asked Collins.

"Never mind who it is. If you want the information, you will be at the counter of the coffee shop south of your office in thirty minutes."

"Come up to my office."

"No, I don't go to offices. If you want the information, you will be at the coffee shop." Culkin hung up. "We'll see if that works. Get the U-group going."

There were seven detectives in the DA's squad that almost no one knew about. They were known as the U-group. They were undercover officers and worked directly under Sergeant Frank Hopkins. They never set foot in the squad office. They had no relationship with the other squad members and really led strange lives. They liked it that way. They were held in reserve for the most confidential investigations. Frequently they were loaned out to other divisions of the NYPD, but only with strict rules and only under the supervision and control of Frank Hopkins. They knew they were to take no orders from anyone other than Frank, not the chief of detectives, not the police commissioner. Once, the chief of patrol, about the fourth ranking cop in the department, tried to get them to do something for him without going through Frank and he lost his job. No one was to know they were undercover cops or that they even existed.

Frank was meeting with them at their usual meeting place, a warehouse in the old meat market on the west side, when he got Culkin's order. Frank was a perfect commander for this group. He was a loner. He rarely socialized with any of the other squad members. He was plain vanilla, low-key acting and dressing. He blended in with the wall.

Frank told them about their assignment to follow Collins. They knew not to ask any questions. If there was information they needed, Frank would give it to them. They were told about Collins' past, what he did for a living and that he might be up to no good. Frank wanted to know where he went and whom he talked to until further notice. Nothing else mattered. Any other assignments he had given them were to be held in abeyance until he told them otherwise. He was sent photos of Collins that he distributed to each of his men. They were not to be detected. The U-group was very good at this. No one had ever contested the claim that they were the best in the department and maybe in law enforcement. On two occasions they were borrowed by the feds to follow suspected terrorists. They never lost a subject and, as far as anyone knew, they had never been detected. Frank made the last-minute assignments so that Collins would be covered around the clock. He immediately sent four of the team to Maiden Lane.

When the U-group arrived outside the coffee shop, they saw Collins sitting on a stool at the counter looking at his watch, checking who came in the door and looking at his watch again. After about twenty minutes, he gave up and returned to the Maiden Lane office. The eavesdropping monitors confirmed that he had told Jowls about the tipster and that he was a no-show. Collins then left the office and went to Beekman Downtown Hospital. The U-group was with him.

Collins went to Beekman's reception area and had a conversation with the lady at the desk. He confirmed that Burns was there, that he was in intensive care and that he could not receive visitors. He left the hospital, but didn't leave the neighborhood. He walked around the hospital three times, and then headed up to the Bronx.

One of the U-group went to the administration office and was briefed on the rules for family visits to the ICU. They arranged to be alerted if anyone claimed to be a relative or close friend of Burns.

Office Logistics had worked with the Beekman staff to set up a room that "Burns would be transferred to" once "he was released from intensive care." It consisted of all the usual monitors and gizmos beeping away as they were attached to a mannequin lying in the bed.

Bradford got everyone in his conference room. He told them about the shooting and that the police thought it was connected to the work Burns did when he was a cop. He tried to convince everyone it had nothing to do with their present jobs. He succeeded with everyone, but Jeanne Dalton, who didn't say a word. Bradford told everyone the important activity now was the jury selection. He left to go to court.

The next day, Collins reported to Jowls that he wasn't able to find out anything about either Burns or his shooting. There was only general speculation that if you stayed in a division long enough, you were going to piss someone off. Collins told Jowls he had to run an errand and left the office. He was followed to Beekman where he was told that Burns was still in ICU, but improving and might be moved to a room where he could have visitors. Reception suggested he call in and get information over the phone to save himself the trip up to the hospital. Instead of leaving the hospital, Collins took the elevator up to the ninth floor, which was the neurological unit. He acted like he had the wrong floor and went to the stairwell where he went down to each floor and walked around. U-group reported this to their sergeant who alerted Culkin. He called a meeting.

"Ian can't be here for this because he is picking a jury, but I think Collins is up to something and we should *move* Burns out of ICU to a private room. If Collins calls in, he will be told that Burns has been moved. He should be told that Burns still can't have visitors, but it wouldn't shock me if Collins tried to pay Burns a visit."

"Then what the hell are we going to do?" asked one of Dick's sergeants.

"Grab him. Why would he be going to see Burns when he is told there are no visitors, and why is he checking out the hospital?"

"Suppose he has answers for that, or more likely, suppose he doesn't answer any of our questions?" asked the sergeant. "Aren't we blowing Ian's investigation just at the point where we might be getting somewhere? I think we should delay this part a bit."

"Let's take this one step at a time," suggested LoMurko. "If Collins is up to no good, he isn't going to sign in as a regular visitor. He is going to try to get to Burns' room without anyone knowing about it. That will be our first clue. We are going to be following him. If he goes the normal route, signs in, gets a visitor's pass and all that jazz, we have the nurses intercept and tell him there has been a problem, Burns was taken into surgery or something like that. That isn't going to happen. Right?" LoMurko looked around the room.

They agreed they would "move the patient," and see what happened.

61

When Myles Spectrum was breaking his ass at Yale Law School, all those many years ago, he never dreamed he would be getting paid $1000 an hour to sit in a courtroom and watch someone pick a jury. But nothing about having Gus Conti as his one and only client had been what he dreamed. At $1000 an hour, Myles didn't care.

It was a relationship that started back when they were kids. Myles was the brainy one. Gus was the fun lover. Gus told Myles that he was going to be a mobster when he grew up. Gus thought "mobstering" made sense. He would make a lot of money and have a lot of people working for him. He just needed to be careful about who his friends were and what he said and did. It also helped to have a smart lawyer. He told Myles to go to law school and then come work for him.

Myles did. Now he lived in a grand house off of Pelham Parkway in the Bronx, not too far from Gus' warehouse. He made more money than he could ever use. He had a car and a driver. Gus didn't mind that Myles was gay. They never talked about it. Myles kept Gus out of trouble. That was his job, and he performed it perfectly.

Gus had never asked Myles to do anything Myles had a problem with. His present assignment was a pretty good example. He was to sit in court and watch the same jury selection Bradford was watching.

He was to give Gus daily reports. He was to tell Gus about the person whom Bradford picked to save his son. The person whom, Myles assumed, if everything went perfectly, Gus probably would have killed.

Myles tried to keep the end game out of his mind. It was Bradford's job to find the right juror. It was Myles' job to report. That was all he had to do—just report. Of course, Gus would ask Myles for his opinion and Myles would give it. Previously, he had approved of the selection of juror number 11. But picking jurors was not Myles' forte. He wasn't a trial lawyer. If Gus needed a trial lawyer, Myles would find him one. When Gus needed a jury-fixer lawyer, Myles found him one, a good one. Right now, Gus wasn't too happy with Bradford because of that letter he'd written. Myles was confident he would find out who had the letter. He could keep it from being mailed. First things first, which of those jurors looked like they would take money to fix a jury?

Myles had never been introduced to Bradford. He recognized Bradford in the courtroom, but Bradford didn't know Myles. He was damn sure the ADA didn't know him either. He was just trying to blend in with everyone else. If he were asked, he would just say he was a freelance writer doing an article on the case and taking notes. Myles had been with Gus Conti for a long, long time. This was just another assignment. So far, he didn't have much to report.

62

Bob Carpenter was basically a good guy. He was a little down on his luck lately, but that had happened before. His philosophy was, "Mind your own business and things will take care of themselves." Just get up every morning and go to work. Do your job. Don't volunteer for anything. Let others do that. His job was with a small company. It wasn't going anywhere special, and neither was he. He went to work, filled out the orders that came in and went home.

He lived alone now. It was a clean, well-maintained apartment off the FDR Drive in lower Manhattan. It was nothing fancy, but it was all Bob needed.

His marriage had failed, but so what? She was a good egg. They were both happier having gone their separate ways. There were no hard feelings. She had remarried. She seemed happy. She left him alone. It was better this way. Thank God they didn't have kids.

He got paid every other Friday. He was meticulous about how he spent his paycheck. He saved so much for rent and utilities, so much for food, so much for church and charities, so much for entertainment. That was the problem right now, the entertainment. His one entertainment was the ponies, and that wasn't going so well.

Every night, on the way home from work, he would buy the Daily Racing Form. That was part of his entertainment expense. He would sit in his living room and dope out the next day's races at whatever New York track was operating. It had to be a New York track. He didn't trust the other tracks. He had to put up with Aqueduct Racetrack for one more week before the races moved to Belmont. He liked Belmont. He always did well at Belmont. He was sure his luck would change.

After he'd made his selections, he would write out his choices in a 4 × 6 spiral notebook. He would have the date at the top of the page, the list of bets and the total amount bet. He would never bet more than $100 on any given day. Most of the time it was closer to $80, but some days he felt he figured out a "sure thing." He would leave a space at the bottom of the page for the amount of money he won or lost that day. He made sure his losses never exceeded his budget for the week. Most of the time he was slightly ahead of the game.

The next morning, he would review his bets. He rarely made changes. On his way to work, he would stop at the OTB parlor down the block and place his bets. He never used a bookie. He wanted everything to be legal, and bookies weren't legal.

He would save any winning tickets for Saturday morning. He always cashed them at an OTB parlor next to a diner where he could get great coffee and a cinnamon bun.

But this was only entertainment. Bob Carpenter never looked to his winnings for income. He stuck to his budget. If he won, he would put his winnings aside for when he lost. If he won big, he would save it for his vacation. Money was very important to him, and he was very,

very careful about it. When he was having a bad run with the ponies, like now, he would be even more careful.

All that Bob Carpenter needed was his job and his paycheck. He didn't need this jury summons that had just arrived in the mail. It was going to interfere with his job and his paycheck. He knew from past experience that the boss didn't like people taking time from work for jury duty. Bob had to try and get out of serving. It was ok to take a couple of days off to report for duty, but not ok to get picked to sit on a jury. That could take weeks. And more significantly, Bob wasn't going to get paid if he wasn't at work. That would screw up his budget. Everything was meticulously planned.

Suddenly it happened. His name had been pulled out of the wheel, and he was walking up to take his place in seat number 8. He had to get out of this.

Judge Hastings leaned forward, "Well, Mr. Carpenter, you have been here for the last two days. You have heard all that I have said, all that the lawyers have said. You know quite a bit about the case from all the questions. Let's get right to it: any reason why you can't be a fair and impartial juror?"

"Your Honor, I have always tried to be fair and impartial about everything I have done in life, but I don't know that I could be fair and impartial in this case."

"Well, stop right there," Hastings interrupted. "We don't want you saying anything in open court that might be the wrong thing for this jury to hear. Why don't you come up to the bench with the lawyers and let's see what the problem is?"

Bob Carpenter worked his way out of the jury box and walked up to the bench where Ian and Nails were anxiously waiting for him.

Carpenter was scared to death. His hands were shaking. He stuck them in his pocket. He tried to talk in a near whisper, but the courtroom was silent with everyone straining to hear what he was saying.

"Judge, I cannot afford to serve. If I don't work, I don't get paid. From what I can understand, this is going to be a lengthy trial and I just can't afford it."

Hastings had heard this excuse a million times and had no patience for it, but there was something about Carpenter's sincerity that kept the judge from jumping all over him.

"Mr. Carpenter, you know if every judge excused every juror who experienced a financial hardship by serving, we would never have jury trials. Let me ask you this: would it help if I called your employer and leaned on him to pay you?"

"Please don't do that, judge. I'm afraid I'd lose my job. Please."

"Ok, I won't. But I'm afraid I can't excuse you. It wouldn't be fair to all the other jurors who are in the same spot you are in."

"All I can ask, judge, is that you consider making an exception for me. That is all I can ask."

Hastings actually looked like he was considering doing it. Ian couldn't believe it. Hastings paused, but then said, "Nope. I'm sorry. I can't do it. Please take seat number 8 and we will continue with the selection process." Carpenter thought he was going to cry. He answered all the questions honestly and both sides accepted him.

63

Bradford came over the tape machine as clear as could be, "Bingo. We have our mark. Tell your guys to get me everything they can on juror number 8 as fast as they can. Unless they develop something to change my mind, he's the one I'm going after for the fix."

Ian ordered that the tape be replayed four more times. "Did everyone hear the same thing I did? I think we have to assume that Mr. Carpenter is going to be approached by Bradford. We have to find out as much as possible about him without bumping into Jowls' people who are going to be doing the same thing. Make sure we pay particular attention to anything that is said by the investigators. Let me know if you hear something that indicates they may be backing off Carpenter."

There was nothing.

Culkin went into action. He left the monitoring room, summoned his lieutenant and two sergeants and hurried into his office.

LoMurko had a satisfied look on his face. "Well, Mr. Waspecutor, you going to take the chance?"

"You bet. Let's get the Pats. We have to make sure we get to Carpenter before Bradford does."

Culkin put the U-group on the tail. They sat outside Carpenter's apartment building and watched. When they were sure it was safe, they went up to his apartment, told him who they were and brought him over to a safe precinct on the west side. They didn't want to take him to the Hole. The Hole was not for civilians.

Ian took his time trying to get an understandably nervous Bob Carpenter to relax. "You are in no trouble. You have done nothing wrong. Please, just listen to me very carefully because I am about to tell you what was going to happen to you and how we are going to work together to make sure it doesn't happen. Ok? Do you have any questions?"

"Can I go to the bathroom?"

"Of course. Smitty take him to the bathroom."

Bob Carpenter couldn't believe what he was hearing. He may not have liked the idea of having to serve on a jury, but to try and fix a juror? That was crazy. He was hearing how he would wear a wire and record everything that the fixer said to him. He was hearing how there would be a backup team to protect him. Most importantly, he was hearing that he then would be replaced with an alternate juror. He didn't have to serve. He was hearing that he could go back to work if he wanted to.

But he was also hearing Ian say, "We can't make you do this, but we would strongly advise that you consider going into the witness protection program. You will be relocated, given another identity, another job and money for your troubles. You will be safe." That all sounded particularly good after Ian told Carpenter what happened to 11.

Carpenter asked, "Are you allowed to bet on the ponies if you are in the witness protection program?"

"You can do anything that is legal."

The Pats came into the room and met Carpenter. In about two minutes, Patricia was Carpenter's new best friend. He was shown how the wire worked and where he would wear it. He could put it on himself before he went to court the next morning. They made him put it on and take it off several times until they were sure he was doing it correctly and they were getting good reception. Patricia gave him her phone number and made him promise to call her before he left his apartment in the morning.

The rest of the evening was spent in role playing. Carpenter was shown several different pictures of Bradford. He was coached on how to react if approached. They told him they didn't know how Bradford might do it, but they were confident that he would not leave this up to anyone else. Bradford might possibly come to his apartment. He could approach him on the way to court. It was more probable that Bradford would let Carpenter spend at least the morning in the jury box, while jury selection was being completed, so he could see how Carpenter was reacting to things. Carpenter should just sit and listen, do what he would normally do.

If or when Bradford approached him, Carpenter should listen politely. Ultimately, when it became clear what Bradford wanted Carpenter to do, he was to be mildly shocked, but not reject the idea. He was not to be enthusiastic. He was to be cautious. He was to show his interest in money. He would need lots and lots of money. He was to be a little scared that he might get caught. They went through all the things people would do in such a situation. Carpenter was kind of enjoying the preparation. He felt like he was a cop. Ian was pleased that Carpenter was a quick study.

Everyone exchanged appropriate phone numbers, and the U-group arranged to get Carpenter home in a covert way in case Jowls' men were watching his apartment building.

After Carpenter left, they all looked at each other and hoped he didn't get cold feet in the morning.

LoMurko and Culkin took Ian aside. LoMurko told Ian, "We have to talk about something. We have to decide who is in charge. We have been avoiding that question, but tomorrow could be D-Day and somebody has got to be Ike."

"I agree, but as far as I am concerned, this is a police operation until an arrest is made, so you guys figure it out."

"I'll make it easy. I am the homicide captain. This operation has been expertly carried out by Inspector Culkin, and I am honored to be on his team. As far as I am concerned, he is Ike."

There was unanimous agreement.

"If I'm Ike, then let's talk about what could happen tomorrow and who is going to do what. Ian, this may be a police operation, but you have been in on it since the beginning so your thoughts are important. Are we agreed that, if an approach is made and Bradford offers the money, we make arrests?"

They talked for another hour trying to consider various exigencies. When they thought most possibilities were covered, they went home. Ian hoped he could get some sleep. He still had to finish picking the jury.

64

The day began with Patricia receiving a phone call from Carpenter. She was checking her reception and could hear him talking to himself as he was getting the microphone in place. She told him the reception was great, but that he should understand that she could hear everything he said or that was said around him. He asked if he had been talking to himself. She told him he had. He would be more careful and hoped he didn't say anything inappropriate. He hadn't. Then he asked, "Does this mean, if I go to the bathroom, you can hear it?"

"It does. You ok with that? I'm the only one that can hear it," she lied, "and I won't listen. Will that be all right?"

"I guess it doesn't bother me if it doesn't bother you."

"It will be our little secret."

After she hung up with Carpenter, she called her lieutenant and told him that Carpenter thinks she is the only one listening. "So don't screw this up." He understood.

Ian left a message with Judge Hastings that he would like to speak to him as soon as possible. After the judge called, Ian went up to Hastings' chambers and brought him up to date. Ian had never seen the judge so happy. He was walking around his chambers pumping air like he'd just won the Masters. Ian reminded him they still had a long way to go.

Hastings asked that they try to do everything they could without involving the jury so he didn't have to declare a mistrial. If that couldn't be accomplished, he understood, but he liked the jury. He didn't want to lose it. He thought Louie did a good job with his jury selection.

They both agreed that it might help to adjourn court as early as possible at the end of the day.

Carpenter made it to court, and made it through the morning and afternoon sessions. Hastings adjourned court at a little after 3:00 PM and told the jurors to be back by 10:00 AM the next morning when they would begin with opening statements.

Carpenter was walking home, proceeding north on Mulberry Street, when he saw Bradford coming toward him with a woman on his arm. They both had big smiles on their faces. "Mr. Carpenter, have you got a minute?"

"Do I know you?"

"I doubt that you do. My name is Barry Bradford, I'm an attorney and I practice down the street at the criminal courts building. This is my associate, Barbara Banner. She is also an attorney, and she works in my office. Here are our cards." Bradford handed Carpenter two business cards. "I know that you have been stuck with jury duty and I also know that that is a hardship for you. I know that you are not getting paid while you serve on that jury and I would like to do something about that."

"You seem to know a lot about me. How come?"

"Well, that's sort of my job. To hang around the courts and see what is going on with juries. Barbara and I do it all the time. Can we talk to you for a minute over a cup of coffee in that espresso shop over there? The coffee's on me."

"I guess there is no harm in that. I don't drink espresso. I'm a pretty simple kind of guy."

"I'll bet you are, Mr. Carpenter. Their regular coffee is just great. Let's have a cup."

As far as Bradford was concerned, the hardest part of the fix was over. He'd approached the mark, and the mark did not run away. Now came the money part.

"How would you like to turn this expensive bit of jury business into a money-making proposition? I am talking about a lot of money."

"How do I do that?"

Bradford looked at Barbara, and she said, "You essentially do nothing."

Carpenter put a huge grin on his face and exclaimed, "That's my kind of way to make some money."

"Not just some money, lots of money."

"Ok, that's my kind of way to make lots of money. I guess I'm interested."

"How much do you make, Mr. Carpenter?"

"Not much, but I get by."

"Would you like never to have to worry about money again?" Bradford was into doing his thing. He was starting to roll. He knew the buttons to push and how hard to push them. He had Carpenter rolling in money, and all Carpenter had to do was sit in the jury room and do nothing, literally nothing.

Carpenter began to think about some way he could pull this off and actually get the money. He came back to reality and remembered where he was and what he was doing.

"How do I know that you are for real about this, that this isn't some kind of a scam? I was taught you never get something for nothing."

"That's the boy, Mr. Carpenter, great question! We're proud of you, aren't we, Barbara?" Barbara was bursting with pride. "First of all, you have our cards. They have our office address and phone number. Now, we wouldn't be giving you that if we were scamming you, would we? Here is my wallet." Bradford reached into his pocket, got out his wallet and slammed it down on the table. "Open that wallet, Mr. Carpenter, see the driver's license, the New York City Bar membership card, my social security card. See all those cards? Take a good look at them. Some of them have my photo on them. Do you see the photo? Do you want to see Barbara's wallet?"

"No. That's ok. I guess you are who you say you are."

"That's right. Now you see the address of my office on my card? That's the Woolworth Building. Do you know where the Woolworth Building is?"

"Yeah, it's down the street."

"That's right. It is down the street, and I am going to have Barbara go outside and hail a cab and I'm going to take you to my office in the Woolworth Building. Now, I wouldn't be doing that if this was a scam. Would I?"

"I don't think you would, but I don't think it's necessary to take me there. I think I believe you."

"Oh oh, you're disappointing me, Mr. Carpenter. I don't want you to believe me yet. Not until you open this envelope I am going to give you. Hand me the envelope, Barbara." Barbara went into her shoulder bag and pulled out a bulging 10 × 12 yellow envelope. "Here, Mr. Carpenter, this is for you. Open it." Bradford thrust the envelope toward Carpenter, and Carpenter took it. "Open it. It's yours."

Carpenter looked at Bradford and at Barbara. He looked around the coffee shop. No one was paying any attention to them. He lowered the envelope under the table and opened the top. Inside was more money than he had ever seen in his life. He said, "My God," and quickly closed the envelope.

"Some scam, isn't it, Mr. Carpenter? That is $100,000. If you want to count it, you can. Take your time. We will have another cup of coffee while you count."

Carpenter couldn't help it; his hands were shaking. "No, that's ok. It looks like an awful lot of money. I don't need to count it. Tell me what I have to do."

"That's my man, Mr. Carpenter!" Bradford reached across the table to shake Carpenter's hand. Barbara got up and gave him a kiss. Carpenter started to shove the envelope toward Bradford who stopped him, "No, no, no, that's yours. You are going to keep that, and we are going to talk about how much more you are going to get and when and how you are going to get it. You just tell me when you are ready."

"I'm ready now, but do you think, instead of this coffee, we could go across the street to that pub? I could use a drink."

"Absolutely. Let's go."

They crossed the street, and went to a table at the back of the pub. Bradford told Carpenter that he would sign some papers promising to do as they discussed. Upon the signing, he would get another $100,000. He would not vote to convict and remain a holdout until the judge declared a mistrial. At that point, he would get another $300,000. He would be transported to an island in the Caribbean where he would remain for a week without talking to anyone, and at the end of the week, he would get $500,000 for a total of one million dollars. "Can you imagine that, Mr. Carpenter? One million dollars, and you thought you were going into the poor house with this jury service gig. Not bad, right?"

"I don't know."

Bradford was startled. "What do you mean you don't know?"

"Couldn't I get in some serious trouble for this? Am I getting enough money?"

Bradford tried not to show his relief. This jerk wasn't worried about getting arrested and going to prison, like he should be. He was looking for more money. This was Bradford's kind of guy.

"There is a certain amount of risk involved in this. But think about it. Who's to know? We are going to show you how to handle yourself in the jury room. We are going to go over what you say if the judge or someone else asks you questions. It is foolproof. But having said all that, how much more do you think you should get? And don't you be the one who is doing the scamming, Mr. Carpenter."

"I think I should get another, say, $200,000." Carpenter hadn't even thought about how much more he should ask for.

"I'll tell you what. I'll ask the client for another $200,000. I'll even recommend that he give it to you, but in the meantime, you have a guaranteed one million. Do we have a deal?"

Carpenter paused. Bradford could feel his heart beating. Barbara thought she felt herself peeing. Patricia was holding her breath back at the squad. She was squeezing Pat's hand so hard it hurt.

"I want to see the additional money. But we got a deal."

Bradford pulled another envelope of money out of his briefcase. He pulled out some legal papers and a pen, and started to go over the agreement line by line. Barbara excused herself to go to the ladies' room. Culkin and company moved into place.

65

On Culkin's signal, they came in the back door, through the kitchen and into the back room. Several of the detectives had their guns drawn. "On the floor, hands and legs spread."

Bradford let out a loud "Shit."

Banner yelled, "Oh my God!" and started to cry.

Carpenter hadn't been told this was going to happen and thought he was going to faint. Smitty grabbed him, took him out the front door and almost threw him in the back seat of a waiting squad car. They immediately took off.

A group of ten detectives went to Jowls' office. They arrested Jowls, Pete Fusco and Steve Upper. They were told that Leslie Collins had called in to say he wouldn't be at work today. They showed Jowls a search warrant and started to pile all the files into boxes. A call to the U-group revealed that they were watching Collins. He was sitting in his car in the basement parking lot of Beekman Hospital. He had been there for an hour.

Three other detectives went to Bradford's office in the Woolworth Building. They showed Jeanne and Rita a search warrant. Then they started boxing records and took both of the women to the district attorney's office. The game plan was to see who was cooperating and who was not. That would go a long way to determining who stayed arrested and who didn't. Everyone was put in separate rooms. Bradford was in a conference room with Ian, Robbie and Smitty.

"Barry, as you know, I am on trial. I have to give an opening statement and start calling witnesses tomorrow morning. I'm prepared to do that, but I would really like not to waste time with you now. So please, just sit there and listen to me. I'm going to give you your rights which you know as well as I do. Then I'm going to tell you what we have on you, what you are facing and what we want from you. Then, depending on what you have to say, I will tell you the options we have with respect to whether you ever go home again or not. Is that clear?"

Bradford listened to and acknowledged his rights. He listened to what Ian had to say. He sunk lower and lower in his chair as Ian spoke. Ian told Bradford that what he had done as a lawyer, as a former assistant district attorney and as a citizen was one of the most heinous and despicable things a person could do. Ian told Bradford of the bugs and the tapes. He was prepared to play them for Bradford, but he did not want to waste time. Ian did not tell him that Spence and Jeanne were undercover cops. Bradford would figure that out soon enough.

Bradford interrupted Ian, "For God's sake, Ian, stop. Tell me what you want. Whatever you want, I'll give you. There is no point in fighting this. What do you want?"

"We want the truth, and we want old man Conti."

"You got it."

Ian called for David Sean.

By the end of the evening, Rita had cooperated and was prepared to cooperate further. She went home. Steve Upper was prepared to tell Smitty his life history. He went home. Jowls, for the time being, was exercising his right to remain silent. Ian was certain that would change. He was arrested. Pete Fusco was trying to get in touch with the law firm that represented DEA agents. He had used them before. Barbara Banner was in a room with Patricia and had not shut up since she was arrested. She lapsed in and out of hysteria. Bradford gave a complete statement and, as a result, Culkin was authorized to go to the Bronx and arrest Gus Conti. That was going to be a big deal because of who Conti was.

Bradford called his trust and estate lawyer, told him he was cooperating with the district attorney and asked him to hand deliver his letter to Ian. Bradford and Banner were told that, because of their cooperation and the ongoing Conti trial, there would be no publicity about the case for the time being. Ian was going to ask for high bail. If they made it, Ian would be notified. Ian would seek to make another condition of bail, that both Bradford and Banner surrender their passports and make themselves available whenever Ian wanted them.

Ian made a call to Vince O'Rielly and told him Culkin's men were on their way to the Bronx hoping to arrest Gus Conti. O'Rielly told Ian that he didn't feel obligated to call Harper until all the arrests were over. "Things are in progress. We don't know the final tally yet. I think I should wait," he said with a hint of mischief.

Ian called Judge Hastings, and then he called Nails. Nails told Ian he was going to ask for a mistrial first thing the next morning. He was convinced that there was no way this would remain quiet. Ian made two other quick calls: one was to Purns and the other was to the former ADA in the Bronx. They were both shocked at the news about Bradford. Ian made a note to himself about arresting the juror from the Bronx case who was in Florida.

The Office of Organized Crime gave Culkin all they had on Gus Conti. The detectives went to his home, his warehouse and a social club he was known to frequent. They did not find Conti. Ian called O'Rielly to give him the news. O'Rielly concluded that he had to let the DA know about the arrests, Conti or no Conti.

Ian's last call was to Adele's burner. It went to her message machine. That meant that she was awake and working. She would call back. Ian wasn't sure he would be able to stay awake long enough to answer the phone. He stripped down and got ready to jump in the shower when his burner rang.

"Hi Adele," he answered.

"What are you doing?"

"I'm standing here naked, about to take a shower and talking to you. What are you doing?"

"I'm thinking of you standing there naked wishing I didn't have to take care of this appendicitis that just came in. When can we see each other? This is starting to suck."

Ian gave her a rundown of the day's events. "We are getting there. I don't know what Conti will do when his father gets arrested."

"You mean if his father gets arrested."

"It is just a matter of time. When one of these mob guys starts to bleed, the wolves begin to circle. They will want him out of the way. Someone will give him up. He probably realizes that. Anyway, that's all the good news; now I've got to give you the bad news."

He told Adele that he anticipated that Harper would jump at the chance to have a press conference no matter how much pleading anyone did with him. He asked Adele if she would have time to call her family and warn them that Mary's case was probably going to hit the papers again. He knew that would be upsetting to Maggie.

"I'll call my folks and let them know. I'm very proud of you."

"Thanks, Adele. You are the greatest."

"Honest?"

"Honest."

The only man not accounted for, Leslie Collins, finally got out of his parked car. He was wearing a white doctor's coat. A stethoscope hung around his neck. Culkin, who was striking out up in the Bronx, was notified. He, in turn, alerted his sergeant who was about to hide in the closet of Burns' hospital room. Two squad detectives were hiding in the bathroom.

Collins went directly to the doctors' elevator and took it to the sixth floor. He exited the elevator, turned right and walked past room 615 with Burns' name on the patient card outside his room. The U-group watched and notified the sergeant in room 615. Collins walked to the end of the hall and looked out the window. He whispered to himself, "That fucking Burns is an undercover cop and he is a dead man."

He stood there for about thirty seconds, took a deep breath, spun around and started walking back down the hall. When he got to room 615, he stopped, opened the door and went in. As the door was closing, he pulled a revolver out of his coat pocket. It had a suppressor on it. He fired two shots into Burns' head. *Pffffit Pffffit*. The detectives sprang from their hiding places and, with their guns pointed at Collins, ordered him to drop his gun. Collins raised his gun toward the sergeant. Simultaneously, the sergeant and the two detectives shot him. He was dead before he hit the floor.

Ian had just fallen asleep when he got the call from Culkin. They would send a car to pick him up. Ian contacted the ADA on homicide call to give him a heads up on what had happened. They both agreed that Ian was too close to the case and should not be involved in the investigation of Collins' death. There wasn't a hell of a lot to investigate.

66

Ian had finished up at the Wall Street precinct, and was walking out with LoMurko looking for LoMurko's car for a ride to the DA's office. Danny, who was driving past them, blasted his siren when he saw his boss. Shootings by police officers always brought out the press, but the story coming out of Beekman Hospital was a showstopper. TV vans were all over the street. Ian never would have made it to LoMurko's car without help. Danny put the siren on at full blast to get the reporters away from the car so that they could get going.

Vince O'Rielly and Frank Carney were already in Vince's office preparing to see the DA. Ian gave them a quick summary of the death of Leslie Collins. They both congratulated Ian on the Bradford case, and expressed their relief that no one from the squad had gotten hurt in the hospital.

Vince left a message with the eighth floor to be called as soon as Harper got in. It was decided that it would be best if Ian didn't go with them to see the DA. The excuse was that he was in court where he was on trial. This way, they could plead ignorance about some of the details, and Harper might decide he should wait until Ian was available.

No such luck. As they were considering their options, an office-wide announcement was made that the district attorney would be having a press conference at ten o'clock. Almost at the same time, Vince got a call to come up to Harper's office.

Ian wished them good luck and went to his office to call Hastings' chambers. He wanted the judge to know what had transpired.

"So that's we're we are at, judge. We have to assume that Vince is going to be unsuccessful in his efforts to talk the DA out of a press conference. You have told the jury to be here by ten. As they are filing into the courtroom, Harper is going to be blowing this thing sky high. Nails is going to move for a mistrial, and in my humble opinion, you don't have a choice. You must grant it."

"You're right. It may seem like we have wasted our time, but we haven't. As far as I am concerned, it has been well worth it. You have done an incredible job. You have an airtight case against that son-of-a-bitch Bradford and his entire crew. All you have left to do is find old man Conti. And you will. You know the way that world works. There is always someone who would like to get rid of him. He can run, but he can't hide. I'll put the case off for one week, and we'll see how things shake out. My sense is you could use a bit of a break. You've been a tad busy."

Hastings got up from his chair and walked over to Ian to shake his hand. "Great job, Ian. You are a credit to your office. See you down in court."

Vince and Frank gave a draft press statement to Harper's team and emphasized that one of the main culprits, Gus Conti, was still at large. Having a press conference was not going to help find him. They respectfully requested, once again, he postpone it.

"I don't give a shit about Conti. I'm going ahead. I'll have another press conference when we pick up Conti. Where is Ian? We are going to need details."

"He is in the courtroom."

Harper said, "Why is he in a courtroom? Why isn't he here?"

"He is doing what you pay him to do: trying a case."

Nails was waiting outside the courtroom with Bunny. "Hello there, Ian. Why would the street outside be filled with TV and communications trucks? Could it be that your shy and humble boss is going to get his mug before the cameras yet again?"

"I think you may be correct, Nails. I want you to know that I tried to avoid this. It does not help matters. You make your motion. I'll oppose it for the record, but I have the feeling you might win this one."

The motion for a mistrial was granted. The jurors were excused and went home. The case was adjourned for a week.

Pete Rusk couldn't believe what was happening. They were going to have to start all over again. Thank God Maggie had stayed home.

What about the gun? Pete concluded it would stay right where it was. There was no point in moving it. No one was going to find it. He would see what the system could do. If the system sent Conti away for the rest of his life, Pete would do nothing. He had faith in Ian. Anything short of going away for the rest of his life and Conti was a dead man.

Shortly after Bradford and Banner were arraigned, Bradford's father put up his huge estate in Bedford Hills, a Westchester suburb, as collateral to the million-dollar bail bond for both Bradford and Banner. They were home before Ian was.

67

Myles Spectrum hated everything about the tombs. It stunk. There was an overwhelming odor of Lysol. It was degrading to enter the place, even when you were going into, what was obviously marked, the visitors' entrance. This was not a place for a Yale Law School graduate to be seen. It was depressing. He had to sign all sorts of things and was subjected to all sorts of searches by correction officers who seemed to be equally unhappy to be there. And then he had to wait in a waiting room with a smell even the Lysol couldn't cure. Myles decided that the minute he got out of there he would go home, shower and take his suit to the cleaners.

"Counsellor Spectrum to the front," the loudspeaker announced. Myles got up and went over to the officer who was waiting to take him to the attorneys' room. Myles had bad news to give young Mr. Conti, and the little shit was probably going to cause a fuss.

Culkin had flagged Conti's prison card. He was to be told if anyone visited Conti. Now the inspector was getting a call from the tombs that one Myles Spectrum, counsellor at law, had registered to visit Conti.

Culkin put a call in to Hopkins. The U-group sat outside the tombs' entrance where they could wait for Spectrum. Soon they got a radio message that a short man dressed in a three-piece grey flannel suit and wearing a Panama hat was on his way out. They spotted Myles. He looked like he had been in a cage fight. He walked directly across the street to Manny's Bar, and got himself a scotch on the rocks. It was only eleven twenty in the morning. They watched Myles down his drink, order another one and go over to a pay phone on the near wall. He made an animated five-minute call, finished his drink and came out to the curb. In ten seconds, a limo pulled up to Myles and he got in. The U-group followed the limo to a large mansion off Pelham Parkway in the Bronx. The limo pulled into the circular drive. Myles got out of the back and ran into the mansion.

The team stayed on the mansion, and in a half an hour, Myles came out dressed in a golf shirt and slacks. In addition to his briefcase, he carried an overnight bag. He got back into the limo and headed toward the Hutchinson Parkway.

Ian went to Culkin's office when he heard the news. Culkin wanted to grab Spectrum and squeeze him.

"Dick, he's a lawyer. He's going to claim the privilege. We can't make him talk." Ian knew that the inspector was pissed about missing Conti the night before. He was also pissed that the DA held a press conference.

"We can follow him, can't we?" Culkin asked. "He may lead us to Gus."

"Sure you can follow him. I wouldn't count on him leading us to Gus."

There were two teams of the U-group now involved in the tail. They were taking turns and giving a blow-by-blow as to where

Spectrum's limo was going. "Looks like he is turning into a Comfort Inn outside White Plains," one of the teams reported.

Myles' limo pulled up to a room at the end of a row of several attached units. Myles went into number 8, and the limo took off. The detectives waited. One of them got out and started walking past all the rooms. He paused outside number 8 and gave a thumbs up. He hustled back to their car and reported that two men were talking in the room, but he couldn't make out who they were or what they were saying. They found that the room was been registered to one John Smith. Another trip past room number 8 fifteen minutes later produced sounds wholly inconsistent with the second man being Gus Conti, unless Gus Conti was having an affair with Myles Spectrum.

68

Ian went down to O'Rielly's office to give him a briefing. Frank Carney was there, and he said, "Something's up. I have been asked to be at the governor's office at one this afternoon. Vince called Harper to arrange to tell him about Conti. He was told that Harper was up at the governor's office now."

"Please God, let it be what I hope it is," Ian prayed. "I can't think of a better first press conference than you announcing Conti's arrest as the new district attorney."

Vince O'Rielly had a huge grin on his face, and added, "Amen."

The governor explained how important it was for Harper to fill a vacancy on the Appellate Division of the First Department. He needed Harper on that court. Harper was shocked. "But I like being DA. I think I can go places."

"I am asking you, as a personal favor, to do this for me."

"I have to think about this."

That did not please the governor. After Harper left his office, the governor called Judge Dickerson. "Bernie, he is resisting. Time to let him know where he stands. Meet with him."

Dickerson did. He told Harper that he would not receive the support of the regular Democratic organization in Manhattan if he were to run for election. His appointment had been a mistake, and the governor was saving him from an embarrassing oblivion by offering him the judgeship. He should take it.

Harper continued to resist. "I like the job. I have a great staff. They work very hard and make some great cases for me."

"That's just the point, Ferris; they are not making the cases for you. They are protecting the citizens of New York county and you use it for your own ends. You don't even take their advice and hold off on going public when it is in the best interest of the case to hold off. You are an egomaniac. You can't be an egomaniac when you are the DA. There have been too many complaints about the way you run the office."

"From whom? Not from the people on my staff?"

"From your entire staff. Your press guy has been driving everyone nuts and is universally hated."

"Am I surrounded by a bunch of babies?"

"No, you are surrounded by a bunch of professional, experienced prosecutors to whom you and your team refuse to listen. I am giving you the political facts of life. Take the governor's offer of a judgeship, and he will be grateful to you. Turn him down and try to run for election, without the support of the governor and the party, and you will soon be a nobody, knocking on doors of law firms looking for a job. No one is going to hire you because they don't want to be perceived as crossing the governor. Am I making myself clear?"

Harper sat and fumed, and then jumped up. "God damned bunch of babies." He actually knocked over one of Dickerson's lamps. "Who the hell wants to work with a God damned bunch of babies anyway? Fuck 'em all. It'll be great to get out of there. Tell the governor I'll take the judgeship."

"No, Ferris, you call the governor and you tell him how grateful you are to have this important opportunity. Tell him that you would be delighted to be appointed to such a prestigious position."

They agreed that next morning at ten the governor would announce Harper's appointment to the Appellate Court and Harper's career as the district attorney would be over. He had the rest of the day to get his stuff packed.

Carney was summoned for a meeting with the governor. He was told that he would be appointed the district attorney. He was asked if his family and a few select friends could be at the governor's office next day, at noon, for the ceremony. The governor didn't want to make too big a deal out of all this in order to save some face for Harper. He promised that after Carney was elected in the special election, he would have a full-blown inauguration with all the bells and whistles. Carney told the governor he didn't need any of that. He was honored to have the opportunity to serve, and he thanked the governor. He used the governor's phone to call his wife and give her the news. Dina told Frank how proud she was of him and that she would keep the girls out of school so they could attend. As predicted, things had moved fast.

When Frank got back to the office, he went directly to Ian's office. As usual it was in a "trial preparation" mess. He chased everyone out of the office and told Ian, "The governor is swearing me in at twelve noon tomorrow. I know you are in the middle of a lot of stuff, but I will not go through with this unless you can be there."

Ian jumped up from his desk and started shouting. Smitty barged into the room thinking someone was hurting Ian.

Frank said, "Be quiet. You can't tell a soul about this. The governor is keeping this hush-hush."

"What governor is keeping what hush-hush?" asked Smitty. "What's going on, Ian? Are you all right?"

Carney spoke up. "I'm sorry, Smitty. It's all my fault, but Ian can't tell you a thing. Do me a favor and pretend you didn't hear a word. Be in my office at two tomorrow afternoon. I'll explain everything then. Ok?" Smitty waved as he shut the door and left.

"Why do I think that Smitty knows?" asked Carney.

"Because Smitty knows everything that happens south of 42nd Street. So what happened?"

Carney told Ian of his meeting with the governor.

The next day Ian was up at the governor's New York office with the other members of the Homicide Bureau, Frank Carney's wife and daughters, the Dickersons, a few other Carney family members and a few of Frank's friends. The governor had asked him to keep the guests to under thirty, and Frank did that. After looking around to see that there was no one present from the Harper camp, the governor became extraordinarily gracious. He praised Frank and promised to work for his election.

The governor had sworn Harper into his judgeship earlier in the morning before several of Harper's family members. It had been like attending a wake. Everyone knew what was going on. Manhattan was getting rid of a mistake. It was hoped that Harper would see that his political career was over and he would devote his time on the bench to being a decent judge rather than promoting himself. Carney arranged to meet with Harper the next day to go over any pending issues. He decided to go to Harper's new office out of deference to the new judge.

69

The Bradford investigation became the "Find Gus Conti" investigation. All efforts were focused on that goal. Bradford and Banner had fulfilled their obligation and reported to Ian the moment they were released on bail. No one was more interested in Conti being located than was Barry Bradford.

Jeanne Dalton was in charge of making sure everything of evidentiary value was taken from Bradford's office pursuant to the search warrant, as now that Bradford was out on bail, he might want to return to his old office—though no one could imagine him ever practicing law again.

Rita had continued to cooperate and had been back to the DA's office two more times. She had several contact numbers for Conti that she had used to get in touch with him during the first trial: a social club, a country club, places like that. Culkin had been busy checking them out. So far all efforts to locate Conti had failed.

Rita still could not believe that Jeanne Dalton was a detective in the New York City Police Department. "She looks younger than my niece." Rita asked if she could go back over to the office. She had left some makeup and personal items in her desk, and if she could retrieve them, it would save her some money. Jeanne cleared this with Ian, but

Ian wanted Jeanne to go with Rita. He was pretty sure that Bradford wouldn't do anything stupid, but he didn't want to take any chances. Together, Jeanne and Rita walked over to the Woolworth Building.

Rita still had a key that she used to open the door. As she pushed open the door, she let out a horrible scream. Jeanne pulled her automatic and pushed Rita to the side. Barbara Banner was lying in the doorway to the conference room. She had been shot in the head. Jeanne cautiously walked deeper into the office and found Bradford slumped over his desk. The top of the desk was full of blood. Jeanne felt Bradford's neck for a pulse. He was not only dead. He was cold.

Jeanne called Ian.

It didn't take long for Smitty and Robbie to get to Bradford's office. They were followed in short order by LoMurko and his men, and then the forensic people and the morgue people. The medical examiner's preliminary determination was that Bradford and Banner had both been shot three times in the head. Much the way 11 had been shot in Jamaica.

Ian was called down to Vince O'Rielly's office. When he got there, he was greeted by a somber Vince, Culkin and LoMurko. "Uh-oh," Ian observed, "This does not look good. What's happened now?"

Vince ran the meeting, "Our friends from the department thought that we should have a little discussion and I agreed. Jim, why don't you tell Ian about your concerns?"

"Make that our concerns," Dick Culkin put in.

LoMurko took over. "Ian, this comes from Dick and me, both of us. At this point we do not know who shot and killed Banner and Bradford, but we do know that it was an execution done by professionals. They were both killed by three gunshots to the back of the head, at close range. Bradford and Banner had been out on bail less than twenty-four hours. We know that when they made bail, Bradford took Banner to his family's home in Bedford Hills and told his father that they were going over to Bradford's home in New Rochelle. We have been there, and it is hard to tell if they were taken from there down to the city or if they went on their own. No one can recall seeing the two coming into the Woolworth Building or seeing anyone with them.

"At any rate, the shooters were able to get into Bradford's office and kill both of them without being seen. We are assuming from the powder burns that they used suppressors on their guns that silenced the shots.

"Jeanne and Rita found the bodies at about two thirty in the afternoon and the ME thinks they had been dead about three hours, so we are putting the shooting at around 11:00 AM.

"The point of all of this is that this was a hit and we are concerned. We don't know where Gus Conti is or what he is up to. We want you to be careful."

"You don't think he would come after me, do you? I thought the prosecutor was always immune. It's not going to do him any good to get rid of me. Someone just takes my place and has, I hope, even more incentive to be successful."

"You're thinking like a rational man, Ian. Conti is a desperate man. We know Bradford told him about the letter he left with his lawyer. He has to assume we have that. It sets forth the killing of 11, and even if it might not be admissible in court, it gives us a roadmap.

"But more significant is the world he lives in. Once he is perceived as crippled by his colleagues, he knows he is in trouble. There are always those waiting to take his place, to take over his organization and to assume control of his money machine. It is the greatest liability a family boss has. He wants to make a statement before he hides, and he wants to hide well before someone rats on where he is. We are afraid he is making his statement: 'Don't mess with me. I still have power. I can still hurt you.'"

O'Rielly added, "The bottom line, Ian, is that we want to put some protection around you until we know where Conti is."

"You mean I have to have a bodyguard, Vince?" Ian's tone showed his disappointment. "I can't stand that idea. Do I have a choice? Can I refuse?"

"I guess you can, but I guess that this would then also have to go up to the new DA. I have absolutely no doubt in my mind what District Attorney Carney is going to decide once the inspector and captain give him their opinion.

"None of us who know you and work with you wants to be in the position of not having done all that we can do to protect you."

LoMurko spoke up, "Look, Ian, it doesn't have to be too onerous. We have guys in this department who do it all the time. They are trained. They know what to look for. They are discreet. Most of the time you won't even know they are around. And with you it's going to be a piece of cake. You never do anything but work, go home and sleep, get up and work, go home and sleep. You have absolutely no social life. You don't do anything any normal person does. You are very, very weird." A smile came across LoMurko's face.

"Alright, alright, enough. I'll do it, but arrest this guy, please. Are there any more leads?"

Culkin answered, "Some minor stuff. We are sticking on this Myles guy. He is close to Conti. We are hoping he gives us something.

Look Ian, thanks. It is much better this way. I'll call the chief of detectives and they will send a detail over to meet with you." The meeting was over.

There was a message that the new District attorney wanted to see Ian. This was Ian's first trip up to the eighth floor to see his friend in his new office. He fixed his tie and went into the men's room to comb his hair. This was kind of a big deal, and he wanted to look his best.

"Hello chief. You look great in this office. How do you feel?"

"I don't feel like any chief, that's for sure. I have been meeting with the various bureau chiefs making sure they know I want them to stay on. It is amazing the level of discontent that had developed under Harper."

"Why are you amazed? Look at how we felt."

"I thought that was just the Homicide Bureau. I thought we were the only ones with problems. Everyone was having problems."

"Well, you know that everyone now thinks the problems will soon be over. There is a feeling of relief throughout the entire office. You also know that if there is anything I can do to help you, I'm here. Just say the word."

"I know, Ian. Now we have to talk."

"That sounds ominous."

"I am aware of the security issues, and I am delighted that you have agreed to the bodyguards, but what about Adele?"

"Oh my God, what about her?"

"Well, if Conti knows what I know about you and Adele, and Conti wants to hurt you, that is the way to hurt you. Right?"

Ian was stunned. He turned pale, fell silent and looked down at the floor. "I can't imagine Adele being hurt," he managed to say.

"The question becomes: who knows about you and Adele?"

Ian thought for a long time. "I think that she has mentioned me to her mother. I don't think her mother has said anything to her father or anyone else; I suspect that there is a religious issue holding her back."

"I know about that. Dina and I suffered through that same stuff."

Ian continued, "I mentioned Adele to my father and I'm sure I left the impression that I thought she was something special. He is a pretty smart man. But he isn't going to talk to anyone. He's out in Middle Pennsylvania.

"I suspect that Adele's roommates at the hospital have been given an earful. Nails suspects something and asked me once if anything was going on. I told him there wasn't and he told me he would never do anything about it in the trial. I trust him. Smitty is always suspicious about everything I do and don't do. Robbie cares. They probably wonder. I don't know. Please don't tell me you think she is in danger."

"I guess I don't. That is a pretty uninteresting list. Congratulations, you have been quite discreet. You might tell Adele what is going on and emphasize the importance of continuing to be discreet. You never know what the talk is up at the hospital. When do you start the retrial?"

"In three days."

"I guess that is too soon to insist that someone else try the case?"

"Please, let's see how things shake out."

Ian returned to his office and called Adele. He got the answering machine and left a message: "We should talk."

His phone rang five minutes later. He grabbed it expecting Adele, but it was the main entrance security officer. "Hi Ian, we got a busload of cops down here to see you. Can I send them up?"

Ten of the best-dressed and fittest-looking plainclothes officers came into Ian's office. It was clear that this was a highly select group of the department.

"Hi Ian, I'm Captain Pete Luther. I'm in charge of confidential security. Meet your new best friends." The captain made the introductions, and then jokingly challenged Ian to repeat all the names. "Don't worry about it. You will all get to know each other. Let us explain what we do and how we do it. The first thing for you to understand is that you are in charge. If you . . ." Luther spent the next fifteen minutes going through what Ian should expect. He explained what Ian's responsibilities were and what their responsibilities were and how the work was divided up.

Then the men started asking questions about Ian's daily routine. "Hi Ian, I'm Ned. I'm in charge of sex. You talk to me about your partner/girlfriend. We don't want to get these other guys involved. It's none of their business."

"I'm afraid I'm a little dull." Ian told them about Adele and his concerns for her. How little he saw of her and how he was waiting for her to call. You had to like these guys. They were pros. They had obviously been through this many times and had to deal with all sorts of people who thought they were very important. Ian was going to make it as easy as possible for them. The men relaxed. They could tell this was going to be a pleasant assignment. Ian's phone rang. They all got up and left his office to give him privacy. The captain asked Ian to call him when he was off the phone. It was Adele. Ian didn't want to get her upset so he tried to lowball the whole bodyguard development. That didn't work. She was immediately concerned. "This is scary. I don't want anything to happen to you. I'm very happy you have these guys protecting you. We are just going to have to go deeper underground for a while. But you know what? This is all going to end. Then we GP."

Ian called everyone back in, and told them about the call. Ned said, "Now that comes under the category of sex. You are not supposed to be talking about that in front of these lechers. Captain, speak to Ian."

They gave Ian a list of phone numbers and a schedule of who was doing what and when. They only asked that Ian let them know where he was going. They also decided to discreetly, without her knowing, put a detail on protecting Adele. They didn't tell Ian either.

70

Next day, Davey Garr called Ian and asked him to come up to the courtroom. When Ian and his bodyguard got up there, Davey handed him an envelope. "Some guy I've never seen before handed me this envelope and said, 'Give this to ADA MacDonald as soon as you see him.' I didn't know if I would see you today; that's why I called you. It's all yours. Open it out in the hallway please, in case it explodes."

Ian took the envelope and held it up to the light. There was nothing but a piece of paper in it. The bodyguard took it and opened it. He looked at it and handed it to Ian. On the paper was written:

WESTCHESTER COUNTY AIRPORT

PRIVATE PLANE

They left the courtroom and went directly to Culkin's office. The inspector was elated. "This is just what we have been waiting for. Now let's hope it pans out and we are not getting this too late."

Culkin called the guy in charge of passport control at the general aviation side of Westchester County Airport. That was the side of the airport where all the private planes were fueled and boarded. They had helped each other before and were friends. "I can give you the flight manifests of all the private planes that have left here for the past week.

There have been no suspicious flights during that time period. Most of them are corporate guys that I know. There is a certain sameness to who goes in and comes out of this side of the airport. Do you want to send some of your guys up here and I can show them how we operate?"

"They are about to leave, Harry. Thanks. I'll have my guys look for you. We will be in touch." Culkin put his lieutenant in charge of a group that headed for Westchester.

Smitty came into Ian's office and shut the door. "I have some good news for you."

"You have arrested Gus Conti."

"No. It's even better news than that."

"What could be better than that?"

"You don't have to worry about Pete Rusk and his gun. It is a non-issue and a non-problem."

"Oh my God Smitty, that is great news." Ian stretched back and took three deep breaths. "I can't tell you what a relief that is. What happened?"

"You don't want to know. I've told you all you need to know. Except I made a promise that you have to keep."

"I'll promise anything, Smitty. What's my promise?"

"No one can ever tell his family about this. He is too embarrassed and ashamed. You can't tell Adele. Ok?"

Ian gave Smitty a long, hard look, and then said, "I'm ok with that. Just tell me that you are ok and that Pete Rusk is ok."

"I'm ok and Pete's ok."

71

All private planes flying out of Westchester County Airport were required to file a flight manifest as early as possible. Culkin's men were being shown the flight manifests for the rest of the day and whatever existed for the next day. It was mostly corporate stuff like IBM and GE. There were many corporations that were headquartered in Westchester County and the neighboring Fairfield County in Connecticut, who found it convenient to use Westchester for their flights.

On Friday afternoon, a flight manifest was filed for a 6:00 AM flight Saturday morning from Westchester to New Orleans on a private Gulfstream jet. The passengers were Mildred Conti, Gus' wife, and his sister Betty. Ian had no reason to stop them from flying, but requested immigration to make certain there was no one else on that plane. Culkin called the New Orleans authorities and let them know what was going on.

As Ian was about to leave the office, his phone rang. When he answered, a woman in tears said, "Assistant District Attorney MacDonald please."

"This is ADA MacDonald."

"Oh Ian, this is Deb Spence. It's about Bill." There was a sob. Ian's heart sank.

"My God, Mrs. Spence, what's happened?"

"About an hour ago, Bill opened his eyes and smiled at me. He put out his hand and grabbed mine and said, 'How we doing babe?' I screamed and called for the nurses. This is what we have all been waiting for. Bill is out of the coma. He is going to make it. I had to call you." Deb Spence broke down in tears.

Ian had trouble controlling himself. "Wow, this is fantastic. Can I come up to the hospital?"

"I don't see why not; you're family."

Ian got LoMurko on the phone, and he was at the entrance to the DA's office in five minutes. In thirteen more minutes, they were at Bellevue. Danny had been laying on the siren all the way uptown.

By the time they got upstairs, Spence had been moved into a private room. He was a little groggy, but greeted them when they came in. Deb Spence came over and hugged both Ian and LoMurko. "Isn't this the greatest day? The girls will be here in a few minutes."

Spence weakly raised his right arm and everyone got still. "It was Collins. He had a ski mask on, but it was Collins. He called me a rat bastard cop before he fired."

LoMurko and Ian looked at each other as if to say, "Which one of us is going to tell Bill what happened to Collins?"

"Jim, tell Bill what has happened."

LoMurko ran through the details of the killing of Collins, and then he picked out two evidence envelopes from his coat pocket. He held up what looked like a pint-sized baggy. "This slug was taken from your upper back muscle." He held up another pint-sized baggy. "These two slugs were taken from a mannequin that was shot by Collins at

Beekman Downtown Hospital. Ballistics has confirmed that they were fired from the same gun. It's the gun Collins had when he was killed."

Spence just closed his eyes and said, "Good detective work, inspector."

Ian thought that it would be best for Spence to rest, but asked if anyone had called Culkin. At that moment, Dick came into the hospital room. "You've been moved. I couldn't find you." He gave Spence a gentle embrace.

At 11:00 PM on Friday night, Myles came out of his mansion and got into the backseat of his limo. The U-group hung way back. Two days before, they had placed a tracker under the spare wheel bin of Myles' limo. There was now no need to follow too closely.

They went over the George Washington Bridge and started down the New Jersey Turnpike. Their concern that they might be driving all the way to New Orleans was alleviated when the limo turned off the Turnpike onto the Garden State Parkway. They then exited for the Long Beach Island Causeway, a road that took summer vacationers to one of the barrier islands off the New Jersey coast. It was off season, and there were only a handful of year-round residents on the island. Once on the island, the limo traveled south and then made a left-hand turn toward the ocean.

Since the island was so deserted, the tail car stayed way back and then followed the tracker to a huge beach house that was right on the ocean. Only sand separated the front door from the surf. Every light in the house was on, and three cars were parked in the driveway. Every other house in the neighborhood was closed up, dark and empty. Myles got out of the limo and went inside.

Frank Hopkins checked in with his inspector. Culkin had already started a second car heading south. He didn't know where this was leading, but he wasn't going to lose Spectrum. When Dick heard about the beach house, he called his contact at the New Jersey State Police. They were sending support.

Two of the U-group were about to work their way over to the house and do what they could to figure out how many people were there. When they were two houses away, the lights on the porch over-looking the beach suddenly came on. At the same time, two flood lights lit up the sand from the house down to the surf. Two men came out onto the porch, stood there for a while talking and then walked down the steps to the sand. They walked toward the surf. They stopped and conversed, and then returned to the house and went inside. One of the two men was Spectrum. A debate ensued over whether the other man was Conti. It looked like him, but there just wasn't enough light to be sure.

About five seconds after the two men went into the house, two other men dressed in black overcoats came out onto the porch and took up positions at either end of the porch. A third similarly dressed man stood by the entrance to the driveway. The detectives retreated to their tail car.

This new information caused Culkin to call his friend at the state police again to tell him he was about to get on a helicopter for a flight down to the island. He should be there within the hour.

The Jersey State Police decided to surround the beach house with troopers. They would stay about a block away until the arrival of the New York authorities. There was no way to leave the beach house, unless Conti was an Olympic swimmer.

12

It took Culkin about forty-five minutes to get down to the island. A field office was set up at the local Beach Haven police department. It was now close to five in the morning, and the first hint of a lightening sky was developing in the east. It was agreed that everyone would hang back to see if anyone left the beach house. The only activity was at 6:00 AM: the three men wearing black overcoats left their posts and went back inside. Everyone waited.

It was now daylight, and at 7:30 AM, a man came out the back door, walked quickly to a Toyota Tundra pickup truck and pulled away from the beach house. When he got a block away, he turned a corner and stopped abruptly before running into two New Jersey State Police patrol cars. He was taken out of the Tundra and searched. He maintained that he was on his way to pick up a donut order at the local bakery that was about a half mile away. He would not answer any other questions. Attempts to find out the numbers and names of the people in the house were unsuccessful. A check at the bakery revealed that the order was for two dozen donuts and three elephant ears. More telling was the order for two gallons of coffee.

SWAT teams arrived from Trenton. The small army of officers surrounding the beach house moved in closer to the house.

Loudspeakers were set up. Culkin was soon announcing to the occupants what was going to happen.

He told them that the house was completely surrounded and it was going to remain that way until he had gotten what he came for. That was Gus Conti. If Gus Conti came out of the house unarmed and surrendered and there was no violence, there would be negotiations as to the other occupants of the house. If any shots were fired from the house, or there was any other form of resistance, all bets were off. Everyone would be subject to arrest and prosecution, and there was no guarantee that the house would not be stormed by the SWAT teams that were present, standing by, and champing at the bit. It was now 8:00 AM and they expected an answer by 9:00 AM. Culkin gave them his cell number that the occupants could call should they have any questions. The number was repeated every five minutes.

At 8:20 AM, the phone rang. It was Myles Spectrum. He said he was Conti's lawyer and Conti was going to surrender, "We will be coming out the front door onto the front porch. We will have our hands over our heads. We will have no weapons. We will come down the steps to the sand, and then walk to the north side of the beach house where we will stand on the driveway and await instructions. Do not shoot us."

Culkin wanted to know how many others were in the house.

"There are twelve more: seven men and five women."

Culkin ordered, "They are to come out of the house after you do and lie down on the sand in front of the house. If they have weapons, they will be shot. If they do not have weapons, cooperate and do not resist, they will live. Is that clear?" It was.

The front door opened. Conti and Spectrum came out onto the porch and proceeded down the steps to the side of the house. At that point, they were told to lie face down on the driveway with their arms and legs spread out. While they were in that position, all the remaining people in the beach house, seven men and five women, filed out the front door. They walked down to the beach, and assumed a similar position on the sand.

They were quickly surrounded by the SWAT teams and searched. None of them had weapons. The SWAT teams then went into the beach house, and in five minutes came out and announced that the house was cleared. There were no other occupants. Culkin and his men went to Conti and Spectrum, and removed them to the Beach Haven Police Department for questioning. Conti would answer no questions.

There would be the usual paperwork and official proceedings involving the extradition of Conti back to New York. After lengthy discussions about the propriety of his actions, Myles was permitted to return to New York. Ian was anxious to have Spectrum break the news to Gino Conti about his father's arrest. Spectrum was going to the tombs as soon as he got back to New York City.

Two days later, ten guns of various make and caliber were found at the bottom of a water softening unit in the basement of the beach house. To no one's surprise, none of the recently vacated occupants of the beach house had any knowledge of where those guns came from or who owned them.

73

Spectrum arrived at the tombs as early as possible. He wanted to get this over with. He told Gino Conti his father had been arrested. Conti became hysterical, and they had to get one of the prison doctors to come in and give him a sedative.

Later in the day, Nails responded to a request from Conti and went to the tombs to visit him. By now Conti was calm and deliberate. He told Nails to keep his mouth shut and listen. He didn't want any arguments. Monday morning, he was going to plead guilty. His father's arrest had sealed it for him.

Without his father to help, Gino Conti knew he was sunk. He had done nothing but cause trouble for his family. He had driven his mother to drink. She hated him. He, frankly, did not care much for her. But he loved his father's power and money. Now that was gone.

Nails tried to reason with Conti, but got nowhere. He told Conti that he was in shock over his father's arrest and that he should not be making decisions until some time had passed. He suggested they talk again on Monday when they were to begin jury selection. That way he would have the weekend to think about what had happened and to reconsider what he might do.

Conti was adamant. He told Nails that it was all a waste of time and he wanted no part of it. He was going to plead. Nails explained to Conti that, if he pleaded guilty, the judge would most likely give him the maximum sentence. He might as well go to trial and take his chances. He had nothing to lose. Conti would have none of it.

Conti wanted Nails to tell the ADA to get Mary's family there. He wanted to say he was sorry. He wanted this over on Monday morning. Nails told him it wouldn't be over on Monday. The judge would adjourn the case for sentencing, and it wouldn't be over until then. Conti slammed his hand on the metal table.

Ian had been in the office since 6:00 AM that morning. He was up in the squad room following the developments from New Jersey. He wanted to fly down with Culkin, but the security detail talked him out of it. He kept in touch with Vince O'Rielly and Frank Carney, and they both arrived at the office around 10:00 AM.

Spectrum called to say that Gus Conti would waive extradition so Louie Balzo didn't have to prepare those papers. Louie started on a different set of papers setting forth Conti's consent to be moved to New York. Nails called and left a message that he wanted to speak to Ian.

When Ian spoke with Nails, he learned about the meeting with Conti. Nails could not have been happier that this case was about to end. He told Ian that Conti wanted the Rusk family in court Monday morning and that he planned to apologize.

"Now listen to me, Ian. I am not responsible if on Monday morning this jerk gets to court and changes his mind. I don't want you blaming me. I tried to talk him out of pleading guilty, but he wouldn't listen to me. But who knows what he is going to do on Monday.

Understood? I just thought you ought to know and maybe you could enjoy your weekend."

"Nails, I appreciate the call, but I'll believe it when I see it. I can't tell the Rusks about this and get their hopes up just to have Conti change his mind. He has hurt them enough already. Let him enter the plea before the judge. The Rusks can be there for the sentencing and Conti can make whatever statement he wants to make then. I do not trust the bastard.

Ian concluded with, "As far as my plans are concerned, we are starting jury selection on Monday."

Ian put down his phone, paused and decided to call Adele. He asked her what she was doing.

"I'm about to end my shift. I'm going home to get some sleep. Why? What's up?"

He told her about Gus Conti's arrest and the call from Nails. "Tell your family that there is a chance that Conti may plead, but that I don't want anyone counting on that. Tell them that if he pleads, the case will be adjourned for sentencing and, on that date, they should be in court and prepared to tell the judge anything they want to say. They should not bother to come to court on Monday. Am I making any sense?"

"Sure, I'll handle all of that."

"When do you start your next shift?"

"Not until next Wednesday. I get a swing break."

"What's that?"

"Extra time off."

"So if the case pleads on Monday, would I be able to take you out for dinner on Monday night?"

"I would love that."

On Monday, Gino Conti pleaded guilty. Judge Hastings questioned him extensively about why he raped and killed Mary Rusk. Conti's answers displayed the callous disregard he had for another human being. Hastings also questioned him about juror number 11. Conti laid all that at the feet of his father. He admitted he knew it was going on, but claimed he had nothing to do with the details. Hastings ordered Ian to present a jury tampering case to the grand jury. The judge assumed that Conti would plead guilty to that charge also. Hastings would then have a consecutive sentence opportunity ensuring that Conti would never leave prison. At the conclusion of the proceedings, Hastings asked Conti if he realized that he could sentence him in such a manner that he would never be released from prison.

Conti's reply was, "I hope you do."

To which Hastings said, "I'll try my damnedest to make you happy." He then adjourned the case for two weeks for sentencing.

Ian and Louie Balzo returned to Ian's office. Ian asked Louie to take a seat. Ian spent some time thanking Louie for the work he did on the Rusk case. "You have been terrific. I could not have had a better second seat."

"Ian, I feel like I should be paying tuition. You have taught me so much."

"Well, we make a pretty good team. Let's do it again."

Ian remembered having the same sort of conversation with Frank Carney several years ago.

After Louie left, Ian picked up his burner. Adele answered on the second ring.

"The case is all over except for the sentencing. We can GP."

"Yippee!" yelled Adele.

"So how about, instead of me picking you up at the dorm, you come down to the apartment? We can go to dinner from there after we have a drink or whatever."

"Oooh, I think I like 'whatever.' Just what is 'whatever'?"

"You know, whatever."

"I'll bring my toothbrush."

"Honest?"

"Honest."